⊰⊱ Mariah Mundi ⊰⊱
THE MIDAS BOX

G. P. TAYLOR

❋ Mariah Mundi ❋
THE MIDAS BOX

G. P. Putnam's Sons

G. P. PUTNAM'S SONS
A division of Penguin Young Readers Group.
Published by The Penguin Group.
Penguin Group (USA) Inc., 375 Hudson Street, New York, NY 10014, U.S.A.
Penguin Group (Canada), 90 Eglinton Avenue East, Suite 700, Toronto,
Ontario M4P 2Y3, Canada (a division of Pearson Penguin Canada Inc.).
Penguin Books Ltd, 80 Strand, London WC2R 0RL, England.
Penguin Ireland, 25 St. Stephen's Green, Dublin 2, Ireland
(a division of Penguin Books Ltd.).
Penguin Group (Australia), 250 Camberwell Road, Camberwell, Victoria 3124, Australia
(a division of Pearson Australia Group Pty Ltd).
Penguin Books India Pvt Ltd, 11 Community Centre,
Panchsheel Park, New Delhi - 110 017, India.
Penguin Group (NZ), 67 Apollo Drive, Rosedale, North Shore 0632, New Zealand
(a division of Pearson New Zealand Ltd).
Penguin Books (South Africa) (Pty) Ltd, 24 Sturdee Avenue, Rosebank,
Johannesburg 2196, South Africa.
Penguin Books Ltd, Registered Offices: 80 Strand, London WC2R 0RL, England.

Design by Marikka Tamura.
Text set in Cochin Medium.
Library of Congress Cataloging-in-Publication Data
Taylor, G. P.
Mariah Mundi : the Midas Box / G. P. Taylor.
p. cm.
Summary: In 1886, in England, when fifteen-year-old Mariah
begins working at the Prince Regent Hotel,
and discovers many previous workers have disappeared, he tries to
solve the mystery, only to find that nothing is as it appears.
[1. Missing persons—Fiction. 2. Magic—Fiction. 3. Mystery and detective stories.
4. Great Britain—History—Victoria, 1837–1901—Fiction.] I. Title.
PZ7.T2134Mar 2008 [Fic]—dc22 2007043140
ISBN 978-0-399-24347-9
1 3 5 7 9 10 8 6 4 2

To Suzy and all the team at Faber —
without your help and support none of this would have
been possible — you are the people who turn
my dreams into a reality.

Also by
G. P. TAYLOR

Shadowmancer

Wormwood

Tersias the Oracle

The Shadowmancer Returns:
The Curse of Salamander Street

CONTENTS

⋇ Mariah Mundi ⋇
THE MIDAS BOX

CHAPTER

✷ 1 ✷

Mariah Mundi

Mariah Mundi stepped into the long, narrow railway carriage and blinked in the bright light. Swirls of steam and the sound of the stoking engine filled the corridor that appeared to run the length of the train.

It was ghostly empty, as had been the platform where he had waited patiently for the train to the coast. He had watched the old beast shudder along the track out of the dark, stormy night and up to the platform, its heavy engine pulling six grubby-looking coaches.

Now in the glare of the carriage, Mariah hesitated. The coach was much brighter than he had expected, with a gas lamp lighting the drab walls and blinded windows. He looked again at the sign painted on the glass pane of the door. FIRST CLASS. He read the numbers on his ticket and matched them to a compartment. Coach number one, compartment three, seat number two, first class. Cautiously, he looked into his compartment.

In his seat sat a tall man with muscular frame, wearing the uniform of an army officer and carrying a thick scar across his right cheek. Mariah took the seat opposite, holding out his ticket.

"Please, sir," he said quietly. "I believe that is my seat."

"*Your* seat?" the man said, raising a furrowed brow. "I believe this seat belongs to whoever owns this train."

"But my ticket says—"

"Your ticket says that you should sit quietly and not disturb your elders or your betters," the man replied gruffly as he took a penny dreadful from his pocket and opened the creased pages. He grumbled to himself, "And another thing, boy. If I choose seat number two, it is because I like to see neither what is beyond the window nor what is in the passageway. It is a quiet seat, where I will not be disturbed and where I can rest. Now, if you don't mind, save your complaints for the ticket collector and keep quiet."

Mariah sat quietly, holding the ticket. The man buried himself in the dreadful.

There was a sudden jerk as the train started to move. The lamp dimmed as the train pulled away from the platform, steam hissing as it moaned along the track gathering speed.

Outside, the lights of houses flashed like phantoms in the darkness. Faster, called the rails as the wheels of the train clanked and churned, the great leviathan racing into the night.

Mariah had set off to travel north from London early that morning, clutching the ticket presented the day before by Jecomiah Bilton, headmaster of the Chiswick Colonial School, Mariah's home for the past seven years. Mariah's parents had travelled to the Sudan and had never returned. They had paid in advance, and so even after their death two years before, Mariah had been allowed to stay until he had reached his fifteenth birthday. That day had come and gone, along with a further six months of grace during which he cleared the refectory tables and washed the floors. Now he had been dispatched to his new home and place of employment with a third-class ticket, a first-class suit and a writ of worthiness signed by the gentle Professor Bilton.

This morning, as he stood by the ticket office on Euston Road he had noticed an agitated young gentleman strutting along the pavement in a silk top hat, examining his fob watch and looking up and down the street, scrutinising every horse carriage that drew close by. The man had cast him a quick glance and then looked away as several more carriages drew up at the station and left their passengers on the cold sidewalk surrounded by their hastily thrown down cases. The man had inspected the names on the cases from a distance as he pretended to swagger nonchalantly along the wide avenue in the cold December dawn.

Mariah had been fascinated, drawn in by the way the man twitched his head from side to side. Mariah watched the man, and oddly, the man seemed to watch him. The station clock chimed the seventh hour. The gentleman looked up and then pulled a narrow pair of spectacles and a thin piece of paper from his pocket. He perched the glasses on the end of his nose and peered at the tiny writing that was scrawled on the paper.

A tall, dark carriage suddenly pulled up to the station. The man flushed with panic, spun on his heels and dropped his gaze to the ground, marching straight toward Mariah.

"My dear friend," the man said in a strong accent that had not long resided upon those shores. "I beg of you a favour for which you will be highly commended. Here is a travel voucher, first-class, for any destination you choose." He handed Mariah a piece of paper emblazoned with the crest

3

of the Great Northern Railway. "Take this voucher as a gift, but I ask you one thing: tell no one you have seen me and . . . look after these."

The man handed Mariah a crisp pack of playing cards, still boxed and sealed with wax. On both sides was the face of the joker, cross-eyed and holding his wand as if to cast a spell.

"When you reach your destination, send a postcard to Claridges Hotel, mark it for me, Perfidious Albion, and I will make arrangements for the cards to be collected. Tell no one."

Mariah nodded silently as the gentleman dashed off into the crowd. Two men stepped from the black carriage and scurried into the throng, as if following the gentleman.

Mariah exchanged the voucher for a first-class ticket for his journey. As the train ambled to the north he looked from the window of the carriage at the fields that sprawled out before him. They soaked up the cold sun, and as the dark of the winter's afternoon fell, he looked upon the bright stars as they peeked from the high heavens.

Several hours later, he changed trains and boarded the branch line to the coast. Now he sat in the warm carriage, Professor Bilton's writ of achievement still folded neatly in his pocket.

The door to the compartment opened suddenly. A man in a long black coat and tie peered in.

"Compartment number three?" he asked.

Mariah nodded. His companion shrugged his shoulders, not bothering to look up from his penny dreadful.

"A dark, chilly night for us to be abroad," the man said, smiling at Mariah. "Do you travel far?" he said to the boy as he rummaged in his carpetbag.

"The end of the line," Mariah said.

"If I am not mistaken, you're a Colonial boy," the man said as he sat down next to the soldier.

"That I am. Do you know the Colonial School, sir?" Mariah asked expectantly.

"Well, very well. Had a suit like that myself once. The five-pound suit, given for good behaviour." He laughed as he leaned forward and felt the collar of the boy's coat. "Finer cloth than I ever had. Sent into the world to make the best of all they taught me, and now I am a man of leisure, forty-one years of age and taking a winter's rest by the sea. Tasting the waters, with a prescription to bathe in the Oceanus Germanicus every morning, rain or shine . . . Good for the constitution. They say the water is remarkably warm, even in winter." The man took in a deep breath as if he were inhaling the fresh sea air; he then paused and looked about the carriage, talking like he didn't want to be overheard. "Travel from London this morning? Seven twenty from Kings Cross?"

"That . . . that I did; never thought it would take so long or that I would come so far," Mariah replied as the thought of Perfidious Albion flashed through his mind. He slipped his hand into his coat pocket and fingered the deck of cards, which he had pressed deep within, not wanting to give their presence away.

"Strange," said the man. "I should have travelled that train myself, but my companion didn't wait for me. I waited a half hour and caught the next train. Travelling alone can be so . . . tiresome," he said slowly as he tried to peer over the top of the penny dreadful and see the face of its reader. "Do you travel together?" the man asked, attempting to engage the soldier in the conversation.

"Alone," the soldier said monotonously.

"Far?" he asked, smiling.

"'From the ends of the earth, by sea and sail, hackney cab and now by rail,'" the soldier replied, reading the words from the plaque above Mariah's head. "And all in one day . . . now if you would excuse me, my eyes tell me that they desire to sleep, as we will be arriving within the hour." The soldier slumped down in his seat.

"Very good, very good," the other man muttered, gesturing for Mariah to be silent.

They sat in silence for the next nine miles. Mariah held his arms across his chest, holding himself against the thick-piled seat. The man stared at him as they listened to the soldier's heavy snoring. The long journey north had numbed Mariah's mind. He wanted to join the soldier in slumber, but some inner thought kept his eyes from closing, not trusting the other man. Mariah looked at him—he clutched his large carpetbag, carefully balancing it upon his knees. The man looked back at Mariah and smiled a sheepish smile through his thin lips.

"You know a lot about me, and I nothing of you," the man said as he fiddled with the strap of the bag. "Do you work at the end of the line, or are you going there to take the waters?"

Mariah hesitated. He snuggled back into the deep pile of the seat as the carriage rattled back and forth along the shaking track. "I'm going to work at the Prince Regent," he said slowly.

"Well, well, well . . . bless my soul. If that isn't a coincidence beyond all coincidences. I too shall be a guest in that fine place. The Tower Suite, a reservation until the end of March. They say you can see the castle and the harbour and on a clear day the windmills of Holland . . . And you, in what capacity will you be employed?" He spoke quickly, not giving Mariah time to reply. "Perhaps you will be my butler. Now that would be a fine thing, meeting like this in a *first-class* carriage and you being a servant." The man stopped and looked at the ticket that Mariah held nervously in his fingers. "You do have a ticket for this compartment, don't you? It wouldn't be good order for a Colonial boy to be thrown on the platform of the next station for riding without the proper papers." The man leaned forward and snatched the ticket from Mariah's hand. "Aha," he said as he examined it. "You appear to be in order. First-class suit and first-class ticket, things certainly have changed since my time at the Colonial School . . . certainly have changed." He sat back in the seat and cast a glance at the soldier sleeping next to him.

"Men . . . men . . . ," the soldier shouted, twitching like a sleeping dog. "Line of fire, line of fire," he screamed, waking himself from his dream with a sudden start. He picked up the penny dreadful from the floor of the carriage. He gave a deep yawn and shook his head, rubbing his face in his hands and chomping his lips. "Not used to the English weather," he said to the man, who had leaned away from him and now clutched the carpetbag even tighter. "Haven't had a decent sleep since the Sudan; couldn't sleep on the ship, too hot by day and too cold by night. No place better than a train carriage to rock you like a baby, though . . ."

"Sudan?" Mariah said without thinking. "My parents were in the Sudan."

"I take it they are not there now?" the bagman asked before the soldier could speak.

"Lost . . . missing . . . dead . . . ," he said slowly, the words coming in the order of events that had broken his heart two years before. Mariah stared with his piercing blue eyes at the leather bag thrown into the luggage rack above the soldier's head; he read the words etched in black on the tan hide — CAPTAIN JACK CHARITY. "It was in the uprising, a mission post. My father was a doctor and my mother a nurse. At first we heard they had been taken prisoner," he said. "But later, Professor Bilton told me that news had come that they were . . ." Mariah couldn't get the words from his mouth.

"On your own, boy?" the soldier said.

"Now that I have graduated from the Colonial School . . ."

"Any family?"

"Not one left," he said as he looked at the floor.

"A hard life, but still . . . worse things happen at sea . . . ," he said as he leaned back in the seat and opened the penny dreadful.

"A story like my own," the other man said as he took a packet of thick toffee from the carpetbag and gave a piece to Mariah. "Whatever your circumstances, let it be known that despite your present station in life, by virtue that we are both old boys of the Colonial School, we are practically brothers. Isambard Black . . . Here is my card." He held out an empty hand, then with a twist of his wrist, a neat gold-edged calling card sprang out of the air to the tips of his fingers. "Take it," he said with a smile. "If you are ever in London and need gainful occupation, then call upon me. You never know, the coast may not suit you and the London smog may be a place to hide." He chuckled to himself, twisted his hand again and brought forth an old playing card. Mariah gasped.

"I have a friend at Claridges; he could help you. In fact, I was supposed to travel with him today, but he never came." The man held out the card to Mariah. "The fool, the joker without jest, behind his smile is great tragedy and malice, not one to be trusted."

Mariah couldn't speak, Albion's command to tell no one echoing in his mind. He swallowed hard as the sight of the joker with its telltale cribbed edge and bright-coloured mantle flashed before him, spinning in the man's hand as he made it bob back and forth, then twist on his fingertip in some elaborate conjuring trick. It disappeared suddenly.

"Gone," said the man as he reached toward Mariah, who pressed himself harder against the seat, one hand firmly in his pocket clutching the pack of cards that Albion had entrusted to him. "And now . . . ," he said as he reached into the top pocket of Mariah's new suit and pulled forth the card as if it had been there all the time. "Aha!" he exclaimed. "The card dances about my new friend."

"Party tricks," muttered the soldier, who had returned to his reading. "Next you'll be littering the carriage with rabbit droppings and pigeon feathers from all the beasts hidden in your dangerous undergarments."

"Such a trick would be too crass. I am a magician — part-time, of course, but sleight of hand is my passion. I travel the world collecting the most audacious illusions that I can find and using them to bring mirth to those I meet."

Mariah sat wide-eyed, twisting strands of his thick, dark hair in his fingers as Black balanced the joker on the tip of his finger once more. Then in a puff of smoke that blew from the palm of his hand, it vanished.

"Where does it go when it disappears?" Mariah asked.

"That I cannot tell you. I am bound by oath never to divulge the secrets of the Order of Magicians. It would be on pain of death to give such vital knowledge to the uninitiated."

"You can buy those tricks on any street corner where you're going, boy," the soldier said without even raising his head from his paper.

"There is one magic trick that cannot be bought and is not an illusion," Black said quietly to Mariah. "A magic box that turns anything placed within it to the finest gold. That would quench all of my desires; it would surpass any sleight of hand. If I could have the Midas Box, I would be a happy man."

"You could turn anything to gold?" Mariah asked.

"Anything . . . and everything," the man replied as the whistle blew and the train was consumed by a tunnel, disappearing into the blackness.

CHAPTER

❧ 2 ❧

The Prince Regent

Mariah peered through the side slat of the heavy blinds that were firmly pulled over the carriage window to keep out the night. Squinting into the blackness, he could see the twinkling of the lights from a thousand windows as the train slowed over the high viaduct that took the track into the heart of the town at the end of the line. Below him were the roofs of the fine houses that snaked along the contours of the railway leading the train to the sea. It was as if there were an enquiring face at every window as the train slowly ambled along, steam billowing from the engine, brakes squealing as it panted to a halt.

Neither Captain Charity nor Isambard Black had spoken another word since the train had left the tunnel many miles before. Mariah had sat in silence, trying to avoid the grinning face of Mister Black as Captain Charity had slept again, this time silently, the penny dreadful folded over his face to keep out the light from the gas lamp that hissed above his head.

The carriage shook violently as it came to an abrupt halt, the engine clanging against the iron buffers that marked the end of the track. Mariah was catapulted forward, tumbling headfirst into the lap of the captain and waking him awkwardly from his deep sleep.

"Never . . . ," he shouted as he grabbed Mariah by the arms, picking him up and throwing him sideways to land upon Mister Black. "Never in a million years will you take me . . ."

"It was the—," Mariah protested as Black struggled beneath him, compressed by the carpetbag, his head squashed against the back of the seat.

The train rolled back from the buffers, throwing Mariah to the floor of the carriage. Black jumped to his feet, dropping his bag upon the boy, and then stumbled and fell backward into the captain's lap.

Charity pushed Black off of him, giving him a sharp jab in the back with his tightly clenched fist. "Once more," he barked, "and I will pull the ears from the side of your head . . . and . . . and . . . make you eat them." Black fell forward, tripping over Mariah and landing face forward into the seat, spilling the contents of his coat pocket to the floor.

"I have never been so treated in all my life," Black complained as he tried to collect himself. "If this is the North, then I shall find myself on the first train back to the city—"

"END OF THE LINE," shouted a voice in the passageway outside the compartment. The guard walked the long corridor tapping on every window. "CARRIAGES AND OMNIBUS AWAITING ALL."

"At least I will get a civilised journey to the Prince Regent," Black exclaimed as he picked up several silver coins and the chain from a broken fob watch from the carriage floor. Mariah stared up at him as he scowled. "Move, boy, you're in my way. Come on . . . out of the way and help me pick up the things I've dropped. Move . . . move," Black commanded angrily as Captain Charity took his bag from the rack and pushed past them both, sliding open the stiff door.

"It's time you went," Charity said as he grabbed Black's coat collar and tried to pull him from the compartment. "The boy has helped you enough. He doesn't work for the hotel yet, so leave him be."

Black was lurched into the corridor, fob chain and coins in hand. "My bag," he yelled in protest as he was dropped unceremoniously. Charity leaned in and grabbed the old carpetbag that pressed Mariah to the floor and threw it at Black, who put his hand to his head to protect himself from the blow.

"I'll have you arrested, taken from the train in irons and transported to Australia, never to see the light of day again," Black grumbled loudly as he grabbed the bag and scurried off backward. "Never . . . never have I known anything like it," he said as he quickly pushed through the door and onto the platform.

Charity turned and looked down at Mariah, who lay motionless as the captain stared down at him, his immense frame filling the door and casting a dark shadow across his face.

"What shall we do with you?" he bellowed as he grabbed Mariah by the collar and lifted him to his feet. "We never did get introduced; I'm Captain Jack Charity. Too tired to talk, and that imbecile would have driven me mad with his chivying . . . so come on. Who are you?"

"Mariah Mundi," he said sheepishly.

"Well, Mariah Mundi, you have reached the end of the line, and from what I can remember, you have an appointment at the Prince Regent." Charity laughed as he rubbed the side of his sharp nose. "Not a place I'd like to stay, so watch yourself. Better seen in daylight, and too many tales of devilish doings for my liking. There's rumour that a madman walks the streets in these parts, taking the children and leaving no trace. Never go out alone, especially after dark." Charity rummaged in his pocket. "If they give you a day off, come and see me. Just look from the Regent to the harbour, and on the quayside you'll see my place." Charity beamed proudly as he handed Mariah a gold-edged calling card. "The Golden Kipper, the finest place to eat on God's earth. I have a chef who can cook the most luxurious fish that man has ever eaten, and if you get yourself along, there's one waiting for you." Charity held out his large hand, and Mariah squeezed it firmly. "Done," said Charity as he stepped back into the compartment, pulled up the blind, opened the window and leaned out. "Careful what you do with my trunk," he called down the platform to the luggage van. "Break a single thing and you'll end up the same, mark my words." He looked at Mariah, who cowered back into the seat. "Doesn't do to be nice to everyone," he said with a slight, lopsided grin. "Got to keep them on their toes. Now, boy, pick up your things and off you go. I'll see you to the street and point you the right way."

Mariah didn't reply, his eye caught by a small trinket that dangled from the seat where Black had fallen. He picked it up and held it to the carriage lamp. There on a fine chain was a golden skull the size of a honeybee. Two green jewelled eyes stared at him, twinkling in the light. Its jaw dangled open, set on the tiniest hinges he had ever seen, a full set of intricate diamond teeth sparkling like drops of morning dew.

Mariah held out the skull to Charity. "Not mine," Charity said. "Could belong to the madman, dropped from his pocket when he fell over." He laughed. "Give it to him when you see him at the Prince Regent."

"What is it?" Mariah asked as he twisted it in his fingers, allowing the light to shine upon its fine jewelled eyes.

"Never seen the likes of it before. Once saw an earring of a skull, but that had been shrunken by pigmy headhunters, and it certainly didn't have jewels for eyes. Best you keep it safe. Doubtless if it belonged to Black, he'll be squealing for it by the morning."

Charity turned and stepped from the carriage, holding his bag on his shoulder. Mariah clumsily lifted his bag and followed, balancing it on his head as he staggered along the corridor to the platform door.

The cold night air cut sharp against his skin, taking away his breath, the smell of the sea as strong as if he were being wrapped in a blanket of seaweed. The flagstone platform glistened with a sheen of frostlike grit that crunched underfoot. He and Charity marched on, protected from the strong sea gale by the station canopy, which rattled, glass upon steel, high above their heads as small whistles of breeze pushed the sand around their feet in thick swirls. A row of small shops stretched out in a long parade, each lit by its own gas lamp. Even on this winter's night, they bustled with the business of the late hour as inside, brown paper and string wrapped objects of every kind.

Charity beleaguered the porter who dragged his sea chest along the platform as quickly as his stunted legs would carry him, trying to keep pace with the captain's stride. "Quickly, man," Charity harassed him. "I've been away for seven years and I want to see how this town has changed. My eyes eagerly await the delight that is before me, and your poor provision of limbs holds me from that enchantment." The porter tried in vain to run faster as he dragged the case behind him, red-faced and wheezing, past the row of shops to the station's iron gate.

By the gate stood a tall, thin ticket collector, a pair of the neatest spectacles perched on the end of his hooked nose, held in place by a thick strap that circled the back of his head. His hand was held out as if he were a fine waxwork or shop manikin dressed in pin-striped trousers and a thin overcoat with tattered elbows.

"Train tickets, please," said the man, his lips never moving, as if he had trained his nostrils to speak. Mariah handed him his ticket.

Charity pressed by, ignoring the man and signalling for Mariah to walk on. "Too busy to pass the time of day with you, Postill," he bellowed at the ticket collector. "I'm in the service of the Queen, and if a queen doesn't need a ticket, neither do I."

Postill grunted as they marched into the dark night. High above, the station clock chimed midnight. Tall railings surrounded the station like the bars of a prison, stopping all from escaping to distant shores. Beyond was a row of houses that soon petered out into the fields of the North Way, which gently sloped away to the pleasure ground of Northstead and the deep cut that bit through the cliff to the open sea. Paint flaked from the boardinghouse in the corner of the square just past the gate. The hackney stand bristled with fine black carriages and tired drivers. The horses chomped in oiled leather nose bags.

"There she blows," Charity shouted as he pointed to a carriage etched in a silver outline, the name of the Prince Regent emblazoned upon the door. "Hey you," he shouted to the cabby, who had perched himself, rug-wrapped and double-coated, upon the driving plate above the cab. "I have a guest for the Prince Regent, stand and be made ready."

Charity pushed Mariah forth and into the station yard. The cabby looked down, unwilling to offer even the slightest hand of friendship as Mariah scurried across the gravel under the harsh moon, his back beaten by the strong wind that gusted from the sea.

"He is a Colonial boy, sent to work. Treat him well or you'll have me to deal with," Charity hollered as he humped his sea chest into the back of the cab, tipped the porter with a penny piece and patted him heavily on the back.

Mariah held fast to his bag and looked up at the driver, who looked down with cold grey eyes that peered out from underneath a heavy wool hat.

"Get on the back . . . You're late. Already got a guest and have to wait for the servants, not a good start to your life at the Prince Regent," the cabby muttered as he flashed the wand above the horses' heads, dangling it like a menacing summer fly as he ushered them on with a tug of the reins.

Mariah jumped onto the back of the coach, grabbing the cold brass rail as the carriage pulled into the cobbled street and turned sharply right.

"How long to the hotel?" Mariah heard Black ask impatiently from inside the carriage.

"A couple of streets and then to the cliff top, sir," came the bored reply as the cab made its way slowly through the empty streets, past shuttered inns, shut drapes and coffee shops. It turned past a sandstone church with rain-cut carvings running through each stone, then left toward the cliff top as the sound of the roaring sea grew louder and louder and the salt spray billowed up from the beach far below, churned by the violent tide.

"Not a night to be out," the driver shouted as the horses brayed like donkeys against the wind. "Get yourself down and under the oilskin; as soon as we turn the corner, the gale will be upon us."

For Mariah it was too late. The sudden gusts blew harshly against the carriage, quickly bringing a damp dusting of sea and sand that lashed against his face, filling his eyes and nose with coarse grit. Rain blasted against the carriage and smashed against the ground, surrounding the horses' hooves as if they were walking in boiling lead.

"Quickly, man, I'm drowning in here," Black said, tormented by the stinging rain that broke into the front of the carriage, dowsing him.

"Only go as fast as the horses will take us," the coachman muttered under his breath as he cracked the whip. "You, boy. You hailing well?" he shouted.

Mariah cowered against the gale as he gripped the carriage straps and balanced himself on the back box. He had pulled the oilskin over his head and curled up his legs as he was bounced back and forth.

"Fine," he said as another turn in the cobbled street threw him sideways.

"Not much farther, the Regent isn't far away," the coachman shouted again, his voice fading into the whining of the wind, which howled and moaned in and out of the dark alleyways that ran back and forth between the houses. "There it is."

Mariah peeped from the side of the oilskin as cold drips trickled down his back. He gasped. There before him stood the finest, most gracious building he had ever seen.

The hackney stopped, the horses slipping on the stone slabs that had been laid to form a long courtyard in front of the Prince Regent. Mariah slipped from the carriage, clutching his leather bag as he pulled up his collar against the wind and chill of the night. His eyes were dragged upward, on and on, almost to the pinnacle of the sky as they searched out the high towers that perched on every corner of the building.

A golden sign lit by bright limelight hung above the large doorway, glowing in the darkness like the gateway to some strange magic kingdom. Letters a yard high read

PRINCE REGENT

Mariah stood in the drizzle as Black stepped from the hackney and pulled a floppy felt hat from his pocket, squeezing it upon his head, tugging the brim over his eyes. He glanced at Mariah and grinned, his smoke-yellowed teeth illuminated by the phosphorescent glow of the limelight. "Be seeing you again," he said slowly, as he began to walk the twenty paces to the steps of the Prince Regent. "This is for guests. I'm sure you will find your way in somewhere." Black disappeared behind a large marble column that towered like the trunk of a giant tree. Mariah looked up; there in the domed vault of the entranceway and topping every column was a tight growth of marble palm branches, dripping with gold leaf and pomegranates. Staring back at him was the face of a blue monkey, teeth bared and snarling, clutching the pillar as if it were life itself.

"You'll be in the staff quarters, up there," said the cabby as he slammed the door to the carriage and pointed to the heights of a tower high above them.

Mariah looked up, his eyes straining to see the pinnacle that touched the black, rain-filled sky. "I've never . . ." He stopped in amazement.

"They all say that when I drop them off, every one. The biggest pile of bricks in the known world," the man said. "Just think of the view, almost in heaven. Thirteen floors, three hundred and sixty-five guest rooms and four towers, one year old on Christmas Day and still standing. Wait till you see it from the other side, makes a man know where he stands in the universe."

"Can you see the windmills of Holland?" Mariah asked as the drizzle wet his face.

"Some say you can, though I have never dared to go up that high. But watch the storms rolling in to the land. A thousand white horses chasing the ships as they run for harbour, and then in an instant it'll be flat like a millpond. Don't let looks fool you, lad. All that glitters isn't gold. Keep your wits sharp and watch out for Mister Luger. Been a lot of disappearing and dying around here lately—some say it's a curse from what was here before the hotel was built, the curse of the Prince Regent."

Mariah turned to ask him to explain, but the cabby was gone. The horses stood stock-still, braving the rain as the door swung on the empty carriage. In the wall below the high tower, a door opened suddenly, slamming against bright red bricks. "You, boy," shouted a girl's voice louder than the rain and wind. "Stand there and you'll die of cold. Get yourself in."

Behind Mariah the hackney lurched away with the crack of a whip and the clatter of hooves on wet stone flags. He jumped, startled. The girl laughed, a bright smile gleaming across her face as her laugh echoed from the terrace of large houses that lined the clifftop square.

"Colonial boy," she shouted again. "I was told you were coming—get in, you've work to do."

CHAPTER

❊ 3 ❊

The Steam Elevator

The door slammed behind Mariah and he was alone; whoever had called him from the dark doorway had gone. He stood dripping wet in a shadowy corridor that seemed to stretch for miles ahead. A gas lamp was posted by the door, a sentinel of light in the dark chamber. He shook the rain from his coat and folded it over his arm, and started walking slowly along the passageway toward the ever-darkening gloom ahead of him.

"Colonial boy . . ." The sharp voice came from somewhere behind, rolling along the passage like a storm wave crashing to the beach. "Colonial boy." It came again, louder than before. "This way, can't you see?"

Mariah turned and saw the girl. She had dark hair that was pulled tightly back and tied in a strict knot at the back of her head. To her right was the outline of an entrance that had been hidden from view when he had stepped into the tunnel.

"It's this way," she said. "I've been sent for you—we're working together." She looked Mariah up and down. "First job, fresh out of Colonial School?"

At first Mariah couldn't reply. He felt as if he were on display as the girl's eyes inspected every crease of his white shirt and focused upon the blue school tie that was tightly wrapped around his neck. She raised a dark eyebrow in disdain at what she saw as a wry smile crept onto her face.

"Do ya get paid for wearing that outfit?" she asked in a broad Irish accent. "Looks like you've stolen the pants from an old man."

"It's a first-class suit. I earned it at the Colonial," Mariah replied softly as he looked at the green tiles beneath his feet, not wanting to look her in the eye.

"Well, you'll get the pick of what you want here; the wardrobes are full of things to wear. One day a prince, the next a pauper. Look at me . . . Today I was a housemaid." She smoothed the creases in the white pinny that covered her long black dress with its tidy cuffs and ruffled collar. "We'll get you started in the morning and you'll be ready for tomorrow night. Better be quick—a steam elevator never waits."

The girl turned and vanished through a narrow doorway that Mariah wouldn't have noticed if he hadn't seen her disappear through it. He quickly followed, turning sideways between two narrow walls of green tiles that opened out into a large room. The girl stood waiting at a tall gate, a lattice of metal that formed a flexible iron grid. It was covered in shiny brass rivets, and behind it was a deep shaft that sunk into the depths below. From high above, he heard the sound of laughter and distant music echoing down the shaft.

There was a sudden hissing of steam and the whirring of

a large flywheel. The gate rattled as the sound got louder and louder, shuddering the floor beneath his feet.

"Don't worry," the girl said. "It's only this loud here because we are close to the engine. When you get upstairs, you can't hear a thing."

A bright light appeared in the shaft, coming closer and closer as billows of steam oozed from the blackness and filled the room like a thick London smog.

"Only a minute and it'll be here," the girl said loudly, above the clanking of the steam generator. "It was built by Mister Luger—he's an inventor, owns the Prince Regent, designed it with his own hand."

"I've never seen an elevator before," Mariah said nervously as swathes of thick steam swelled about his feet like a rising tide.

"There're many things I had never seen before until I came here," she said as the elevator chugged from the bottom of the deep shaft, winched by a steel wire the thickness of a man's arm that vanished upward into the darkness, pushed by a steel piston that powered it higher and higher.

"Is it . . . is it . . . safe?" he asked as the shaking intensified.

"Safe, no. Fast, yes." The light grew brighter, illuminating the walls.

The elevator ground to a sudden and noisy halt before them. The girl turned the brass handle and slid the metal gate open, stepping into the elevator and beckoning Mariah to follow.

"Thirteenth floor," she said. "That's where you're living. Nothing special, but you can call it home."

"What will I do here?" Mariah asked as the girl slid the door shut and pressed a button.

"Work in the hotel's theatre, general dogsbody . . . that's until you learn the ropes, and then, like me, you'll walk the boards. Best job in the place. Lucky you came when you did.

Felix had the job until he went . . . *missing*," she said, gripping the brass rail that was heavily bolted to the wall of the elevator.

Suddenly, the elevator was thrust up the shaft, the open wall speeding by too quickly for Mariah to count the floors, his ears popping as the steam pushed them higher. "What happens when we stop?"

A bell pinged and the elevator hit the thirteenth floor as if it were crashing into a stone wall. Mariah was lifted from his feet, momentarily weightless, and then smashed against the floor. The girl never moved, braced against the wall of the elevator, her foot hooked beneath a discreet handle in the corner.

"Should have warned you," she said. "But I had to see the look on your face . . . priceless."

"Glad you think it so amusing," Mariah said as he got to his feet, picked up his bag and brushed the dirt from his damp shirt. "So that was a steam elevator."

"Not only that, but the fastest in Europe, Mister Luger told me. He should know; he built every one of them," she said as she pulled back the metal gate and stepped from the elevator into a small corridor with three narrow wooden doors that formed a semicircle before the elevator gate.

"Lodgings?" Mariah asked.

The girl pointed to the doors, "Mine, yours and the stairs. Yours belonged to Felix."

Mariah looked at the first door. There was a tiny scrap of paper that had the smallest handwriting etched in jet ink. "Sacha," he said as he read the paper. "Is that you?"

"My short name; you're English, so you could never pronounce what I'm really called, so you call me Sacha—do you have a name yourself?" she asked without drawing a breath.

"Mariah—," he began.

"Never tell your last name," Sacha interrupted. "I don't

want to know it, and if I did, I would know you too well. Who's to say you'll be here in the morning? After all, you may run off and hide, like Felix. Here three weeks, then goes off without telling anyone. So keep your name for yourself; Mariah will do for me and for old Bizmillah. You're taking over Felix's job, so you're his assistant." Sacha gestured toward the door. "There isn't a lock, so hide your things well. We clean our rooms ourselves and get fresh sheets on the first Sunday of the month. We eat where we work, and Mister Luger wants to see you at first light."

"What exactly will I do for Bizmillah?" Mariah asked as he pushed open the door and stepped into the dark room.

"You'll be a magician's apprentice," she said excitedly. "Cleaning his illusions, polishing his boots and allowing him to cut you in half in the Sunday matinee. Better than scrubbing floors and doing dishes, but then again, you did come from London in a *first-class* suit." Sacha laughed at him as she took a lucifer match from her pocket and lit the mantle of the gas lamp that hung over the small fireplace. She saw Mariah look at the empty grate. "You'll never be cold, not in this tower," she said as she brightened the room with a turn of her nimble fingers. "We have water heating, the finest in Europe—"

"Mister Luger says," Mariah finished for her.

"It's true," she protested. "Gurgles like a great dragon. Hot as Hades, winter and summer. Everything runs from steam, everything. The cooking, washing and even the harmonium in the theatre. There's nothing better." Sacha laughed.

Mariah looked about the room. It had a fusty smell, like an old church he had once visited with his mother. It had smelled of musty, unopened books. Yet even that gave his room a familiar feeling that caused a pang of sadness to shadow his thoughts.

The chamber had a small bed with clean but tatty blankets folded back beneath two duck pillows. By its side was a small cupboard next to the fireplace. A fine wax candle was pressed neatly in an old brass holder by the bed, with two matches and a striking pad lying in the wax gutter.

Mariah could hear the howling of the wind, which blew round and round the high turret of the tower. Above his head was the cracking of the flag that festooned the tower. It carried the banner of an unknown land, trailing out more as a signal of the gale's strength than of reverence to the state. The grey slate tiles creaked and moaned with every breath of the sea gale that beat against the side of the Prince Regent as if it were battering some ancient cliff. The windows rattled in their frames, shaking the sashes, cords and weights that hung behind the thick, green damask curtains.

"You can take a look," Sacha said as she saw him gaze at the chink in the curtains. "You'll not see much on a night like this, just black of night and a few lights from the harbour." She stopped and thought for a moment. "But you'll see the lighthouse. Keeps me awake. Sends its beam out to sea time and again. Never stops." Sacha seemed reassured by the thought.

"Can you see the windmills?" he asked as he slumped onto the bed.

"No. I was told that when I came here. I looked and looked, but all I saw was the sea and the town." Sacha closed the door to the room quietly. For a brief moment he glimpsed a look of discontent upon her face.

"Do you like it here?" he asked as she stared at the gas lamp and gently turned the knob to dim the light.

"These are for you," she said as if she hadn't heard him, picking up a suit of clothes from the door back. "Hope they fit. We wear black in the theatre during performances so we cannot be seen as the scenes change. Bizmillah will give you something to wear when he cuts you in two—you're the same size as Felix and his never got too . . . bloodstained," she said, laughing.

"So I am to be cut in half every Sunday matinee?" Mariah

25

asked as he poured himself a small glass of water from the bedside jug.

"Every Sunday, three o'clock. That's after he has plunged five long daggers deep within you *and* put your head in an iron mask . . . all for a silver shilling and six pence in the balcony."

"Is that why Felix ran away?"

Sacha was silent. She laid the black coat upon the bed and stroked the sleeve dreamily. "The truth is, Mariah, no one knows what happened to him. The night before he went missing, I heard him arguing with Bizmillah. He shouted at him that he would tell Mister Luger what had happened, and Bizmillah said that whatever went on, he would take a pound of flesh from Felix as payment for his lies. Then he was gone. I came to the room the next morning and his bed was unruffled and unslept in. This suit of clothes hung behind the door, and everything was as it had been. There's . . . there's a rumour in the town that a kraken, an evil creature from the sea, has been taking the boys who work here. Catching them when they've been out on their own. Felix was the fifth one." Sacha stopped and looked away.

"You must go on," Mariah said as he reached out to her and jabbed her arm.

Sacha looked back and forth from window to door uncertainly. She grasped the bedpost, twisting the wood in the palm of her hand. "How do I know I can trust you?"

"I'd never even heard of this place until Professor Bilton gave me a note saying I was being transferred," Mariah said as he rummaged in his pocket for his writ of worthiness. "Look at this. It'll tell you who I am and why I'm here. You can trust me," he said as he handed her the folded velum tied with a red ribbon.

She held it, unopened, and looked at him. "Promise me one thing, Mariah. Whatever you hear tonight stays between us."

Mariah nodded, hands in pockets, fingers secretly crossed. "Promise."

"Not long before Felix disappeared, he told me he had found something. It was more of a secret than something precious, but he wouldn't tell me what it was or where he had discovered it. I asked him again and again, but he seemed afraid to tell me. The only thing he said was that the secret was hidden in the Prince Regent, somewhere people would never think to look but go past every day."

Sacha paused. "The night he vanished, I heard something at the door of my room. I lay in bed as the door slowly creaked open an inch or two. There was no light. Whatever it was had come by the stair and turned off the gas lamp by the elevator." Sacha spoke slowly, looking about her, keeping her voice to a whisper for fear of being overheard. "I pulled the covers over my head; I didn't want to see it, whatever it was. I thought if I didn't look, it would go away and find someone else to torment . . ." She stopped and took a breath, her hands feeling the ruffles of her collar, pulling them from her reddening skin. "I couldn't move. I wanted to scream, but no one would have heard me. Whoever . . . whatever it was, came into my room and looked at me. I could feel its breath panting against the bedclothes over my head. Then it slowly walked back to the door. Whatever it was, I could smell it . . . It was like old mothballs and gin mixed together. I had to look, so I took a peek — I couldn't help it, I had to see, . . . and . . . and . . . there was nothing. I heard the door pull shut, but didn't see anything. There was a clang as the door to the elevator shut and a whizzing of the engine, and the next morning Felix was gone."

"Do you think it was Felix who came into your room?" Mariah asked, gulping the lump from his throat, shivering as if a cold hand were touching the back of his neck.

"Why should he? I have nothing to steal but a few old postcards from Ireland, that and a trinket or two."

27

"Did he leave anything for you, a note, a gift?"

"Nothing . . . When Mister Luger searched his room, he found nothing, even the mantelpiece had been dusted and the grate cleaned. All that belonged to Felix was gone except this stage suit," she said as she brushed the sleeve again and again. "That had been put on the hanger and placed inside the closet."

"What about his family?" Mariah asked, nervously twisting a strand of his hair.

"No one . . . He spoke of no one. Mister Luger only takes orphans, boys from the Colonial School and the workhouse," she said. She saw Mariah look at her with enquiring eyes. "Did you know Felix? He must only be a year older than you."

"Felix . . . no, . . . can't say I did. There were so many of us," Mariah replied slowly. "Have you worked here long?" he asked, hoping to change the subject.

"My father got me the job here. I'm the eldest of nine children and there's no room at the inn." She laughed at her own joke. "My mother keeps the Kent Arms in Paradise. It's a bar by the harbour—we get Saturday afternoon to ourselves, so I'll take you. My father's a coastguard. In the morning you'll see the castle; look to the street below and that's Paradise."

"So you lived in Paradise?" He laughed.

"But some parts of Paradise are so full, I now have to live here." Sacha lost her smile as a distant church clock struck midnight, its shrill chimes carried by the wind. "Best be leaving you," she said as she opened the door. "Since Felix disappeared I've taken to blocking my handle with a chair. Haven't slept for so long . . . I'm glad you're here; I'll sleep tonight," she said as she turned to go, shutting the door firmly to keep out the night.

Mariah crept to the window, opened the thick curtains and looked out to sea. The room appeared to be at the very top of the hotel, in the top of the tower. It was as if it were the height of the clouds that swirled about the round turret and rattled the glass panes. Through the rain-streaked windows he could make out the square shapes of bathing machines on the narrow strip between the Prince Regent and the sea, two hundred feet below. They looked like miniature houses strapped to the backs of old horse carts and wheeled out into the sea. The scene was clearly lit by the gas lamps from three hundred windows and several cones of limelight that illuminated the hotel, so it could be seen far out to sea.

Far below, the lighthouse poked like a thin white finger through the rolling waves that broke over the pier, drenching the fishing boats that clung to the harbour wall. Wave after wave crashed from the darkness, briefly phosphorescent in the glow of the light, then plunged black-dark into the night storm.

Mariah turned the element of the lamp until the mantle glowed with the strength of a firefly, barely lighting the palm of his hand. He then sat on the bed, wrapping himself in the wool blankets as he listened to the storm beating against the windows and crashing against the beach below.

CHAPTER

✵ 4 ✵

Galvanised Bathing Machine

Since the supposed death of his parents, Mariah had tried to sleep as much as he could. When he closed his eyes, he lived an interior life only known to him. In his dreams he would see his mother, talk to her, know her again. They would fill each second with chatter, always in the same place. They would be on a bridge by a river, staring at each other's reflection in the changing waters. There was no sun, just a radiant light that edged its way around the high grey clouds blanketing the sky.

He had never looked at her face-to-face in his dreams. It was only her shimmering reflection that he had seen, often broken by the wisps of breeze that blew through the tall oaks and cedars surrounding them. Then his dream would slip away, and he knew that soon he would wake, holding fast to the hope that he would see her again.

Waking was always the same. It snatched away her life and allowed the memory of her death to return. Sleep was, for Mariah, a great comforter.

But morning came quickly. The storm had ebbed into a gentle December breeze that chased mountainous white clouds across the sky. Mariah was wakened by the scream of the seagulls that lodged on his roof well before the rising of the sun. He dressed quickly in the black shirt and suit left for him by Sacha. They fit well, as if they had been tailored just for him. In the dirty brown wardrobe he found a pair of black, pointed boots with silver buckles — they fit like a glove. While he waited for Sacha he stared out the window, captivated by all that was before him.

To the north he could see the castle with its bombarded keep, high walls and a garrison house, which proudly flew a Jack from a stubby flagpole on its grey slate roof. Mariah looked for Paradise and traced the street with his eye, follow- ing his finger across the windowpane as he drew its length from the castle to the sea. Far below was the harbour, every inch of water crammed with small boats that even in the first light of dawn jostled with each other to flee to sea. On the slipway a large brig stood half-built, its ribs and keel open to the elements like the carcass of a dead whale. It crawled with men, who from that distance looked like small black ants.

Mariah never expected it to be such a beautiful sight. The crisp blue morning sky was edged in gold thread from the rising of a southern sun, which skipped across the horizon, shedding its light below the high clouds. It was the first time he had seen a dawn such as this. From his tiny room in the Colonial School, he had only ever witnessed the drab rising of a foggy orb that would, with its feeble arm, scatter the smog by late afternoon and allow its return as it quickly set to the west. The sky and the sun had always been but a backdrop to his life, but now they commanded his time and attention

31

as they stretched out before him to the distant horizon of the German Ocean.

Mariah tidied the room. He felt as if it were not yet his, that Felix was closer than he could imagine. He set about searching the room for some clue as to the disappearance of the boy and why so many had vanished before him. He looked everywhere, but it was as if every trace of Felix had been totally eradicated. Whoever had done this had been purposeful in their plan, and Mariah could not decide if Felix had been the perpetrator or victim of some elaborate plot.

Then Mariah remembered something he'd been trying not to think about—the penny dreadful that had lain open on Captain Charity's lap as he slept. The black ink cartoon of Fiery Jack snatching the children from their beds and dragging them across the rooftops of London to be devoured in his lair. He checked the window again, feeling the securing bolt to see if it had been tampered with. He looked outside to the small balcony that encircled the tower and wondered if Felix had escaped that way, onto the roof then down to the street. Or, he dreaded to ask, was he carried off by the kraken—the demon creature that plagued the city—across the rooftops, devilishly transporting Felix to another world.

It had been with great care that he had folded his own suit and placed it into the wardrobe, and now he remembered the playing cards wedged deeply in his pocket, kept away from prying eyes. Slowly and carefully he dipped his hand into the pocket and, before bringing the cards and the jewelled skull to the light, looked over his shoulder to see if he was being watched. He stared at the joker dressed in his clown's guise, with his checkered shirt, ruff collar and painted face. He examined the stiff wax seal that held the box lid securely shut. Then he quickly took the cards and the skull and hid them under the bed, wedging them between the mattress and the oak boards.

As he got up, there was a knock at the door. "Mariah," he heard Sacha whisper. "If we go now, I can show you something before you see Mister Luger . . . You have to see it."

Mariah opened the door and stood back to allow her in. Sacha didn't move. She looked him up and down, not speaking. "Cat got your tongue?" he said as he tired of her staring.

"You look just like him," she said, sounding surprised. "Same hair, same eyes, you could be brothers."

He ignored her, uncomfortable in his new clothes and feeling as if Felix were closer than before, that he had never left the room but just changed into dust and now stared down from the thick cobwebs that hung in the corner of the room. "What do we have to see?" he said, reminding Sacha of her excitement.

"Something special. Mister Luger said he'll see you in an hour; Monica's been causing trouble, and Bizmillah wants her cast out of the theater. They're all in his office; you can hear the shouting. She's screaming and . . ." She paused, as if trying to remember her point. "That's it!" she shouted. "I found a Galvanised Bathing Machine; it's incredible. Arrived last night from Luger's workshop, the only one in Europe and destined to cure all of life's ills, so—"

"Mister Luger says," Mariah said.

"Precisely, . . . and it's in the hotel. I found it this morning. Quickly, we'll have to go by the stairs."

Sacha took him by the hand and dragged him through the doorway and into a narrow spiral staircase that twisted down, lit only by slit windows looking out across the sea.

Mariah followed as Sacha ran faster, skipping steps as she ran. Every now and then she would whirl herself around the blind corners, grabbing the brass rail and throwing out her feet, vanishing from sight, then reappearing as Mariah chased after her. The sound of their footsteps echoed, drowned only by the vibration of the elevator as it went up and down, shivering the shaft and gargling steam from the many vents that crisscrossed the wall.

Every so often, they passed a small landing, each with a wooden door marked with the floor number. Mariah counted the landings as they spiralled down, his hair blowing in the strong draught that blew from the depths of the shaft.

"Much farther?" he shouted.

"Another five floors and then we'll find it," Sacha gasped as she ran.

They were now below ground level. The lower they descended, the hotter the shaft became; the handrail was warm to the touch, and the sound of hissing steam filled the staircase.

"Don't worry," Sacha cried out above the noise of the steam engine, "only two more landings."

Mariah didn't know what time it was, and he felt a growing concern that he would be late to see Mister Luger, that this unseen master of everything would pack him on the first train back to London.

"We're here," Sacha shouted, out of breath. "This way for the experience of a lifetime."

Mariah followed her through the door and into a long corridor. He suddenly realised that they were not below ground, that because the hotel was built on the edge of a high cliff, one side of the Prince Regent was built into the rock face. The corridor was lined with large windows that ran its length and carpeted in fine green wool inlaid with golden crowns. Mariah overlooked the narrow beach covered by the high tide and peculiar bathing huts. A hoard of shabbily dressed urchins, barefoot and ragged, searched the strand for the washing of jetsam that had been brought in by the storm.

Sacha beckoned him to follow her. "Not far," she said. "Just at the end is the spa; drink the water and you'll turn green . . . People pay good money to swallow the stuff, smells of whiskey and devils belching. You should see the look on their faces after they've been made to drink a gallon of the stuff." Sacha grimaced, opening her mouth and sticking out her tongue.

She stopped at a double door crafted from the finest dark wood and etched with carvings of holly leaves. "This is it," she said, looking both ways along the passage, then stepping quickly inside.

Once inside, Mariah stood in an incredible water garden. A large swimming pool stretched out before him, lit with blue gas lamps that shimmered a rainbow upon the purple water. It looked like a huge cavern made of blue and white tile mosaics, and large parlour palms shot forth their long green branches. Around the pool were several large wicker sofas with curiously shaped backs, humped at one end like a camel. Immediately, the heat made his face sweat, and the heavy black suit felt out of place.

"Not far," Sacha said as she went on her way through the spa, looking for a gathering of tall tropical plants that protected a small doorway in the tiled wall. "In here," she whispered as she slipped under the branches of a minute tree laden with yellow fruit, with a large bat dangling by its thin claws from one of the branches. It slept in the morning sunlight, which streamed in from the high windows that reached all the way up to the glass floor of the terrace above.

"What is this place?" Mariah asked, wide eyed in amazement.

"People come here to swim, take the waters and sit under Mister Luger's health lamp. After a week they turn brown. Some of them look like boiled lobsters, *and* they pay," she said incredulously. "But if you want to be amazed, wait until you see this." Sacha's eyes lit up with excitement as she pushed open the door and dragged him into a large room clad in fresh pine planks and smelling of a freshly cut forest. "Look."

Mariah stared at a large brass dome. From the dome three large pipes came out. One went into the ceiling; the others bit into the enamel bath next to the dome like giant spider fangs. Over the bath was a wooden hood, like an upturned boat, with a tidy, circular hole padded with red leather. On the side of the bath was a large green lever and brass indicator, which at that moment pointed to the word *resting*.

"Steam powered," Sacha said proudly as she stroked the soft wood. "This really does become a wonder: one flick of the handle and it's filled with steam; two flicks and gallons of freezing salt waves are pumped from the sea and sprayed inside; three flicks and hot water bubbles all around. Mister Luger says it invigorates the soul and cleanses the mind, the only one in Europe." Sacha looked at the handle and smiled. "It's a Galvanised Bathing Machine. I overheard Mister Luger saying the water was mixed with a secret ingredient that gave it curative properties. He said he would pump it from under the streets and mix it with the seawater, called it kuck," she said, her eyebrows raised. "Every bath adds an extra pound to the bill, so people wouldn't pay if it weren't worth it. Shall we see it work?"

"I wouldn't do it, Sacha. What if we are found here? I have to go, got to see Mister Luger."

"So . . . Mariah *is* a coward. I knew it. When I saw you last night, *Just like Felix*, I thought to myself, *all talk and nothing in his britches*. No one will know, Mariah; we are the only ones here." Sacha fumbled with the starting handle. "There's a swimming robe in the back room, get changed and get in; it'll be the best thing you've ever done."

Mariah thought for a moment; he was torn between pleasing her and running away. He looked at the Galvanised Bathing Machine; it sat on the tiled floor, dead. "You can do what you like, Sacha, but I'm not getting into that thing — I want to see it working first."

"If *that's* what, you want, then *that's* what you'll get," she said quickly as she slipped the handle from RESTING to ACTIVE.

The large brass bubble made a sudden gulp, then began to gurgle and simmer, quietly shaking the floor and making the bath tremble as it sucked in kuck from a huge vat far below. It belched a breath of salty steam through the leather-clad hole. Mariah watched, glancing toward the door, the only means of escape.

"What if somebody comes?" he asked anxiously as the bathing machine's sulphurous breaths came faster and faster. The room began to stink like a sewer.

A sudden loud shudder shook the whole room, and the brass bubble belched violently. It rumbled as more and more thick brown steam billowed from the top of the bath.

"Ready?" Sacha shouted as she flicked the switch once and stood back from the machine.

A large guzzling of bright white steam blew through the pipes and into the bath, like the smokestack of a steam train at full speed. It gave a deep, loud roar as it rushed into the air, hitting the ceiling and blasting across the room.

Sacha panicked and hit the switch again. This time the Galvanised Bathing Machine trembled violently as the pipes rattled. Then with a sudden and desperate moan, it began to spew forth a torrent of bright green salt water into the bath, filling it to the brim, spurting from the leather neck hole and showering the room.

"Stop it," shouted Mariah as he leaped out of the way of a charge of spray. "It'll drown us!"

Sacha hit the switch again; the seawater ebbed back, sucked down the sluice, glugging as it disappeared down the plughole. But then they heard the blasting of the hot-water pipe as it rattled its welcome to the world.

Before they had time to think, a torrent of boiling hot water filled the machine like a swirling vortex. It shook upon its clawed metal feet, nearly knocking Sacha to the floor as she gripped the handle, vainly attempting to stop it.

"Run," Mariah shouted as he scampered to the door, leaving Sacha hanging on to the machine as the stinking vapour darkened the room. "Let go and get out," he hollered above the sound of the steam. He turned and saw Sacha being pulled back and forth by the intense vibrations of the machine, which appeared to have developed a life of its own, intent on destruction.

"Mariah!" Sacha screamed as the handle began to glow with the conducted heat from the steam bubble. "I'm stuck!"

He saw that her coat sleeve was caught on the handle. He ran to her, avoiding the frothing of the machine and holding his breath. Quickly he grabbed her sleeve, tearing it as he pulled her free. "Now run," he said as he dragged her to the door. "If we get caught now, that'll be the end of us both."

"Mister Luger would understand," Sacha pleaded as she skidded through the kuck that had spat from the machine and now covered the tile floor in large puddles.

"He'd kill us . . . feed us to the seagulls . . . sack us if we were lucky," Mariah moaned as he pulled her through the tiny door and into the shade of the tropical palms, quietly closing the door behind him and looking out across the spa from the cover of the undergrowth.

Quickly and quietly, they crawled through the palms that lined the side of the spa, keeping to the shadows in the hope they would not be discovered. Within a minute they were alongside the large wooden doors that opened out onto the long corridor leading back to the staircase. Mariah looked at Sacha, thin-lipped and tight-eyed, hoping she would see his irritation. She looked back with bright eyes, a wicked smile breaking the side of her mouth.

"Wasn't that fun?" she asked.

Mariah was about to reply when the door swung open and a head covered in long, greasy hair peered into the room. A man stepped into the spa dressed in a long white bathrobe that trailed along the floor. He walked cautiously across the tiles, his bare feet squeaking with each step. He inspected every inch of the wall as if he were looking for something hidden.

Together they watched as he stopped, looked around and waited, then turned away. Mariah and Sacha cowered deeper behind the plants, hoping that he would not hear the Galvanised Bathing Machine.

Then Mariah saw his face. "*Isambard Black*," he gasped, the sound echoing slightly in the chamber.

Black jerked his head at the sound. He dived to a chaise lounge by the side of the pool and sprawled upon it as if he had been there for some time. He slipped the white towel from the back of the sofa, put it over his head and began to grunt like a pig, feigning sleep.

Mariah seized the moment. He grabbed Sacha by the arm and dragged her from the cover of the palms, pulling the door open and pushing her through into the passage. He looked back; Black snatched the towel from his face and sat bolt upright as the door to the spa swung shut.

"Quickly," Mariah pleaded, "we mustn't be caught."

Together they set off toward the staircase, running along the crown-encrusted carpet as fast as they could. He knew that Black would be close behind as soon as he realised what they had done; they had to reach the stairway before they were discovered. Mariah knew there was something more to Black than taking the waters; he had seen it in his eyes on the train and now in the spa.

They raced to the door, Sacha grabbing the handle and diving into the darkness of the stairwell. Mariah allowed the door to almost close, keeping a fingerbreadth through which to peek into the long passageway.

He could see Black peering out of the spa door, looking back and forth, his lips twisted into a foul grin.

CHAPTER

❋ 5 ❋

The Importunate Otto Luger

Otto Luger sat in his large gold-leafed office, on the ground floor of the Prince Regent. He rolled an old quill pen in one hand as he attempted to perch his monocle in his left eye with the other. The gold-rimmed glass balanced precariously in place. His breath seethed, and his thick, unnaturally black moustache twitched angrily.

"It's not that bad, Mister Luger," the Great Bizmillah said as he stepped back toward the door, trying to escape before Luger exploded. "Whatever you want is what you will get. She can stay, but all I ask is that you don't allow her to throw knives at the audience again. They were only laughing—when she fell over, they thought it was part of the act; that's why they laughed."

"No one laughs at Monica," Luger screamed as he got to his feet, "not even the guests. If

41

they laughed, then they deserved what they got. Monica is an *artiste*, a creative genius. Believe me, Bizmillah, the name of Monica Momzer will be known throughout the world . . . Understand?"

"Indeed, Mister Luger, we all understand, and I will do everything in my power to . . ." Bizmillah stopped speaking as he saw the look on Luger's face.

"I'm glad you see it my way because that is the only way there is around here," he said sharply in his Texan drawl. "I came here penniless, and everything you see belongs to me. Monica stays in the act or you don't stay in the hotel . . . Understand?" Luger shouted as he raised one eyebrow, his monocle falling to the desk. "If Monica's happy, then I'm happy, and if I'm happy, that means you get paid . . . Understand?"

Bizmillah didn't reply; he bowed his head and looked at the floor as his hand rummaged for the door handle behind him. Several beads of sweat trickled across the top of his bald head.

"One more thing," Luger said as he again sat at his desk. "The boys . . . Any questions being asked as to why they keep disappearing?"

"Not that I've heard, Mister Luger, not that I've . . ." He stopped and thought for a moment, his mouth poised as if he had been suddenly silenced. "There . . . there is one problem," Bizmillah went on, fumbling for words.

"Speak, man." Luger motioned with his hand.

"Professor Bilton at the Colonial School said this would be the last boy. He asked where they had all gone, five in a year, and I told him we had lost them and he thought that rather clumsy. He said for the price we gave him, he couldn't give us any more and Mariah Mundi would be the last."

"Mariah Mundi?" Luger said as he looked up at the enormous castle-shaped clock that hung above the door, its axehead pendulum swinging menacingly back and forth. "I was supposed to see the boy half an hour ago . . . the last one . . . Mariah Mundi . . . Understand?" Luger seemed confused. His hand ruffled the papers on the desk; he seemed to be looking for something important, something lost in the depths of his memory that he tried to find in the reality of the cluttered world before him. "That's it," he exclaimed as he grabbed a piece of paper. "Monica wrote it here. She wants to cut him in half . . . in the matinee . . . on Sunday . . . Said you do it every week and now it's her turn and I had to ask you." Luger stopped and looked at Bizmillah as he joggled the tiny scrap of paper before him like a small fan. "It will be fine, won't it? I don't want to upset Monica, do I?"

Bizmillah rustled in his green silk suit, grabbing the billowing cuffs and wrapping them around his wrists anxiously as he clenched his teeth together. "Fine," he said, grimacing. "Whatever Mister Luger requires."

"So glad, so glad," Luger said softly as he again looked at the pendulum, lost in its motion, dreamily watching the axe go back and forth as it gently struck midday, the hands coming together at the pinnacle of the castle keep.

The front of the clock burst open and a fanfare of tiny figures leaped on fine silver rods, with a blast of little trumpets, appearing to dance about the parapets and along the finely etched castellation that surrounded the clock. There was a whooshing of steam as the chorus began to blast a reveille of miniature notes, which shrilled loudly across the room with great brio, rattling the wineglass that balanced precariously on Luger's desk. A team of horses and armoured knights leaped from a small door, suspended upon long fanned arms, galloping in tune to the music as the clock's doleful bell chimed twelve.

Luger sat charmed as Bizmillah cowered, fearing what was to come. Above his head the pendulum suddenly dropped, the axe swinging close to the floor as he leaped out of the way.

High above, the clock took on a life of its own as the castle keep was filled with minute figures that danced and swirled with every bugle note. Luger looked, bewitched by the spectacle. With the final stroke of midday, the tower door opened and a small, jewel-encrusted executioner slid out on a small brass stand to be met by a silver-plated king, who buckled at the knee, bent toward him and met the axe across the back of his head.

"Such a sight, such a sight, Bizmillah, and you missed it," Luger said excitedly. "Come back tomorrow. You can sit at my desk and watch it again . . . Better still, come back at midnight and you will see something even more spectacular."

"The boy, Mariah Mundi?" Bizmillah asked, desiring a reason to escape Luger's ramblings.

"Why should I want to see him?" Luger asked as he waited for an encore from the gold clock.

"You invited him. Every boy sees you on his first day . . . a tradition, all part of the process. You see him and then you send him to me in the theatre," Bizmillah reminded him.

"Yes . . . yes," Luger replied, still distracted. "Send him in, . . . and remember, Monica will cut the boy in half at the Sunday matinee."

Bizmillah turned to the door, taking hold of the brass handle as he glanced upward at the golden clock that hung high above him. It had been a strange journey that he had taken to that place. He remembered first stepping from the boat at Dover two years before, mumbling his intentions in broken English as he was questioned by the guard. He had amused him with card tricks and sleight of hand, twisting a living frog from his fingers and allowing it to spring upon the man, landing on his shoulder. From there he had gone to London, where he had spent a year in a small theatre, standing before the limelight and casting doves from his open hand to a sleeping crowd huddled before him, there only to escape the cold.

One night all that changed. Otto Luger had stepped into the darkness dressed like a fine London gentleman, a fat cigar between his lips, fine silk gloves in his hand, and a long black cane. He had sat by the door of the small theatre and laughed loudly, carousing with the singers, laughing at the jester and standing in awe, clapping frantically in appreciation of every single dove that Bizmillah had squeezed from the sleeve of his coat. Later, Mister Luger had sidled his way toward him, forcing him to sit at his table and offering him something that he could not refuse.

"I like you," Luger said as he sipped a bottle of fine brandy, clutching it by the neck with his thick hands. "I have always been fascinated with magic, but something that takes you beyond picking a pigeon from your coat sleeve or twisting a card from the back of your hand." He stared into Bizmillah's eyes, holding his gaze. "I searched for something for many years, something that made me leave Texas and come to this cold, foggy, grubby city. I knew it was here, and it cost me a fortune to find it."

"I too search for something," Bizmillah said as he flicked a card into the air and watched it vanish, the trick unseen by Luger, who took a swig from the bottle. "A pack of cards so amazing that to touch them would be all I would ever desire. In the right hands, the cards know your very heart and show your future in dancing pictures."

"Dancing pictures, you say?" Luger muttered through a mouthful of brandy.

"Whatever is in your life will come from the cards. They are not marked, and have no trickery of any kind. It is as if they had a will of their own and an understanding of the human heart."

"And who has these all-seeing knights, knaves and queens?" Luger asked.

"They vanished many years ago, taken from Vienna. They

have travelled across Europe, and now they are somewhere in London. In every city I hear stories that they have been seen, that some great deception has been performed, and every time I am a month, a week or a day behind. Once, in Paris, I even knew the man who had found them. I went to his apartment and discovered he was dead and the cards were nowhere to be found."

"How much would I have to pay to get my hands on them?"

"Priceless, totally priceless. The only way to get them would be to steal them," Bizmillah whispered as he looked over Luger's shoulder and around the room to see if they were being overheard.

"Then that's what we'll do, my friend. Nothing should keep a man from his desires, and if we have to steal them, so be it." Luger slapped Bizmillah heartily on the back, grabbed his hand and squeezed it in a crushing handshake. "I have two men, detectives, Grimm and Grendel. They *found* something for me, and I'm sure they could accommodate a little investigation into your poker deck."

"Poker . . . ?" Bizmillah exclaimed as a look of disgust crossed his face. "Nothing so crude as that; they are the Panjandrum. The finest deck ever crafted, life breathed into them by their creator."

"Whatever you say," Luger replied. "One thing, Mister Bizmillah. I own a hotel, newly built and the grandest in Europe. Come and work for me and I will find your Mister Panjandrum and get you his cards. All I ask is that you help me."

Now that seemed such a long time ago. Luger had not kept his promise, and all talk of the Panjandrum had faded. Every night, Bizmillah had entertained the guests of the Prince Regent with an ever-decreasing supply of magical doves and disappearing frogs.

Luger had taken to inventing all manner of strange steam-powered devices to bring health to his clients. From deep in the depths of the hotel, where maids and porters would fear to walk alone, he had spent many days and nights in his laboratory. The sound of his pounding iron reverberated through the elevator shaft to the very pinnacle of the hotel.

"So you'll send in the boy?" Luger said as Bizmillah stepped from the room. "I have things to do, so don't let him keep me waiting."

Bizmillah smiled submissively. "Very well, Mister Luger, whatever you say."

Mariah sat on the chair outside the office. He watched every guest who passed by, looking for Black. He had bought a picture postcard of the Prince Regent in the lobby, and now he scrawled the words *Perfidious Albion — Claridges Hotel — London* as neatly as he could before placing the card in his inside pocket. He knew Mister Luger would ask for him at any moment.

That moment had already come and gone several times as Mariah looked out of the window at the busy marketplace that by day sprung up outside the hotel. He had watched the coming and going of several fine carriages, dropping their elegant guests, who were swarmed upon by wasplike porters in blue suits and yellow braid. They gathered up the suitcases and breezed in and out of the hotel through its grand, oversized revolving door, which hissed like a snake as it went around.

Mariah had watched as fine gentlemen walked the wide, sweeping staircase to the gaming room on the first floor, their ladies leaving to look at views of the endless sea from the glass-topped veranda. No one paid attention to him as he sat waiting patiently, hoping that the muffled conversation would soon be over and he would be admitted to Mister Luger's sanctuary.

"Mariah Mundi," Bizmillah said as he stepped out of the room. Mariah sat up straight and stared at the man, surprised

47

to see him wearing a silk suit with green embossed dragons and thick gold thread. Bizmillah the Great looked Italian, with sun-warmed skin and dark hair that spiralled in eccentric wisps around his ears and to his shoulders. "Mister Luger will see you now, and later . . . I will teach you how to be a magician."

Mariah smiled, stood up and walked into the room. Luger sat at his large, cluttered desk pretending to write on a piece of paper, his pen going over the same three words. He didn't speak; Mariah waited, watching him trace the name again and again. From where he was standing, he couldn't make out what was being written and rewritten, but Luger made him wait until the last drop of ink had dried from the tip of his old quill pen.

"Sit," Luger shouted, his eyes fixed on the piece of paper. "I am a busy man and not one to be kept waiting. I said nine o'clock. What's your excuse?"

"I was outside," he said quietly. "It must have been . . ."

Luger shook his head and looked at the clock and then at Mariah. He pulled a large gold fob watch from his waistcoat pocket and held it to his ear, checking to see if it was still working. He raised his eyebrows, a look of puzzlement cross-ing his face. "Waiting for me?" he asked, unsure of himself. "Outside?"

Mariah nodded as he bit his lip, trying to keep a straight face. "Sacha said that you were busy, so I waited."

"Waited," shouted Luger as he rose from his seat. "Do you know what happens to the man who waits?" Mariah was si-lent. "Nothing . . . That's what happens, nothing. Life charges by, and he wakes up one morning and his life is over; that's what happens if you wait."

"Sorry," Mariah said softly as Luger began to pace about the room, looking at the floor and pummelling his fist into his hand. "I won't wait again."

"Time waits for no one. Already the morning has gone; soon it will be the afternoon and that will die and become the evening, and you know what comes then, don't you?" He spoke frantically, not giving Mariah a chance to speak. "*The night* . . . dark and cold and miserable. Filthy, thick black night . . . and I lay a wager that you expect to sleep?"

Mariah nodded hopefully.

"And you know what happens when people sleep? *They die* . . . that's what happens. I've seen it a thousand times: old men get into bed, close their eyes, and then they are gone. So what's the answer, boy?"

Mariah stared back vaguely, not knowing what to say as Luger waved his arms erratically.

"*Don't sleep* . . . I haven't slept in years, never go to bed, and all I allow myself is to close my eyes for five minutes each hour. Whenever I am indoors, whatever the place, as soon as the quarter of the hour comes, I sit and close my eyes for five minutes." Luger walked back to his desk and sat in the large, worn leather chair. He looked Mariah up and down, and then pulled a piece of velum paper from a brown folder that lay on the top of his desk. "Says you're a Colonial boy? Know Professor Bilton well, do you?"

"Very well," Mariah replied as he fiddled with the button on his jacket sleeve.

"You are the last in a long line of boys from that school, and I have heard there will be no more. All the others have . . . *run away*, gone without a by-your-leave. Will you do the same, young Mister Mundi?"

"No, I —"

"It would be a shame to lose someone as bright as you." The clock struck a quarter past noon. Luger looked up, then looked at his fob watch, setting a small gold lever on the side, and then sat back in the leather chair, closing his eyes. Instantly, he began to snore, his broad chest heaving under his fine gold waistcoat, his head tilted back against the chair.

Mariah hesitated, unsure if he should wait or leave the room whilst Luger slept. He looked at the desk; there in the middle was the piece of paper that Luger had scrawled upon. He edged closer, trying to make out the words, intrigued as to what the owner of such a fine place should want to write again and again. He reached out and turned the paper toward him. *The Midas Box* was scrawled in thick black ink.

There was a sudden shrill clanging as the bell in the fob watch rattled in Luger's hand. He leaped from the chair, dropping the watch and grabbing the front of the desk with both hands to steady himself. He looked about the room, and then fixed his glare on Mariah.

"Yes?" he asked madly, as if he had never seen the boy before. "Do you want something?"

CHAPTER

✳ 6 ✳

Perfidious Albion

An hour later, Otto Luger released Mariah. His fob watch had jangled in his pocket to remind him it was time to sleep again, and Mariah was despatched with a quick grunt and told to make his way to see his master . . . Bizmillah the Great.

Mariah clutched a guide to the Prince Regent, a fine brochure etched in silver and giving him a plan to every floor. It was like an exquisite little book, marked in several different colours, showing him where he was allowed to go. Luger had warned him severely about breaking the purple code — purple was the colour of the rooms for guests only. "Instantly," Luger had said, "will you be thrown from the building if you break the purple code."

As Mariah walked along the fine corridor that led from the grand office to the theatre Luger's warning rattled in his head. He came to a pair of tall oak doors. Next to them was a small sign painted in gold lettering with the words THEATRE CLOSED. He flicked through the pages of the brochure, his eyes searching for the colour purple. Near the back of the small booklet he found a page with a drawing of the swimming pool and the room that contained the Galvanised Bathing Machine. The room was distinctly coloured purple. On the facing page was a drawing of an attendant's jacket with an introductory note.

> Staff can always be identified by their type of dress—here in the spa you will be attended by our finest staff—gold-braided jackets edged in a purple stripe. We are always on hand for your every need. Try the Galvanised Bathing Machine, the only one in Europe, guaranteed to invigorate the most weary of bodies.

Mariah took a sharp breath. He had been but one night in the Prince Regent, and if Luger found out what had happened to the bathing machine, he knew he would be on the train to London with his first-class suit, a third-class ticket, nowhere to go and no one to help him. He found himself missing his parents more than ever. But this was his home now, like it or not, and he would have to make the best of it.

He looked up. Towering above him on a dividing wall that held the two sides of the passageway together was a gigantic portrait of a medieval prince seated on the back of a large white horse. The prince stared down at him. Mariah walked backward. The eyes followed him. He took a quick step to the side; the eyes followed him again. Everywhere he walked, it was as if the painting were looking at him, its cold, staring gaze burning into his head. Mariah looked at the painting, convinced that he was being watched. Then he realised that the face of the prince was that of Luger, his crooked smile peering out from behind the thick black moustache. Mariah wondered if someone would walk this way—he thought he would wait and see if the picture followed them as it had him.

There was a small alcove recessed in the oak panelling that clad the wall of the dark passageway at head height. Set on a tall wooden stand was an aspidistra in a brass pot, its long green leaves darting from the black earth like dragon's teeth.

Suddenly, the oak doors rattled as if they were about to be thrown open. Startled, Mariah darted behind the large plant. The thud of feet upon the tiled floor echoed along the corridor. Two people walked hurriedly toward him.

"They can't stay here; they'll have to go on the first ship next week," a woman's voice said in time with the tap, tap, tap of her high heels against the tile floor. "That last one nearly got away. If I hadn't seen what he was doing, he'd have been long gone and the peelers would have been on to us. Bizmillah's a blind old bat. You're going to have to do something about that man—what does he have on you, Otto, that you keep him on, anyway?" The man walked silently at her side. "Let him go back to wherever he's from and entertain some old lady on a station platform in Transaldovia. You want this to be the finest show in Europe, don't you? Get rid of the guy." The woman spoke without taking breath.

"He knows too much, Monica," the man replied, blowing out a huge breath of cigar smoke. "It's better to keep him here where we can see him than to let him go around the world looking for those stupid cards."

"Yeah, just like your stupid box . . . I remember when I believed in you, Otto. Now I just think you're a fool. Who'd believe anyone would think there was a box that could turn anything to gold."

"It's not just any old box, Monica, it's the *Midas Box*, and it really exists."

"Then show me. Let me see it for myself, and then I'll believe. Just look at you," she said as she glared at the painting of the prince that regally stared at her from its golden frame. "Every picture in the place has your face on it; everywhere I go, there's your gawping face."

"It's my hotel, I can do what I want," he replied. "Come on, Monica," he drawled impatiently as he pounded on along the corridor past Mariah's hiding place. "There's been a problem with the Galvanised Bathing Machine. Someone has been messing with the controls, *someone* who shouldn't even be down there."

Mariah listened from behind the aspidistra. Monica grumbled to herself as she clattered on behind Mister Luger. Then, peering from his dark hiding place, Mariah saw her. It was as if he had discovered a creature never before seen by human eyes. More catlike than human, it was as if Monica were from an unknown world.

Clattering on a pair of the finest patent leather high heels was the most elegant thing his eye had ever fallen upon. Every inch of her was festooned in black and green ostrich feathers, which fell to the floor like two giant wings that trailed behind her. She wore long silk gloves that glistened with innumerable silver and green jewels. The tip of every finger was cut through with a long red fingernail. Upon her head was a crown of bright peacock feathers tied in a silver band that twisted around her fine, shimmering white hair.

Monica stopped, turned and looked at the aspidistra. For the briefest moment Mariah thought she had seen him as he stood deathly still in the blackness of the deep alcove, trying to keep himself hidden. He dared to peek out, realising that she was preening her bright red lipstick and powdering her ghostly white cheeks in the shine of the brass pot. He wanted to reach out and touch her, to see if she was real. She puffed her face in a blizzard of white powder. From her tiny snakeskin bag she took a bottle of deep brown perfume and fired a sudden breath of dank musk onto her long, thin, translucent neck.

Mariah held his breath as the air around him was filled with the thick perfume that clung to his skin. Monica smiled as she raised an eyebrow, as if pleased with what she saw, and turned and walked off.

"Hey, wait for me," she crowed again as she sped after Mister Luger. "I wanna be there when you sort out Bizmillah. *This* time, Otto, give him what for."

"Get in the elevator, Monica," Luger replied coldly as the thundering from the elevator shaft came closer and the hissing of steam filled the passageway. "First we sort out the sabotage, and then we sort out Bizmillah. He's already agreed for you to do the Saw Trick—hey," he said as if he'd almost forgotten the morning. "I found you a new kid. A Colonial boy. Kind of gawky looking, with crazy, piercing eyes and swirly hair, but not a care in the world and no relatives to know if he ever went missing." Luger laughed direfully as he closed the door to the elevator and pressed the button. There was a sudden whooshing as the steam piston sucked the elevator far below.

Mariah slumped to the floor behind the plant stand, his heart pounding in his chest from being so close to Monica. He closed his eyes to stop the vision from disappearing, but like any ghost, it slowly faded.

Slowly and quietly, he looked around the edge of the alcove and into the long hallway. The painting of the prince with Luger's face stared down, his eyes still following Mariah's every movement. He could hear the distant panting of the elevator far below. He stepped cautiously into the passageway and followed the way of Luger and Monica. He stopped by the elevator and looked into the cavernous black depths that belched wisps of sulphurous smoke that swirled in the gaslight and in the sun's rays, which broke in through the row of coloured glass panes that ran the length of the passage.

Without thinking, he pressed the button to call the elevator. There was a jarring of metal and a spurt of steam that billowed up the shaft as the steam piston began to expand, forcing the cage higher and higher.

Quickly, he rushed back to his hiding place and listened for the elevator to arrive. There was a clatter as the cage stopped. Mariah waited; there was no familiar sound of the gate sliding along its metal runner. He looked out; the passageway was empty. In ten paces he was at the gate. Mariah unhooked the latch and slid the gate open, forcing it back as far as it would go and then, taking the chain that hung loosely inside the cage, hooked it there. He knew that the elevator wouldn't move until the gate was shut. If Luger and Monica wanted to come back up right away to question him about the bathing machine, they would have to use the stairs—all three hundred and sixty-six of them.

Mariah then took the brochure from his pocket and looked at the floor plan. At the end of the passageway was a door that read STAFF ONLY. The theatre, he thought as he read the plan, then looked up once more at the painting of the prince to see if the eyes were staring directly down upon him.

Then he saw something that he thought he must be imagining. The horse on which Luger rode so proudly had a strange fetlock that had suddenly doubled in thickness and resembled a long, thin hand pointing back toward the aspidistra. Mariah stepped back, wondering why he had not seen this before. Then, just as suddenly, it changed back into the front leg of the horse.

He looked at the aspidistra, then back at the plan, and for the first time noticed a small golden lion painted in the margin just where the plant stood on its fine wooden stand.

Taking a step forward, he looked up again and as he moved nearer to the painting he saw the fetlock change back into a hand. He realized that it could only be seen from that angle and at no other place in the corridor, and wondered why it was there and if anyone had seen it before. If Mister Luger had the picture commissioned, then surely he would know about the hand, hidden in such a way. Mariah ran to the aspidistra and turned and looked at the painting. All he could see was Luger staring down from the horse, clutching the reins as the beast rose up on its hind legs as if to leap to the ground.

Mariah checked the monstrous plant and stared into the brass pot. Then he saw the red lip paint smudged upon the mirrored surface, where unbeknown to him, Monica had kissed her own reflection. The heavy scent of her perfume clung to the aspidistra, and traces of white powder tipped the leaves. It was as if she were still there, those dark, burning eyes staring at him in the darkness. He closed his eyes, remembering her.

The sound of the elevator bell being rung far below woke him from his reverie. It clanged harshly, growing from a faint echo to a loud buzzing that vibrated through the shaft and into the passageway. The cage rattled as it tried vainly to close itself and answer the call of the bell.

Mariah looked at the alcove one last time, his eyes trying to pierce the darkness and see if there was anything hidden in the deep recess. Nowhere could he see the lion's head that was shown on the map. All he could see was the plant, sitting majestically on its stand, enclosed on three sides by the bright oak panelling. Then as the bell pushing grew more frenzied he saw a glint of silver in the shade of the pot. It glistened in the lamplight, hidden between the brass vessel's clawed feet.

Mariah quickly attempted to lift the pot, but some hidden thing held it in place; it was as if the claws were digging themselves into the wood, holding fast to the secret beneath it. He reached underneath, getting tantalisingly close as he touched the cold metal of the hidden object. With his little finger he nudged it slowly toward him and into the light.

It was a grand key, made of gold and engraved with the letters CCCLXVI. Mariah looked both ways, checking the oak doors and the elevator. He glanced up at the painting of the prince. Luger stared down at him. Mariah quickly grabbed the key and slid it into his right boot, checking to see if anything else had been placed beneath the dragon teeth of the plant. There was no reason to steal the key, he thought to himself as he turned to walk toward the theatre doors. But he couldn't help himself; he wanted to show Sacha and find the door it would fit.

Mariah told himself that Monica had left the key for him, knowing that he was in the darkness of the alcove and that the kiss had been a present of welcome to a new friend. As he walked by the elevator he could hear Luger shouting at Monica far below, his words rising higher like his anger. Mariah unhooked the chain and the door sprung shut, almost trapping his hand. The shaft rattled as the elevator was suddenly sucked into the depths in a gush of hot steam.

CHAPTER

❧ 7 ❧

The Great Bizmillah

The Prince Regent was like a fine oceangoing vessel; every corridor was etched in
gold leaf. Every door was made of the finest oak and everywhere was the gentle hum and
rumble of the steam engine deep in the basement.
On a high tide, when the waves lapped viciously
around its foundations, the Prince Regent looked
like a man-o'-war in full sail and set for sea, billowing steam from its fine chimneys.

Deep within its cavernous belly and far
above the line of the highest tide was the theatre.
Mariah pushed open the doors and stepped inside. It was pitch black, all but for the limelight
that shimmered upon the painted stage-boards.
There was not a sound, not a person in sight. In
front of the high proscenium arch were row upon
row of bright red velvet seats, edged in cold iron
and burnished with gold. Before the stage was

a deep pit, where, in the shadows, he could see an array of musical instruments.

He took the liberty to sit upon the end seat on the farthest row from the stage, and his sight grew used to the darkness. He plucked the key from his boot. In the half-light he looked at the key, holding it close should he have to hide it quickly if someone were to find him. He ran his fingers along the warmed edge and felt the raised lettering with his fingertips. "What have I done?" he said louder than a whisper. A sudden flush of guilt swept across his face. The key trembled in his hand. Mariah thought of running back and placing the key beneath the plant stand and leaving it for whoever had placed it there. He knew that he might get caught and that whoever had hidden the key would soon know it had vanished.

Then he had a sudden thought. "Felix," he said out loud as the thought came to him. "Felix hid the key, . . . but why?" He took the key and slid it inside the cuff of his coat sleeve, and all thought of returning it quickly went from his mind. Possessing it suddenly became extremely important and deeply exciting. It was as if he were repeating a course of action that had started before and had never been completed

He smiled to himself and patted his jacket, knowing the key was in a safe place. He sat gazing up at the highest point of the theatre, where a thousand tiny sparkles dimly lit the ceiling like a night sky.

"He was supposed to be here an hour ago." A voice echoed around the theatre as the sound of heavy rumbling thundered across the stage. "How can I teach someone if they are not here?" Bizmillah asked as he pushed a long trunk from the darkness of the wings and into the limelight.

"Delayed," said Sacha as she followed, carrying a large saw and two square silver knives double the size of dinner plates. "Mister Luger could have sent him somewhere; he could be along presently," she chirped hopefully as she scampered behind him.

"But I am to cut him in half," Bizmillah moaned as he stopped and set up the box in the centre of the stage. "How can I do that if he isn't here?" He paused and looked about him as if he had forgotten something. "Doubtless *she* will take over and this will become her trick. Would be a fine thing if *she* made a mistake and we ended up with two halves of the same boy." He grinned menacingly. "Blood on her hands . . . and she would be away from this place for good. Can't escape the gallows when you have three hundred and sixty-five witnesses to murder," he said to himself in a whisper.

"Sorry, Mister Bizmillah," Mariah shouted as he leaped from the velvet seat and ran down the steps toward the stage. "Mister Luger had much to say and insisted on sleeping whilst I waited."

"Typical, typical," Bizmillah moaned as the boy ran toward him. "I don't want you to become a last-minute boy. Young Felix had that as a very bad habit and look what happened to him."

"What did happen to him?" Sacha asked as she set the saw and the knives on the boards of the stage.

Bizmillah coughed nervously. "Ran away," he muttered. "They all run away, never can stay the distance, never last more than a few weeks. I think *she* eats them." He glared at Mariah. "Now that you are here, I can show you what you have to do. It is quite simple. I provide the *magic* and you provide your lovely bones . . . for me to cut in half."

The magician signalled to Sacha to get ready as he opened the box's lid. She ran into the wings and brought back a chair, onto which she quickly climbed and stepped into the box. It had a hole cut for her neck and, at the other end, two smaller holes for her feet. Sacha lay down as if she had done this a thousand times before. She turned and smiled at Mariah, who by now had walked up the small flight of steps at the side of the stage. He looked on anxiously as Bizmillah closed the lid with great ceremony and locked the top with a large golden key that appeared in his hand as if it had been plucked from the air.

"Now the lock," Bizmillah said as he turned the key and then made it vanish into thin air. "Ladies and Gentlemen," he said as if he were before a full house, "I, the *Great Bizmillah*, bring you something so magical that you have never seen the likes of it before. Tonight, I will cut this young girl in half and restore her to full health. I demand one thing . . . *silence*!"

Mariah stepped back, unsure what was to come. He looked at Sacha, trying to catch her attention as she lay peacefully, a smile upon her face.

Bizmillah took two large knives and, one by one, thrust them into the top of the box. Sacha screamed and writhed, her face contorted, her feet kicking, and then suddenly was still. Her head flopped to one side, eyes closed as if she were dead.

"*See*," Bizmillah shouted. "*Death* . . . and now to prove to you that she is truly cut in two, I will saw through the box for all to see."

He grabbed the saw and began to frantically cut the box in half. Mariah couldn't contain himself any longer. He ran to Sacha, who, hearing his footsteps cross the stage, opened one eye and winked at him. "It's a trick, Mariah—I'm not dead."

"Help me, boy," Bizmillah called to him as he finished sawing the box in two. "I need you to turn the box, and all shall see that the *Great Bizmillah* has worked his wonderful magic yet again."

Together they turned the box to show everyone that Sacha had been cut in half. From one end her head flopped from the hole. From the other her feet stuck out, her shiny black shoes and white stockings in plain sight.

"Now," he shouted, "I will bring her back to life." With that, he blew upon his hand. Sparkles of silver dust shot from his fingertips, and purple and blue flames danced like fireflies across his palm, then exploded in a bright white light, engulfing the box in its shimmering, cold flame.

Sacha moaned and wailed as if in great agony. She tilted back her head and looked to Mariah, then she looked to her side and saw the box with the feet next to her head.

"Are you alive?" Bizmillah asked, though it was obvious to the entire world that Sacha was very much alive and in great pain. He didn't wait for her reply. "Then wiggle your feet."

Mariah gawped as her feet moved from side to side then up and down.

"See . . . even though she has been cut in half, by the power of the Great Bizmillah she has power over her feet." Bizmillah took the box and spun it around on its casters, her feet still moving, separated from her body. "A wonder of magic, the human frame cut apart and yet through the tendrils of the imagination she has control over her body."

Mariah stood back, amazed at what he saw, unsure if this was magic or some kind of dark sorcery. Bizmillah noticed the look of surprise on his face and gave a gentle laugh.

"*Now*," he said in the loudest voice he could gather, "the magic of the ages will take the girl and, by spiritual forces, knit every piece of flesh together again." He nodded to Mariah to turn the other box toward him as he moved the two halves together and pressed them firmly shut. Bizmillah began to pull on a long red cloth that slipped from his sleeve and covered the two boxes with an ever-growing mound of red fabric. He fumbled beneath the cloth, his hands slipping the two flat knives from their place and throwing them to the floor. "It is time," he said as he threw two white doves high into the air, having magically appeared from inside his jacket. "The girl will be joined together," he shouted as one of the birds flew high into the air circling around his head whilst the other fell to the stage twitching and unable to open its wings.

Bizmillah magicked the key into his hand and plunged it into the lock, releasing the catch and setting Sacha free. She leaped to her feet and gave a majestic bow. Mariah began to applaud, enthralled by what he had seen and taken in by the power of the moment, unsure if he had been part of some miracle or magical spectacle.

"Your first lesson in magic," Bizmillah boasted as he stepped forward and took Sacha by the hand to join her in the encore bow she gave to the empty theatre. "Tonight, it will be your turn—to see if you're ready to take over the role at the Sunday shows. Do you think you can do as well as Sacha?"

"But what if my guts won't join together again or I cannot tell my feet what to do when they are set so close to my head?"

Sacha laughed. "It's a trick, false feet that move mechanically. Look."

She lifted the lid of the box. A complex mass of wires and springs filled the bottom of the trunk. By their side was a pair of faux feet, dressed in a pair of shoes and socks identical to what she was wearing. Next to them was a large cogwheel and coiled spring.

"Clockwork," she said as she wound the key and pushed the feet through the two holes. "See this, this is the catch that the Great Bizmillah presses when he brings you back to life. Watch the feet dance." Sacha pressed the switch and the spring whirred into life, pushing the feet up and down, jangling the shoes on the end of the narrow wooden ankles. "Who would know the difference?" she said as she reached into the box and pulled out a black pair of boots. "Look, we have these to match your boots, all you have to do is get in the box, and as you do, push the feet through the hole."

"That's not what bothers me," Mariah said as Bizmillah

busied himself picking up the stunned dove from the floor and trying to shake the life back into it. "What happens about being cut in half?"

Sacha smiled. "As soon as he puts the lid on the box, lift up your feet and curl them against your chest. When the knives go down, you are already out of the way. When he slices through with the saw, there's nothing there to cut in half. At the end of the trick, you come back to life . . . Don't forget to pull back the feet. Felix once left them sticking out of the box, and everyone laughed."

"Apart from me," Bizmillah growled as he attempted to revive the dove. "I don't like to be made a fool of. I am the star and you the puppet; never forget that and we will be the best of friends."

"I'll never . . . ," Mariah replied. "What else do I do?"

"Sweep, clean, polish and feed," Bizmillah said as he put the dead dove into his top pocket like a handkerchief. "You are in charge of the doves."

"And the snakes," Sacha interrupted quickly.

"And the snakes," echoed Bizmillah. "You also clean everything I use. But don't touch the frontier pistol. It was given to me by Mister Luger and only *I* can fire it."

"Very well," Mariah said as he looked at Sacha, hoping she would take him away. "What now?"

"Desperate to get away from me?" Bizmillah asked. "Sacha can take you to the cellars and show you what to do. There is a place for everything. Set the traps and the drops, and make ready for the performance. Tonight is your big night. There is nothing like the roar of the crowd to fill the heart with passion. It is more potent than any sorcery I know."

Together they pushed the sawing box into the storeroom at the side of the stage. Sacha motioned for Mariah not to say a word, putting her finger against her lips as she kept an eye on Bizmillah. He paced the stage, gesturing to himself as if he were addressing a large crowd. She led Mariah down a long flight of stairs lit by faint gas lamps on every landing.

Mariah could smell the sea as they descended ever deeper. It was a strange red brick staircase that went one way then another without a fulcrum or any visible means of support. Fingers of brine hung down from the ceiling like icicles and shuddered with the rumbling of the steam engine. He wanted to speak, but every time he opened his mouth or made even the slightest sound, Sacha gestured for him to be silent. It was only when they had gone down several levels and the walls began to drip with long drops of foul salt water that she stopped and turned to him.

"We are below sea level," Sacha said, the damp green algae around her feet cladding the step like a slippery glove. She turned to face a dark, stained door with rat-gnawed edges. "This is where we keep all his tricks." She pointed to a dark passageway that led off into the blackness. "Sometimes the tide seeps its way down there and you can hear the water flooding the passageway."

"You can go down farther?" Mariah asked in disbelief.

"Three more floors," she said proudly, as if it were a great achievement of hers to have such a fine building. "Mister Luger has his laboratory down there, although I've only been once. I'm not allowed in. You can only get there at low tide. Down the steps, along the passage, then up the other side above the height of the sea. I nearly got trapped."

"What's inside?" Mariah asked, intrigued that anyone could have a workshop so deep underground.

"It's where he makes his inventions, that's all I know," Sacha said as she slowly turned the key in the lock. "This belongs to Bizmillah; no one comes here. If he wants anything, he will send you. Keeps a lot of his stuff in his room, but he'll never let you see it." She stepped inside and lit the gas lamp.

There in the deep cellar was a jumble of boxes; masks; old, discarded conjuring tricks and costumes of princes and pharaohs. In the corner sat a stringed doll with a shiny porcelain face that stared at Mariah blindly with its bulging eyes. It had ruby-painted cheeks that shone in the gaslight and thin purple lips that scowled at him as if he shouldn't be there. He shuddered at the look, feeling that the doll knew who he was, that beneath the fine china skin was flesh and blood, cold blood pumped by a lifeless heart.

Mariah followed Sacha into the room and purposefully turned his back to the doll, making no mention of her. Sacha explained everything in the cellar, pointing to the various items and explaining their use in Bizmillah's Magical Extravaganza.

For some reason, Mariah couldn't concentrate on her words. All he could feel was the stare of the porcelain doll chilling the back of his neck and making every hair stand on end. As she spoke, he was convinced that he could hear someone taking laboured breaths behind him.

Then a large looking glass caught his eye. It hung majestically in a dark wooden frame on the wall before him, dangling from two rusting chains. He glanced quickly at it, more out of curiosity than to see his own reflection. He gasped; the doll was gone. It was as if, when his back was turned, it had got to its feet and walked from the room.

"And one more thing," Sacha said energetically. "Let me introduce you to . . ." She turned and swept her hand in a long gesture, then looked puzzled. "She's gone . . . I'm sure she was here a moment ago . . . Did you see . . . ?"

"A porcelain doll?" Mariah asked anxiously as he edged his way slowly to the door.

"I'm sure she was here . . . sat right there as we came in," Sacha said, pointing to the empty chair. "Someone must have moved her."

"Or she moved herself?" Mariah asked warily as he looked around the room for the doll.

"Impossible," Sacha said as she went to a tall cabinet that stood like an upturned coffin beside the door. "Once I found her in here; funny, the same thing happened then, too. It was the first time I brought Felix into the cellar."

Mariah didn't want to see what was in the upturned chest. He looked at the floor and kicked a piece of driftwood across the stone slabs. He heard Sacha pull open the two wooden doors, which creaked on the salt-rusted hinges.

"Told ya, must 'a been seeing things," Sacha said triumphantly. "Meet Old Scratty—she's from Iceland. Bizmillah bought her from a wreck sale . . . All that was left from a four-masted ship that had gone down on Mascus Rocks. They found her bobbing in the sea . . . All the crew were dead." Mariah looked up warily, greeted by the thin smile of Old Scratty, dressed in her black velvet dress and green silk slippers, hanging limply by a long cord from a metal peg.

CHAPTER

❊ 8 ❊

Similia Similibus Curantur

T he great black curtain fell across the stage as Bizmillah took his final bow. From the shadowy wings, Mariah peeped out of the thin slit that was secretly cut into the panel at the left of the stage. The immense gas chandelier that hung from the gold domed ceiling burst suddenly into light. For the first time he could see that he had played his part to a full house.

Staggering from the theatre was a multitude of finely dressed men and women who had looked on in awe as Mariah had been successfully cut in half and then reunited with the rest of his body. The only blemish to the evening was that Mariah had overcoiled the spring to the mechanical legs. When Bizmillah had asked Mariah to move his feet—the audience fully believing the poor boy had been severed in the trunk—the artificial legs had jumped into action, moving back and forth so quickly that the box shook and Mariah looked as if he would be kicked in the head by his own feet.

Bizmillah, being the Great Magician, had quickly seized the moment and, in his finest Transaldovian accent, had told the audience that the boy had fallen under the influence of his sorcery. After Mariah had been put back together, Bizmillah had even gone so far as to call a fat old man from the bemused spectators to come and inspect the boy to see if he had any visible wounds. This, the man had done with immense enthusiasm, roughly squeezing Mariah around the middle and exclaiming to the world that he didn't leak. Once the inspection had been completed, Mariah was heralded a hero by a standing ovation that lasted for several minutes, turning his face redder and redder. Bizmillah pushed him from the stage into the darkness of the wings. He threw a dove from his hand, and it circled high above their heads and then exploded into a shower of silver petals that floated down and landed gently upon the crowd.

Now Mariah watched from the wings as the theatre slowly emptied.

"We're not finished," Sacha said from nearby. "Bizmillah leaves everything to us . . . There's no time to stand dreaming."

Mariah was about to reply when he saw a man by himself in the back row of the small side balcony that overlooked the stage. He was wearing evening dress, with a silver bow tie, and constantly brushed back his long hair with his hand as he looked around. He seemed to be looking for someone or something and waiting for the theatre to empty. Mariah squinted through the narrow slit, unable to get a clear view of his face from that distance. Then the man got to his feet, walked slowly to the edge of the balcony and looked down into the stalls, casting his eyes over every empty seat.

"Black," Mariah said as he instinctively ducked back into the darkness.

"Who?" asked Sacha, bending down to catch a white rat that scurried about her feet.

"The man from the spa pool—he was on the train from London—said he was staying here 'til March," Mariah whispered as Sacha loaded the rat back into the barrel of the small cannon from which it would be fired.

"Let me see," she said, pushing Mariah to one side and peering through the narrow slit.

Black descended from the balcony, down a vine-clad column of stairs, into the stalls below. He checked underneath each seat with his hand whilst looking around as if he did not want to be discovered.

"He's searching the theatre," Sacha said too loud, her voice echoing from the stage.

Black stopped what he was doing and hid behind a seat. For several moments he was out of sight. Slowly and carefully, he peeped from his hiding place, looking around for whoever had spoken, not realising that the voice had come from behind the stage. Then he continued searching underneath the seats as he made his way along the empty row.

"You watch," Sacha said quietly into Mariah's ear, "I'm going to ask what he's up to."

Before Mariah could reply, Sacha was gone. Mariah got to his feet and peered out again.

The huge chandelier grew dimmer by the second, as if it were starved of gas to give it light. Far to the right came a sudden flash that caught Mariah's eye as the door jumped open and quickly closed again. Black kept searching, his head down, a sullen grimace upon his face.

Then Mariah saw Sacha sneaking quietly along the row, getting closer and closer to Black.

"Lost something?" she said in a loud voice that startled Black, causing him to jump to his feet, twist around in surprise and then fall backward to the floor.

"I . . . I . . . ," Black said.

"I can help you look if you want," she said cheerfully, as if this sort of thing happened every day. "What are we looking for?"

"A . . . a cuff link," he said, seeming flustered. "Great sentimental value, belonged to my brother, actually . . ."

Black looked at Sacha. She smiled benignly, then took hold of his sleeve and pulled the cuff of his shirt. "Like this one?" she asked, grabbing the gold link on the cuff of his crisp, starched shirt.

"No, quite different," Black said as he stepped back from the girl. "What business is it of yours?"

"Just want to be helpful, Mister Black," Sacha said innocently. "I work here and often find things the guests leave behind. I know how painful it can be to lose something of value."

"Yes . . . painful," Black replied, taking two paces back and looking her up and down. "You work here, did you say?" he asked as he rummaged in his pocket. "Well then, perhaps you would keep a lookout for what I search for?" Black held out his white-gloved hand. "These were once a pair; since coming to the Prince Regent I am unable to find the other. I know my brother will be most disappointed should I have lost it." Black held out a small golden skull. Two green jewelled eyes stared at her, twinkling in the light from the vast chandelier. Its jaw dangled open, set on the tiniest hinges she had ever seen.

"That's a cuff link?" Sacha asked, enthralled by its beauty.

Black saw the look on her face. "You admire that which is well made. Find the other and there will be a crisp five-pound note for you to spend on whatever you want." He dangled the skull before her eyes.

Mariah saw the skull, the match for the one hidden beneath his bed. Charity had been right, it did belong to Black.

"A lot of money for the ransom of a cuff link," Sacha said

as she prodded the jewelled eyes and flicked the hinged jaw with her finger.

"A special piece, the set is one of a kind, and more than that—my brother's favourite."

"Must be special, your brother," Sacha said, sitting down and looking up at the domed ceiling.

Black said nothing. He turned, slumped into a seat four places from Sacha and looked up.

"What do you see?" he asked quietly as the dim flickering of the enormous crystal lamp danced in the golden dome.

"A night sky, angels dancing," Sacha replied.

"That's a good thing," Black said sadly. "I came here to rest, but I haven't yet found any peace in this place."

"My mother said that peace and contentment are found on the inside, and not the out. Just going somewhere different won't change your heart," Sacha replied.

"Then she is a wise woman," he said curtly as he got to his feet, brushing several flecks of shining dust from his coat sleeves. "Now remember, five pounds. I am in room three six five." He stopped and looked at her quizzically. "How did you know my name?"

"You're a guest, here until March—Mister Luger told all the staff."

"Are you sure it was Luger who told you who I was?"

"Who else?" Sacha asked with her best innocent smile.

"Is she bothering you?" came the sharp voice of Bizmillah from the doorway behind them. "You've work to do, and talking with guests isn't part of that, Sacha," he said sternly as he ambled toward them, gripping his black cane. "I will see the gentleman out of the theatre; it can be a very dangerous place late at night, and we wouldn't want an accident to befall you, would we?" Bizmillah gestured with a quick nod for Sacha to go as he turned to escort Black to the door.

"She was only—" Black sprung to her defence.

"And now that *only* is finished and she will return to her work," Bizmillah said slowly as he walked him to the door. "Get Mariah to feed the doves before he turns in and load the cannon . . . and polish the swords . . . , then you can finish for the night," he barked to Sacha as he walked away, pulling Black by the sleeve.

Mariah slid out from behind the curtain as Bizmillah and Black left the theatre. He jumped from the stage and ran across the backs of the seats, leaping like a gazelle, until he reached Sacha.

"Quickly," he said anxiously. "We have to go back to the tower, to my room, I have something you *must* see."

"But Bizmillah said . . . ," Sacha protested.

"We'll come back later; he never said *when* we had to do it. And we've cleaned and cleaned all day . . . Please?"

She looked at the clock that ticked away under the balcony. "One hour . . . Promise?"

The elevator rattled to the top floor of the hotel; in the corner opposite where they stood was a discarded umbrella with a white bone handle.

"Always wanted one of those," Mariah said as he picked up the umbrella. "My father had one just the same."

The elevator rattled violently and began to slow down. Mariah gripped the brass handrail that circled the cage as they jerked and shook. Then the cage filled with gushing steam, making it difficult for Mariah to see Sacha.

"I don't think it's going to make it. Sometimes they turn off the steam for a bit, just long enough to let the boiler cool. We're stuck for now." Her words faded as the elevator shuddered to a complete halt, the gas lantern dimming to a soft glow that hardly filled the cage. "Open the gate, Mariah. We could have made the top floor."

Mariah hung the umbrella over his arm and slid the heavy

gate to one side. The steam elevator had stopped a floor below the tower. He looked into the long corridor, then turned to Sacha as he pointed to a door. "Three six five," he said quietly. "Black."

Mariah stepped out of the elevator and listened at the door. There was no sound. In the centre of the door was a brass plate that could be slid from one side to the other.

"Out," Mariah said softly as he read the sign. "It says he's out."

Footsteps clattered from the stairway next to the elevator.

"Hide," Sacha murmured as she pulled open a small cupboard door at the far side of the elevator and jumped inside. "Quickly . . . inside."

Mariah squashed himself into the cupboard, which appeared to be filled with old teapots and empty bottles.

"Careful," Sacha said as he pressed her against the far wall, pulling the door closed until only a chink of light cast a glow down the side of his face.

The door to the stairs opened. Bizmillah walked onto the dark landing, cane in hand, his tailcoat blustering behind him. He stopped outside the room opposite the elevator and looked down the corridor, unaware that he was being watched from the maid's cupboard.

Looking over his shoulder one more time, he unlocked the door and vanished quickly into the darkened room, closing the door and locking it behind him.

"Bizmillah went into Black's room," Mariah said as another set of footsteps pounded the floorboards of the stairway above their heads. Sacha slithered to the floor of the cupboard to see out into the passageway as the door to the corridor opened again.

Black looked back and forth as he toyed with the cuff link on his left sleeve. He appeared as if he'd been tattered by a savage wind, his long locks forlorn, his dress and manner dishevelled. He gripped his silk top hat, the top crumpled and torn, fine strands of silk hanging down. He rubbed a streak of mud from his face and then fumbled clumsily in his pockets, dropping his hat and turning to watch it roll toward the maid's cupboard.

"If this is life . . . ," Black grumbled. "First my umbrella is missing, and now my hat is ruined." He picked up the top hat, took a key from his pocket and opened the door to his room. A chink of amber light from the wick of the gas lamp flooded into the darkened corridor, illuminating the crowned pattern on the deep runner that went the length of the passageway, edged by dark wood. Black looked back and forth, checking the passageway, then stepped into the room. Before closing the door, he peered out again, making sure he had not been followed.

"He'll find Bizmillah in his room," Sacha whispered.

"We can listen at the door," Mariah said as he grappled with the large umbrella that he now knew belonged to Black. "He'll have found him by now; if he thought Bizmillah was an intruder, it wouldn't be so quiet. This meeting has been planned. When I met him on the train, I knew there was something more to him." Mariah dropped his voice quieter. "In my room I have the other cuff link; he dropped it in the train. And there's something else," he continued, hoping she could be trusted with his secret. "A man at Kings Cross Station gave me a deck of cards, said I should keep it safe, then tell him where I was and he would come for them." Mariah paused and looked through the narrow crack in the door, listening intently for the slightest sound. He looked at Sacha in the half-light. "And something else . . . something that I know Felix once touched . . . I found a key."

"Key? What kind of key?" Sacha asked as she pushed open the door and got to her feet, edging her way toward Black's room. She left Mariah no time to reply as she pressed her ear against the door, gesturing for him to be quiet.

Inside, she could hear muffled voices. She pointed at the door to the stairs and opened her eyes wide to signal for Mariah to get ready for their escape. Bizmillah and Black talked quickly in a language that Sacha could not understand.

"What are they saying?" Mariah asked as he pushed on the door to the stairwell.

A sudden thump inside the room and the sound of heavy footsteps approaching the door told them that they had been overheard.

"Quickly," shouted Bizmillah, "unlock the door—someone is outside."

At the same time, footsteps came from the stairwell.

"Twice in one day," Monica moaned, her words tapping faster than the heels of her stilettos. "Fix that elevator, Otto; it's killing my feet."

Sacha looked at Mariah, her face lined in panic as Black's door handle began to rattle.

"The elevator," Mariah seethed through his teeth as the door to the stairwell burst open.

Sacha jumped from the door to the open gate, quickly followed by Mariah. He slammed the gate shut and closed the door, hoping that there would be enough steam to take them down at least one floor.

Sacha pressed the buttons for the floors below, frantically banging them as Black finally opened the door to his room.

There was a loud hiss and a sudden grunt as the elevator woke from its sleep. It shuddered and groaned as the feeble pressure rose in its pipes. Suddenly the carriage dropped several feet in a split second. For that brief moment Mariah and Sacha took off from the floor and floated like dandelion seeds, and then crashed into the deck of the carriage as the elevator stopped dead.

Mariah looked at Sacha as she rolled on the floor. "Do you think we got away?" he asked as he got up, brushing the dirt from his trousers.

Sacha scrambled to her feet. "Open the door," she said quickly. "They'll have heard the elevator and be down the stairs after us . . . We have to get out." Mariah grabbed the door and slid the gate quickly to one side.

This was not the hotel; it was somewhere far different. On the wall opposite was a large clock the size of a man; a long golden second hand swirled around its wooden face . . . backward.

CHAPTER

✻ 9 ✻

Antithetical Accumulations

In two steps Mariah had left the elevator and Sacha behind him. The clicking of the huge clock and the swirl of the second hand had drawn him into the long, brightly lit corridor. Sacha followed quickly, picking up the umbrella and slamming it into the track of the gate so that it couldn't close. She looked for the staircase that she knew should be on the right side of the shaft. To her surprise, all she could see was a wall covered in flocked wallpaper picturing large red swans with piercing black eyes. Several dark oak doors were spaced evenly along the far wall, each one edged in brightly polished brass. They had neither handles nor locks. Just circular brass plates, each with a small jagged slit.

"We have to get away from here and back to the tower," Sacha said urgently, pulling on Mariah's coat sleeve. He was transfixed by the whooshing of the clock; the large golden hands spun around and around, counterclockwise.

"Where are we?" Mariah asked as he stared at the small gold numerals that edged the clock face.

"I've never been on this level. I thought I'd seen the entire hotel, but . . ." She looked surprised, staring at the row of silver-spanned crystal lamps that dangled from the ceiling and lit the passage. "They shine without gas . . . They're so bright." Sacha looked away from the brilliance of the light. "We can't stay, Mariah. If they come down the stairs, they'll find us."

Mariah didn't reply. He stood before the clock watching the hands spinning faster and faster. The hour blade flashed brightly in the dazzling light of the chandeliers. The second hand spun like a whip, its tip bending back with its furious speed.

"Mariah!" Sacha insisted.

Mariah broke free from his trance. "What?" he murmured.

"Bizmillah . . . Black . . . They'll have heard us get in the elevator—we have to get away." Sacha left him standing by the clock and searched the corridor for a door to take them to the tower. "It must be here somewhere."

Mariah followed, his mind feeling numbed by the whirring of the clock.

"Find a door out of here," Sacha cried as she pushed against the doors, none of them opening.

Mariah was still in a daze. He stood near a window, partly covered with thick velvet curtains printed with swans. "There's nothing here . . . nothing," he muttered.

"There has to be. We have to get out!" Sacha shouted as she pushed past him, running to the window and pulling back the curtain.

The brass-framed window had no glass. Where each pane should have been was a black-painted square wedged with fresh putty. Sacha tapped a panel with her fingers and it clunked with the dull thud of thick metal. She grasped the brass handle at the side of the frame and pulled it creakily toward her. There was a hiss of escaping air as if she had opened the lid of a sealed jar. The smell of the sea was sucked up into the passageway and shreds of sea mist fell about their feet.

"It's not a window, it's a tunnel," Sacha said. "Look."

Mariah rubbed his eyes and stared into the blackness. The hole seemed to go on forever.

"That's our way out," Sacha said excitedly. "Let's see where it goes."

"What about Bizmillah?" Mariah asked. "What if he follows us in and it's a dead end?"

"Don't you see?" she asked. "Bizmillah can't find us here. This is a secret floor. The only way to it is by the elevator. We're here by mistake. If the steam pump hadn't failed, it would have taken us back to the theatre. But we're here instead, between floors, on a secret level. And this tunnel leads to the sea; you can smell it."

"Then how do other people get here?" he asked.

"They stop the elevator or come through the tunnel. But Bizmillah and Black wouldn't know of this place. It belongs to Mister Luger."

"How do you know that?"

"It's obvious," she said. "The sign of the swan, it's everywhere. Luger has a ring with the same crest."

"Why a secret floor?" Mariah asked.

"Why not? He built the hotel; he can do what he likes. Now I know where he goes. He often disappears for hours and no one can find him. I bet you he comes here. Look at that," Sacha said, pointing to the door behind Mariah. "That one has some letters on it—do you think it says Luger in Latin? *c-c-c-l-x-v-i.*"

"They're not letters, they're Roman numerals," Mariah

said, looking closely. "I tried to tell you earlier that I found a key under the aspidistra in the corridor by the elevator." He fumbled in his coat sleeve and pulled out the key. "The letters match."

"Let's try it," Sacha said. She snatched the key and compared the numerals. "We can look inside."

"No, Sacha—it's not right to go looking in other people's rooms," Mariah protested.

"Then why did you take it? Gonna turn it in, were ya?"

"Maybe," he said diffidently. "Maybe I was."

"Maybe you were gonna look for the room by yourself and sneak in and see what there was to take," she said. "Now you've found it. So come on, let's just sneak a peek, and then we'll put the key back where you found it."

"I'm not going in. Luger already knows about the Galvanised Bathing Machine. I heard him talking about it this morning. If he finds out we've been here, then . . . then we're finished."

"We're already finished. Better hanged for a sheep than a lamb, and you never know, it might be another way back to the tower," Sacha insisted. "Leave the window open so we can get out if we need to. The keyhole is here somewhere, but I just can't see it."

"It's not in the door, it's here," Mariah said, pointing to the lower edge of the thick brass plate that bordered the door. There, just above the floor, was a small keyhole set into the brass. "You go ahead, Sacha. I'll wait here and look out for Luger."

Sacha looked at him for a moment and smiled. She saw the worry on his face and knew he didn't want to be there.

"Think of it as a game," she said, bending down and putting the key into the lock. "What can they do to us? If we get the sack, then I'll find you another job; they're four a penny in these parts."

"I keep thinking of Felix. It's as if he were here, trying to tell us something. When I found the key, I just knew that he had touched it before me. It was like the key told me."

"Talking keys? What's next, Mariah?" Sacha said as she turned the key and opened the door.

The strong smell of cigar smoke seeped from the room like a thick fog. The door was much heavier than they expected, so Mariah held it open as she creeped into the dark room. He looked at the door's edge and saw that it was made of solid metal.

From the brightness of the hallway, he could see the far corners of the room cast in long black shadows. It was cluttered with furniture. Two high-backed leather chairs faced a large brick fireplace with a smouldering glow in the hearth. Between them was a narrow table embossed with patches of red leather. In the centre of the table was a gigantic glass bowl, filled with musty grey ash. Hanging from the lip of the bowl was the stub of a fat cigar wrapped in a gold band. Over the fireplace was the stuffed head of a tiger that sneered at Mariah, its tongue hanging from the side of its cavernous mouth. In the far corner was another door that had two brass bolts at the top and bottom.

Sacha edged farther into the room, making ready to run. She felt as if she were being watched. Turning, she saw a tall case, a sarcophagus cut into the shape of a man. It was encrusted with gold leaf, and a face was painted upon it in blue and red, with deep green eyes edged in gold. A crown decorated its head, carved into the wood. It stared at her with a sullen smile on its red lips.

"Look, Mariah," Sacha said as she stepped away from it so he could see. "What is it?"

Mariah didn't want to go into the room. It was as if something were telling him not to. He leaned in cautiously, holding on to the door frame. Sacha pointed to the sarcophagus.

"Looks like a coffin," Mariah said. "I saw a drawing like that in the *London Gazette*. One had been stolen from the British Museum. They thought it was filled with gold."

"Shall we open it? We could be rich," Sacha said, already running her hand around the edge of the coffin looking for a gap to pry open.

"There could be someone inside." Mariah coughed, and the thought of opening the coffin made him step back into the passageway. He looked back and forth, peeking into the shaft of the tunnel and then toward the elevator. "Don't do it, Sacha. Come on, let's go. We've seen enough. We can come back later." Mariah edged backward.

"Just one look," Sacha insisted as she pulled the lid, trying to slide her hand into the narrow gap she had found. "It must open."

"Leave it, Sacha. I read that sometimes they're cursed — if you open it . . ."

He spoke too late. Sacha had got a grip on the lid, and it held for a second and then suddenly gave way. She slowly and gently opened it as a cloud of thick dust fell about her feet and then billowed up into the air, swirling around her as if she had been engulfed in a swarm of black flies. Mariah hid behind the door, not wanting to look, the black dust spilling like sand across the polished wooden floor.

"I can see . . . I can see a . . . ," Sacha said breathlessly, stepping back from the coffin as the lid fell from its hinges and dropped heavily. It clattered against the wall, spilling a rack of military swords.

Mariah looked up as the dust settled. Sacha was blackened from head to foot. She stood deathly still, hand over her mouth, staring into the darkness.

"What is it?" Mariah asked, seeing the dread in her face and not wanting or daring to look behind the door for fear of what he would see.

"*Felix* . . . ," she said slowly. Her throat went dry. "*It's* . . . *Felix*. He's . . . dead." Through the slowly clearing dust, Sacha stared into the face of her friend. Felix stared back through open, waxen eyes, his skin pulled tight across his lifeless face.

Sacha held back a scream, pressing her hand against her mouth. She stepped back, pushing Mariah from the doorway, stepping into the light. Stumbling from the room, she fell to the floor and curled herself into a ball. She covered her eyes to keep out the image that had burned into her mind.

"No . . . ," she sobbed.

Mariah hesitated, then slowly peered around the door and into the room. The sarcophagus lay open, its painted lid upon the floor. Several sharp swords were scattered about. In the glow from the fire, he could make out the features of the boy, who stared blindly at him.

Felix had been wrapped tightly in cloth bandages from the tips of his feet to the nape of his neck. The dark brown rags held his arms to his sides. His skin had faded, so that it had a cold, translucent radiance that shimmered in the meagre light. Mariah stepped toward the boy to see more. He gulped back a cough as the dust fell about him. It was as if the body had been covered in a fine, drying lime that now glinted across the wooden floor in small mounds.

Outside in the corridor, Sacha sobbed, mourning her friend. In anger she pulled at her hair and banged her tight fists against the floor. Inside the room, Mariah stepped closer to the body. He looked at its face, knowing something was not right.

He reached out and touched Felix's skin, and felt the soft, warm smoothness. He scratched the skin, peeling from it a long curl of fine pale wax. He took a coin from his pocket and scraped it along Felix's bottom lip. A furrow of red wax peeled off against the side of the coin.

Whatever Felix was, he wasn't dead.

"A waxwork . . . a double," Mariah exclaimed as he wiped the wax against his finger. "It's not Felix but a wax doll . . . a manikin . . ."

Sacha didn't hear; she had pushed herself against the wall, pulling the collar of her jacket around her head, pressing her face into the carpet.

"Sacha, it's not him," Mariah repeated as he examined the wax manikin, pulling out a strand of neatly combed hair from its head. "Listen to me—it's a waxwork."

She stopped sobbing and looked up in disbelief. She got to her feet and stumbled toward him. "What do you mean?" she asked as she slowly edged her way closer.

"See for yourself," Mariah insisted.

The manikin stared at them through sorrowful, blue glass eyes that looked as though they welled up with crystal tears.

"But it looks like Felix," Sacha said as she stepped warily toward the figure.

"Ceroplastica," Mariah said as he gently touched the waxen nose. "The art of taking a human image and creating it in wax. Once read a penny dreadful that told all about it. Never thought I would see one."

She reached out to touch the lifeless skin. "He's warm," she exclaimed as her fingers smoothed themselves against the soft wax. "Who did this?"

"Luger, who else?" Mariah replied as he looked about the room. "I don't think Felix ran away at all. I bet you he's still here . . . somewhere." As he spoke, he looked at the door by the fireplace. It had a solid brass handle that was so polished that it reflected the whole room in an upturned universe. To one side was a key, set into a brass ring within the door. Mariah strode across the room, leaving Sacha staring at the waxwork. "Can't have them coming in," he said, about to turn the key and lock the door, not daring to see what was on the other side. He stopped and listened. Coming through the dark oak panel was the gentle whirring of the steam generator.

"What is it?" Sacha asked as she saw Mariah listening intently. "Take a look—it could be another way out."

Mariah slid back the two brass bolts and twisted the handle at the same time as he turned the key. It gave a sudden and forceful clunk as it jumped home. He slowly and carefully opened the door a hair's breadth and peered into the next room. There was absolute blackness except for the narrow chink from the open door. He sniffed the air; the smell of the sea greeted him. Far away he could hear the lapping of water.

A barb of light pierced the darkness. It reflected like an arrow from wall to wall, jumping back and forth as if being carried by an unsteady hand. He could hear someone approaching, feet scraping against the wet steps.

Just as Mariah started to close the door, it was snatched from his fingers by a sudden draught that slammed it firmly shut. The sound thundered through the darkened room and along the passageway, deeper and deeper to the depths of the lapping waters.

"They're coming," he shouted to Sacha. "To the tunnel!" He ran across the room, bumping into a small table and knocking a tall plaster statue to the floor.

CHAPTER

❧ 10 ❧

Quare Impedit

Moments later, the shining brass handle turned slowly, and the oak door opened a crack. A thin, black-gloved hand appeared, bright red fingernails piercing the dark silk. A feather from a black boa dropped to the floor, and was blown across the wooden tiles until it rested in a faraway corner, in the strands of a large spider's web.

The door opened reluctantly, creaking on its hinges as a black, pointed shoe pushed against it. From the darkness a thin face peered out, the bright eyes circled in thick, dark kohl liner.

"Quietly," Luger said. "They could still be there. I heard him shout as he slammed the door."

"Why am I in front of you?" Monica whispered as he pushed her forward.

"To see what I cannot," he said curtly. "And a good thief would never hit a woman . . ."

Monica walked slowly into the room, pulling her feather dress around her shoulders, and shuddered as she looked around.

"They've gone," she said finally, flopping into the chair by the fire and taking off her shoes. "Who do you think they were?"

Luger didn't speak. With his hand firmly gripping the hilt of his cane, he stared at the sarcophagus, his monocle quivering in his eye socket. He paced back and forth, inspecting the room, trying to piece together what had happened there. Stopping by the sarcophagus, he bent down and picked up a handful of black dust and let it dribble through his fingers.

"We have been meddled with," he said coldly as he watched the small black particles fall to the floor. "Could it be . . . ?" Luger stopped speaking, seeming afraid to continue.

"In the hotel . . . here?" she said nervously, sitting up for a moment, then sliding back into the chair. "That'd be too close for any kind of comfort." Monica sat dozily by the lingering flames.

"He could be here searching for it, too. Maybe someone told him it was here?"

"Maybe you're dreaming."

"Then who did this?" Luger asked impatiently as he flung the last pieces of sand at the wall. "This didn't just happen. Someone broke into my private suite, opened the box and found the manikin. What were they looking for?"

"Did they find your magic box?" She laughed as she idly toyed with the pieces of the broken statue, which were strewn across the floor beside her.

"I wouldn't leave it here . . . not here . . . Has to be kept in the dark, locked away." Luger walked into the corridor. To his right the window that led to the tunnel was tightly shut and covered by the swan curtains, which hung down to the floor. He checked the brass handle. "They didn't go this way," he said as he turned and leaned into the room, where Monica was stretched out like a sleeping cat over the arm of the chair. "Comfortable?" he asked crossly as he looked along the passageway to the steam elevator.

Monica snored in reply, snuggled in a nest of black feathers.

"Do it myself . . . ," Luger muttered as he strode along the passageway to the elevator. The hands of the clock whirred beside him, glinting in the bright light. The umbrella was still wedged in the track of the elevator gate. "Hey, Monica," he shouted, waking her as he pulled it free. "He left something behind, and look, it even has his initials on the handle." Luger traced his finger around the neat lettering. "*P . . . A*," he said slowly. "At least we know who we are looking for, Monica. Check the guest ledger for a P.A. He's our man."

Monica stumbled from the room, shielding her eyes from the bright lights. "How do ya know it's his?" she asked. "Those things are always being left all over the place; he could have just picked it up somewhere."

"I still think it's his *and* he came for the box. I know it, Monica," Luger said. "He knows it's here. Mister Grimm said the man had followed it across Europe and wouldn't stop until he got it back."

"Then let him have it—it's just a tin box."

"It's the Midas Box, Monica. There's nothing like it in the whole world. Soon I can sell this place and just sit and make money. As much gold as you could ever dream of having."

"All I want is my name in lights; gold comes well down the wish list. If you'd ever gotten on that stage, you'd understand. It's not the money that does it for me. It's seeing their faces, knowing you have them in the palm of your hand. That you cast a spell on their hearts that'll never be broken. That's magic, and not the stuff Bizmillah turns out. He's just a cheap trick." Monica leaned back against the wall and put her silk-gloved hand next to the blades of the clock. "This is what I want to do," she said, moving her hand toward the blades. "Watch this, Otto. Do ya think Bizmillah could do this?"

Monica put her hand in the path of the second hand, which flashed by like a steel whip. She held up her palm, waiting expectantly. There was a sudden snap as the blade cut through the bone, slicing her hand. Monica giggled as she waited for it to come again and again, each time slicing through her palm. Luger covered his face with his hands.

"NNNNNO!" he screamed, unable to move.

"Look, Otto . . . Clean through and no blood," Monica said brightly as the blade continued passing through her hand as if she were a phantasm.

Luger peeked through his fingers, then dropped his hands limply and gaped at what he saw. "How?" he asked quietly, his eyes bulging, sure it couldn't be real.

"Magic." Monica giggled as she moved her palm in and out of the speeding hands of the clock. "You spend so much time away from me that you don't know what I can do."

"How did you do that?"

"That's a secret, Otto," she said as she pulled a cigar from his top pocket. "And just to prove this was no illusion, watch this." She thrust the cigar into the clock face and the blade quickly shredded the tobacco into a thousand tiny strands. "See, no trick, Otto. Try putting that back together again."

"But your hand, it never hurt your hand," Luger protested.

"That's what I want to do . . . real magic. Just like your tin box. Lead to gold, cutting people in half. It's all the same to me."

"It was a trick, a sleight of hand, something that old conjurer taught you to do between shows. No one could really do that."

Monica grabbed his hand and thrust it toward the spinning blades. "Then you do it, Otto. Then we'll see if it's a trick."

"No, Monica," he said as he struggled to free himself from her tight grip. "I believe you. It wasn't a trick; it was . . . magic."

"That's right, Otto," she repeated slowly, "it *was* magic, and the sooner you get rid of that old duffer and let it be my show, the better."

"I've told you before, Monica. He has to stay around here; there is a reason."

"Then tell me the reason. What does he have on you that he can do what he wants?"

"He's . . . ," Luger said, trying to remember why Bizmillah *was* the highlight of the Prince Regent. "He's . . . unusual."

"Unusual? So is a one-legged monkey, but we don't have one of them top of the bill."

Luger strained to think. Somewhere in the recent past, there was a gap in his memory. He could remember everything up to that point, and then it seemed as if a gate had been closed.

"I know why . . . ," he muttered as he walked away from her to the far end of the corridor. "I just can't remember."

"Well," said Monica, following him. "If you ask me, it could have been Bizmillah who was in here. If anyone wants your magic box, then why not a magician? It could be him; he could be the man that Mister Grimm told you about."

Luger considered this for a moment; his mind felt split in two at the thought of Bizmillah being the one who would take the Midas Box from him. "I never thought, Monica. He could have followed me to London, and then I gave him the job here. I could have brought my enemy right into my castle." He bit his bottom lip and stared at her, then shook his head, as if to rid it of the thought. "I know the man," he muttered. "He has been a friend to me, here a long time, never a day off. He found you . . . brought you here . . ."

"He could just be patient, biding his time for you to make

one slip, and then he'll find your little magic box and disappear into the night." Monica tapped him on the shoulder as he stared at the wall. "Listen . . . , you tell me about this box every day and yet you never let me see it. How do I know it's real?"

"Believe me, Monica, it's real and it's in the hotel."

"Baloney, Otto . . . It's in your head, and until I see it, I won't believe you." Monica thought for a moment. "Take me to it," she said sweetly. "I'll close my eyes, wear a blindfold, anything, but I wanna see it."

Luger thought about this. "Sunday," he replied. "I'll show you Sunday, but look at this." Slowly and carefully he pulled a tiny golden moth out of his pocket, its thin antennae like two tiny golden wands, its wings outstretched, caught in flight. "This was the first thing I ever transformed. Found it in my office fluttering about the lamp. I plucked it from the air and put it in the box. When I opened the lid, it was pure gold."

Monica snatched it from his hand and held it to the light. "Looks like you made it, Otto. Or you could've bought it from any trinket shop. You want me to believe it was *transformed*?"

"It flew, was a real moth with brown wings, drawn to the flame. I put it in the Midas Box and it came out gold. That's not all. I have this," he said eagerly as he reached into his pocket and pulled out a rolled strand of gold, tapered at each end and wrinkled in several places. "A worm," he said proudly, holding it in the palm of his hand. "A glorious worm, picked up from the mud of Saint Sepulchre Street. I put it in the box as a writhing creature, and then with the closing of the lid, it was stiffened by molecules of finest gold, as if it had been in the grip of King Midas himself."

"Then where is the rest of the gold? If you really have such a magical box, I would expect you to use it every minute of every day."

"That is the problem," he said as he put the worm back

into his pocket. He turned and walked back into the room, and stared at the sarcophagus. "There is only one minute in every day when this can be achieved. The rest of the time it sits there . . . useless. I was convinced that if I could speed up the clock, it would increase my opportunities, give me a minute every hour to do the transformations, but so far nothing has worked."

"Only one minute a day?" Monica snickered.

"There is always the possibility that one day I will uncover the secret of what makes the box work. Then, Monica, then—"

"You'll be very old, and I'll have long since given up on you," she said mockingly. "So what about the kid? When will he be ready for shipment?"

Luger beamed with pride as he looked at the waxen image of the boy. "The best one yet. The finest I have created, a new process with the finest quality wax. The dust keeps them from drying out, but there is always the chance that they will break during shipment." He stared at the manikin, examining its face, seeing the gouge Mariah had made to the lips.

"So where do they go, Otto?" Monica asked.

"That no one must know, not even you, not yet. My waxworks are the finest in Europe, and their destination is a deeply guarded secret." Luger brushed Felix's hair, and taking a cigar lighter from his jacket pocket, he quickly rasped the flint and brushed the burning wick across the waxen lips. With his thumb he smoothed away the mark, then pushed the lip back into shape with his fingernail. "There," he said quietly, as if to the manikin. "All better."

"What about doing one of me?" Monica asked. "I would make a pretty good model."

"Pray that the day never comes. You know there is more to these images than meets the eye. Their cost is greater than most people would imagine." Luger propped the sarcophagus lid against the wall and picked up the swords, returning them to their rack.

"Still, it would be nice to see myself. You never get the full effect just looking in a mirror," she said as she looked over her shoulder to see herself from behind. "I want to see what other people see. What do you see when you look at me, Otto?"

"Something finer than a waxwork and yet from another world. If only you would allow me to see your hands. Always in those gloves, always covered in silk and diamonds."

"It's best that way," she said, curling her arms around herself to hide her gloved hands. "Not my best feature. Don't like looking at them myself." Monica shuddered, as if deeply chilled, ruffling her feathers from head to toe. "They were burned when I was a child, scalded by my mother, and every time I see them, I remember her face and hear her cries."

"Then I shall find you the finest gloves in the world, inlaid with gold and silver, gossamer, as beautiful as your face." Luger took her hand.

The memory of Monica's arrival came to his mind and played as a waking dream.

Luger had stood on the steps of the Prince Regent as her carriage had trundled slowly across the cobbles, picking its way through the myriad of market stalls littering the square that perched near the hotel on the cliff top. The driver had doffed his cap when he had seen Luger on the hotel steps in his black tailcoat and gold vest. The carriage had halted abruptly at the bottom of the marble steps, its narrow oak wheels sinking into the rutted mud, and in the cold sea mist that swirled about its wheels, she had stepped into his life.

As the first light of the morning crept across the hills deep to the south she picked her way through the mud, walked up the steps and held out a gloved hand. Bizmillah had pulled the heavy trunk from the back of the cab and tipped the driver with a silver coin.

"Found her, Mister Luger," he had shouted as he dragged the case behind him. "The greatest assistant for the greatest magician. Miss Monica will be *truly* pleasing."

Luger had held her long fingers as she tiptoed up the steps, guiding her through the revolving door and into the Prince Regent.

"Otto Luger," Monica said, breaking up the dream and bringing him back to the present. "Eyes so far away, not looking at me."

"It's not right, it's not right," Luger said. He dropped her hand and began to search the room for anything that might have been left behind. "I have to know how they got in here . . . I need to know. Only I had the key. Only I could stop the elevator." He looked to Monica for an answer. "There are only two people in the whole world who know of this place, you and I . . . Who told them?"

"Whoever it was is long gone, Otto. They've just had a good look around and messed up a few things. Why worry? Change the locks. Call in Mister Grimm. Maybe he can find him for you—just look for a man who has lost his umbrella."

"Grimm?" Luger echoed. He rummaged in the pocket of his waistcoat and pulled out a curled visiting card with gold edging. "He can find him and put an end to all this, and when he's captured, he will make the finest waxen image ever. Mister Grimm is staying at the Three Mariners Inn—I shall meet him there tonight and have done with this trouble once and for all."

CHAPTER

❖ 11 ❖

Grimm's Law

Inside the tunnel, Mariah clung to the brass handle of the faux window, hoping that Otto Luger would believe it to be sealed shut and leave some other way. He had been eavesdropping, trying to make out the muffled words and enjoying Monica's luscious voice. Sacha had gone on into the dark tunnel, with the promise that she would return. She had crept down the rungs of the cold iron ladder that plunged to the depths of the hotel and the water below. Mariah had not heard her return as she stealthily climbed the three hundred treads back to Luger's secret entrance. Just two feet below him, she was unseen in the darkness as she reached out and tapped his foot. Startled, Mariah looked down, hoping to see something in the crushing black. She tapped his foot again and pulled on his bootlace to tell him to follow.

They climbed lower and lower. Far below, the sea beat against the cold stone steps, filling the tunnel with spray. For ten minutes they didn't speak as they slowly descended. The weight of the darkness pressed against Mariah, taking the breath from his lungs. His legs began to shake as he staggered down the cold iron rungs of the ladder. Flakes of thick rust cut into his hand and fell from the thinning treads. He stopped and touched the wall with the palm of his hand. It ran with cold, dank water, which dripped through the cracks and mortar lines of the intricate brickwork he now traced with his fingers.

Finally Sacha stopped and stepped onto a landing. She struck a long match, its sudden bright flame dazzling Mariah as he gripped the ladder.

"This way. I know how we can get to the beach," she whispered.

Mariah followed, the light from the match flickering over the crisscrossed brick of the tunnel's curved roof. The floor ran like a stream, covered with bladder wrack and sea lettuce. The walls were coated in strands of green algae, which grew from the floor like ivy. Sacha struck another match and held it in her cupped hand, the shadow of her fingers glimmering against the walls. They walked on, Mariah slipping on the wet stone as he tried to make his way. With each step the darkness followed them, the tunnel plunging back into night once they had passed. Mariah struggled to keep pace with Sacha. She hopped back and forth, sure-footed on the small mounds of sand that littered the tunnel floor like tiny islands.

"Nearly there," she said as she lit another match. "I came this way once before, got lost down here with Felix. Never went in far enough to see the ladder. I got this far and turned back." Sacha pointed to a large gouge in the damp brick. "See . . . Felix scratched his initial into the wall. Just along here and we will be out of this place."

Mariah didn't reply. He kept his gaze fixed to the ground as he tried to see his way in Sacha's shadow. Every now and then, he looked behind, his spine shivering as if someone or something were about to grab him from the blackness that lurked at the edge of the light.

Sacha stopped and turned to him, lighting his face with her match. She smiled. "Did they try to follow?" she asked as water dripped from the roof.

"No, but I heard what they said," Mariah replied. "It's a waxwork of Felix, nothing more. They think it was Bizmillah who was in the room. Luger is going to see a man called Grimm—he's staying at the Three Mariners Inn. He wants to see him tonight."

"Then we haven't long," Sacha said, turning and quickly setting off. "If we follow Luger, then we'll see what he's up to."

"But Bizmillah expects us to clean the illusions," Mariah protested.

"No, Mariah, . . . he expects *you* to clean the illusions and me to have them ready for tomorrow." She paused, taking a deep breath of the cold damp air. "Tonight, I am going to find Mister Luger and see who he is going to meet. The last thing Felix said was that the answer to the disappearances could be found with Mister Luger. He said we weren't safe, that Mister Luger had a box that would change everything in the world. I wouldn't believe him, but now that we found the secret level and the waxwork, I know that Felix must have been telling the truth."

"So where is the Three Mariners?" Mariah asked.

"By the harbour, in a back street." She scrunched up her nose—it was clearly not a good place to be. "I know it well. If we go this way, we can soon be past Luger's workshop and on to the beach." Sacha threw the match to the floor, momentarily plunging them into complete darkness. She lit a new one and led Mariah back and forth through narrow alleyways and long cavernous tunnels that echoed with the hiss of the steam generator and the bubble of the sea waves. She stopped by a tall black door that looked as if it had been painted on the brick of the tunnel. It stood at the top of a long flight of steps that went down into the murk. An oil lamp hung on the wall and flickered dimly. Sacha threw her match away and checked the box in the lamplight.

"Not many left," she said. "There's usually a lamp lit for when he comes down here to work—we'll be all right, and then we'll be on the beach."

"How do we get out?" Mariah asked as he instinctively pulled against the door of Luger's workshop.

"No," whispered Sacha as she pulled his hand from the door. "He always locks it, and I wouldn't dare go inside—we don't know what he's been doing."

"Could be where he makes the manikins," Mariah replied, trying to look in through the keyhole. "If Luger made the waxwork of Felix, he could have done it in there."

Sacha urged him to leave the door and follow her, but he refused to go. He held firmly on to the handle and peered through the large keyhole. He could see to the far side of a large room that was lit by the flames of a glowing fire somewhere out of his sight. His eyes flicked from one thing to another, taking in what he could. Behind the locked door was a world of pipes and ropes that seemed to go from floor to ceiling, stacked in tidy rows, strapped to the wall like in the hold of a ship. At the far side was an old sofa of hard brown leather, a gash across its front like it had been cut with a sabre. There, sitting snuggled in the dimpled red silk pillows was a large doll with a pot face, rosy-red cheeks and sombre smile. It stared at the door as if it knew it were being spied upon. It seemed to look directly at the keyhole, smiling at Mariah.

"*Old Scratty*," Mariah mouthed, looking at Sacha. "The doll's here . . . What's it doing in Luger's workshop?"

"Don't try to pull my leg," Sacha said scornfully. "Scratty's locked in Bizmillah's cupboard. I saw her myself before I closed the door, as did you."

"She's here, Sacha, and she's laughing at us." He looked again through the keyhole, and there was Old Scratty, dressed in her black velvet dress and green silk slippers. "See for yourself."

Sacha looked in at the porcelain doll that by now had closed one eye, seeming to wink at the girl. "I do believe . . . ," Sacha said, then paused. "Someone must have put her in there; she can't be doing it herself! Every time I see her, she looks more and more like Miss Monica. Funny thing is, she arrived on the same day Scratty did."

Sacha spoke only to herself because Mariah had wandered off down the steps. He stood on wet sand that had been freshly washed by the winter tide pounding through the grill cut into the bottom of a tall wooden door. Above his head he could hear the whirring and grinding of the steam generator. It was as if the hotel were sighing and coughing like a gigantic beached whale stuck upon the rocks. Coming from far away were the shrill notes of a piano. They seemed to echo through the tunnel. Sacha looked up.

"I can hear it," she said to reassure him that he was not on the verge of madness. "It's from the salon. The holes in the ceiling are vents to the steam room, where they keep the generator. If you stand near them, you can hear sounds from all over the Prince Regent. Sometimes at night you can even hear the guests snoring in their rooms."

"It's like it's alive . . . as if the building were not just bricks but a living creature," Mariah said as he stepped toward the doorway, the Prince Regent sighing and moaning above him.

Sacha slipped open the bolts to the door and pulled the

latch, seeming to have done it a thousand times. As they left the fading light that guarded the entrance to the hotel's cellars they were quickly consumed by the still, moonless night.

They walked together across the sand, surrounded by swirling sea mist. There were moments when the Prince Regent loomed above them, and then, as if conjured away, it disappeared from view as a shawl of mist hid it from their eyes. The sound of the harbour flitted across the breeze, just above the sound of small waves breaking across the beach at the edge of the low tide. Mariah looked back at the trail of soaked footprints they had left behind in the wet sand. He hesitated for a moment, stopping and turning to see the hotel vanish once more. Sacha didn't speak as she bent her head against the cold and pulled up the collar of her smock, wrapping her arms around herself.

"We should go back," Mariah said as she walked ahead of him.

"Not until we find out what Luger is doing at the Three Mariners."

"What if he sees us?"

"In this fog, at nearly midnight?" She laughed and kicked a stone across the sand.

"What of the kraken?"

"The kraken won't be out tonight—the tide is too far out. It can only change into a man when the water covers the drowning post in the harbour. Then it can come from the sea and take children back for a feast."

"Drowning post?" Mariah asked.

"If you get caught thieving at Christmas, you get the chance to be tied to the drowning post the next day; if you live for two tides on Saint Stephen's Day, they'll set you free." Sacha picked up a piece of driftwood and threw it into the mist. "Saw it done one year. The man lasted the first tide, and when we came back in the morning, the post was empty and the man gone. That's when they said the kraken was awake."

"Do you believe in the kraken?" he asked, hoping she would say it was all imaginary.

"Yes," she said plainly, looking around, shivering as the clock from the old church chimed midnight.

They walked across the beach, coming to higher, drier sand, where the sea seldom washed. It was piled against the harbour wall and led them to a row of tar-painted wooden shacks with boarded fronts and gaudy signs. Mariah read each one as they walked by, wondering what delicacies could be bought for the old penny that he rolled in his pocket. Past the huts they crossed a cobbled road that came down from the town to the harbour. It turned sharply left, deep carriage ruts cut into the stones and a fine scattering of sand covered the surface. At the end of the arcade was a bright red letter box stuck to the side of a kipper shed. Mariah burrowed into his pocket and pulled out the crumpled card, and, without saying a word, dropped it into the postbox. He closed his eyes and wished it a safe journey, hoping it would find Albion and bring him to the Prince Regent. Sacha had gone on ahead, along the harbourside.

There, all the buildings that faced the street were covered in nets and ropes, which hung like cobwebs from their hoists as they dewed up in the night air. The roofs were outlined with ridges of silver as the first tongues of frost kissed the dark buildings.

Sacha looked back and forth as a sudden swirl of thick, icy mist rolled around her. For a brief moment she vanished from sight. Mariah chattered with the cold, which ran its icy fingers down his spine. Sacha appeared again, only an arm's length from him in the fog-filled street, but before he had time to reach out for her, she quickly vanished in a sudden spiral. He turned again, the mist clearing and the night sky opening above them.

He looked up from the road to the gigantic sign that spread itself across the white-painted wall of the building in front of them. A burnished board that appeared to reflect all available light, it shone as if with eager anticipation.

Mariah read the sign — THE GOLDEN KIPPER.

"Captain Charity," he said to himself as he remembered the conversation on the train, the invitation for a dinner and the biggest fish he could ever dream of eating.

"You've heard of him, then?" Sacha asked as they entered the long alleyway running from the foreshore into the labyrinth of tunnel-like streets that clustered against the castle hill.

"Met him on the train from London. He gave me a card and an invitation for dinner, then set me on the carriage to the Prince Regent. He was there when I met Black. I could see they hated each other from the first sight. I thought Charity was going to throw Black from the train."

"Sounds like something he would do. I knew him when I was younger, and I've heard a lot about him. Went to fight for the Queen and left this place behind. An adventurer, my father calls him."

Mariah looked through the large plate glass windows of the restaurant. Inside were rows of polished tables, each holding a small candle and bouquet of fine flowers. Upon the front door was a garland of holly leaves and mistletoe with red and white berries. From it hung a small golden fish, a man made of wire and a spurting whale. He took them in his fingers, looking at Sacha in the hope that she would explain them.

"It's Jonah," she whispered. "Wouldn't do what he was told, so got eaten up and taken to the place he should have been and spit out on the beach. The fish is the prize in a fairy tale; in its mouth was a golden coin — spend it and another would come in its place. Its providence would never run out."

"The Golden Kipper . . . ," Mariah said, realising how the place got its name.

"I could never eat here, though," Sacha went on, ignoring him. "Far too fine a place for a skivvy. They say the fish'll melt in your mouth . . ."

"I have a ticket. Eat with me. I'm sure he'll let us both come. Tomorrow's Saturday—we can come here for tea." Mariah spoke excitedly as he looked at the large bowls of exotic fruits that filled the window, tempting him to come inside. He tried the door.

"Leave it, Mariah," Sacha said softly, pulling his hand from the door. "Your man would never leave it unlocked after closing."

A sudden swirl of icy mist filled the street. From the harbour could be heard the bumping of the wooden fishing boats, crammed together on the slack tide. Mariah looked up and shuddered—in his reflection in the glass, he saw the outline of someone standing behind him in the mist, long strands of dank, wet hair matted across his face and, through this mass, a pair of bright red eyes staring at Mariah.

"Seen a ghost?" Sacha asked, seeing the look of fear on Mariah's face.

"In the window," he mumbled, not daring to turn around or speak above a whisper. "It's behind me."

Sacha looked at the window, and then peered into the street. "There's nothing there."

"I saw it, Sacha. The kraken. Like it had just come from the sea."

"Well . . . ," she said slowly, deep in thought. "It's gone now. You must've been seeing things."

"It wasn't in my head. It stood behind us and you never saw it?"

"Not a thing. I was looking in the glass, the same as you,

105

and never saw a thing," Sacha said as she stepped back toward the dark alleyway. "It's this way to the Three Mariners. If we keep along the wall, we won't get lost. To the end, then right and along the Bolts to Tuthill and we'll be there."

"But . . . ," Mariah whispered, not wanting to leave the open sky of the harbourside.

"It's only darkness, Mariah. There's nothing in the night that isn't there in the day." Sacha led the way into the warren of passages weaving between the stacked houses that covered the hillside.

There was something in what she said that made him think of his mother. He had buried his memories of her so deep within his heart that he barely remembered her anymore. Yet the girl's words sent his mind to a night long ago when he was gripped by a fever and his mother cradled him in her arms and spoke love to his heart: *"Faithfulness will be your shield, so you will not fear the terror of the night, nor the arrow of the day. Nor plague that walks in the darkness. A thousand may fall at your side, but no evil shall ever come near you . . ."*

Mariah followed Sacha, slipping from shadow to shadow and then into the utter darkness of the passageway, saying his mother's words to himself again and again.

CHAPTER

✦ 12 ✦

Three Mariners

Mariah's and Sacha's footfalls echoed against the cold, damp walls of the narrow alleyway that ran from the seafront into the depths of the town. Houses were cut into the hillside and cluttered upon each other like a precarious stack of cards. Every now and then, a door had been left open and the glow of a fire came from the room within to light the alleyway. Sacha strode ahead of Mariah, not looking back as she danced from doorway to doorway. Mariah gulped, trying to look ahead and behind at the same time, convinced that the red-eyed creature he had seen in the window now followed him in the darkness.

He stopped at a cottage's open doorway and looked in. There, in the faint light of the fading fire, he could see the tiny front room with its drably painted walls and tattered curtains that stuck to the damp window. A ladder went up through a small hole in the ceiling to a room above. A woman slept by the fire, wrapped in rags and clutching a small child. To her side a small black pot steamed and filled the room with the fragrance of tea. Near the woman, a pair of boot-clad feet stuck out from beneath a short knitted blanket. Unseen by the sleepers, a large brown rat sat upon its curled tail by the fire and rustled its whiskers.

Mariah rolled the penny in his pocket, then, stepping across the threshold, silently placed it upon the arm of a broken rocking chair.

The man snored and gripped his meagre blanket tightly, unaware that he was being watched by boy and rat. Beside the man, all carefully placed upon a small oak stool, were a beer pot, tobacco bag, leather snuff pouch and a copy of the latest penny dreadful.

Looking into the shadows, Mariah saw that far away from the fire and nestled by the wall were a row of sleeping children, covered in old woollen coats and snuggled together to keep out the cold.

Mariah thought for a moment as he looked back at the beer and tobacco. He picked up the penny from the rocking chair and stepped farther into the room. By his feet a sleeping boy scratched his milk white bare arm. Mariah stooped down and carefully placed the coin in the boy's hand, curling up his fingers into a loose fist. He smiled as he made his way out of the cottage, knowing that he would never see the look on the lad's face and hoping that the father wouldn't steal the penny from him.

"Can you do that for them all?" Sacha chided him quietly, having watched silently from the doorway. "I can take you to a thousand houses just the same. Do you have a penny for everyone?"

Mariah shrugged and stepped into the street, pulling the

door closed behind him. "I just thought of the lad waking up and finding a penny in his hand; looks as though his father takes what he wants and they get nothing. Why do they leave the doors open for all the world to see their misery?"

"For the kraken," she said softly. "They believe that if the kraken comes, it will take one of the children and leave a jug of gold pieces in their place."

"Let their children be taken for money?"

"They would do it for a lot less; if the kraken were to give a quart of gin, they would queue the length of the pier to give them away. After all, they can always have another."

"What madness possesses them?" he asked, his voice sharpened by anger.

"Life, Mariah. Cold . . . hard . . . Be thankful it's them and not you," Sacha said brusquely.

They said no more as they made their way through the narrow streets, past the customs house with its barred windows and narrow door, along Tuthill and into Quay Street. They saw no one and heard only the sound of a cawing gull and their own footsteps upon the broken cobbles. Sacha led him down several stone steps. Mariah still looked behind him, sure that somewhere far in the distance the red eyes of the kraken searched for him.

Soon, they waited on the corner of a wide street. Mariah could hear the water lapping against the pier. He could make out the large frame of the warehouse that stood on the quayside. A narrow slipway came up from the water's edge; the outline of a fishing boat was visible against the dark patchwork of crumbling brick and stone. To one side was the Three Mariners Inn—a tall, yellow stone house, much older than any other Mariah had seen that night. It had a large door nailed with black square-headed bolts.

Sacha looked around, as if unsure which way they should take. Then they heard a horse carriage clattering toward them.

She hesitated, then gestured for Mariah to follow her. They stepped into the darkness of a narrow alleyway that was more like a gash in the stone-fronted building. It led, stinking of cess and seawater, back toward the town. They looked out as the coach turned into the street and then stopped by the alleyway that led to the Three Mariners. The coach door opened, and Luger stepped to the ground. He looked about and then waved to the driver with his long, silver-tipped cane, thrusting it into in the air like a magician's wand.

"Did you know he would be here?" Mariah whispered.

"Only way he could come—he'd never walk, scared of getting dirt on his shoes. This is the only place a carriage can turn. Thought if we made quick time, we'd be here before him." Luger disappeared into the alleyway leading to the inn. "All we have to do is wait and then follow him."

"He'll see us," Mariah said as Sacha vanished deeper into the crevasse.

"I'll take you to within a foot of the man and he'll never know you were there. It'll be as if you were but a ghost, listening from over his shoulder."

He quickly lost sight of her as she vanished into the blackness of the narrow alley. He stumbled on blindly, sure he was walking on a living carpet of rats and discarded fish heads. It was as if the ground were moving beneath his feet, squirming around his ankles and over the tops of his boots.

Suddenly, a hand grabbed his sleeve and pulled him into an even darker portal, cut into the sidewall of the long building. Mariah gasped as he was jerked down two stone steps. He stumbled, but Sacha stopped him from falling, holding him up against the dank brick wall until he regained his breath.

"Say nothing," she said as she struck a lucifer.

Mariah looked down a long flight of steps that fell away into the night. Stacked against the wall and blocking the alley to the height of a giant was a hoard of empty wooden beer barrels. Scattered about them were piles of discarded green bottles, which glinted in the match light.

"It's the cellar," Sacha said as she continued down the stairs. "Always left open—a great place to hide and an even better place to listen. From here on, we cannot speak."

Mariah didn't reply as he followed her down in the fading light, which gave out completely by the time they reached the cellar door. Sacha slipped the catch, opened the door and stepped inside. A small oil burner lit a corner of the room, and the sudden sound of raised voices filled the void. Above their heads, many footsteps banged against the thin boards, which in several places had been fitted with narrow metal grates that allowed the light of the inn and the spilled beer to flood into the cellar.

The cellar ceiling was decked with strands of glistening cobwebs, which shuddered with the footsteps above, and billows of sawdust fell through the grates. A stiff bristle broom was sweeping mounds of it back and forth to soak up spilled beer.

Sacha looked up, her face glowing in the shaft of light from the grate above, flecks of wood shavings falling upon her. She edged this way and that, looking for Luger as she peered into the room above, her head almost touching the oak beams. Mariah hid himself behind two stacked beer barrels and listened to the muffled voices that filled the cellar.

Above, the door to the Three Mariners opened and all was suddenly still. The voices of the drunken fishermen hushed themselves, and the hubbub of the barman clanking filled tankards upon the counter ceased in an instant. The click of Luger's steel-capped boots and the thud of his silver-tipped cane made their way across the floor above them. It was as if they could see him taking every step as he walked slowly from the door, stopped, turned and then made his way to the far corner of the room. Then came the scraping of a chair as it was pulled back from a table and the rustle of his thick coat being slid from his shoulders and dropping to the chair back.

Slowly the noise started again, as if each man in turn had recognised his new companion or some secret signal had been given that it was safe to talk in front of this strange gentleman. Sacha edged herself to the other side of the cellar and, propping herself up against a dusty barrel, looked up into the room. Mariah slid to her side and peered over her shoulder. He could see Luger's polished boots and crisp hemmed trousers. There was a man with him, hunched over the table cradling a pot of beer.

Luger was brought a drink without asking, the barman walking to his table as Sacha and Mariah traced his steps above them. They listened intently; Luger said nothing.

The cellar door suddenly rattled as the stiff catch stuck in the saddle. In the half-light Sacha gestured for Mariah to hide. The latch rattled again as someone pulled at the door, then, in frustration, banged a fist against it.

Mariah slid quickly to the floor, pulling Sacha close to him as they squeezed themselves into the narrowest of gaps between the damp cellar wall and the stack of barrels. They were trapped. The door began to open.

"Bodkins," shouted the man as he finally managed to push the door fully open and step into the cellar. He stooped under the low ceiling as he checked each keg, trying to read the fading chalk marks in the dim light. "This'll be the one," he said as he tapped the side of a small, fat barrel that he quickly picked up, pulling it to his chest. "Up ya come and off ya go. Soon be gone and they'll want some more . . ."

The man staggered under the weight of the barrel, grappling to keep upright and climb the stone steps to the dark alleyway. Beads of sweat dripped down Mariah's cheeks. He listened as the man lurched and tottered away from the cellar, leaving the door wide open. Mariah peered from his hiding place behind the barrels and in the dim light saw the open door. Sacha looked up at him, her face cut in two by a long black shadow.

"We better stay hidden," she whispered. "It's old Mathias, drinks more than he sells and he'll soon be back."

At the table above them, Luger remained silent.

"More work?" his companion asked. "I've been waiting in this town for a week, hoping you would come to see me. What is it I can do for you?"

"I have had some trouble, Mister Grimm. Someone messing with my possessions, and I want you to find out who," Luger said as he took a fat cigar from his pocket and lit it from the table candle.

"Just what I'm here for. Want something found, ask Mister Grimm and Mister Grendel. The finest detectives."

"Aah . . . Mister Grendel, . . . and where's he tonight?" Luger asked. He sipped from his glass and puffed his cigar.

"Too much . . . too much . . . " Grimm hesitated and gave a long sigh. "He has taken up a habit that even I cannot pursue. By this time of night, he is slumbering and in a world of his imaginings. It is a malevolence that has pursued him like a deathly hound ever since," Grimm said, clearly disturbed by his friend's condition.

"Not a habit that will affect the way in which he works, Mister Grimm?"

"On the contrary . . . Mister Grendel is helped by his dreaming linctus; it gives him notions that can only be found when liberated from the human condition. In fact, it was such a chimera that helped us track down your little box."

"That isn't to be spoken of in such a place as this," Luger snapped, unaware that ears in the dark, cold cellar could hear his harsh voice. "I paid you well for what you did, and it should be kept in the past. Listen," he said, quickly looking around at the crowd of wind-ruddied faces, "I have had a *visitor* to my

113

private suite. Much was left in disarray, and I need you and Grendel to find out who it was, understand?"

"Investigation is our business, Mister Luger. We will attend the scene of the crime at eight in the forenoon. Leave everything as it is, and we will soon have the scoundrel in our grasp." Mister Grimm paused as Matthias placed another pot of beer before him. "When we find the villain, what would you like us to do with him?" Grimm asked slowly.

"To make him disappear without trace, as if he had never existed," Luger whispered.

"Very well . . . Then I shall wake Mister Grendel and tell him of the details. He will set about his dreaming and find the suspect."

"Good," snapped Luger. He picked up his coat and cane, and stood. "No trace."

"There is *one* thing before you leave me for the night," Grimm said, grabbing Luger's jacket with his grubby fingers. "A slight embarrassment has come upon me. In my waiting, I have drunk more than my wallet would allow, and I was wondering . . . ?"

"It'll be settled . . . and with one more for the road to keep the cold from your back and the kraken from your neck." Luger nodded to Matthias to bring more beer. "On the Prince Regent," he shouted. He threw his cigar to the floor and kicked it into the grate, watching it fall between the iron bars into the darkened cellar. "I wait eagerly for your assistance, Mister Grimm, . . . eagerly."

Mariah watched from his hiding place as the cigar stub fell like a smouldering comet. It landed, sparking upon the top of a barrel, and burned in the gloom.

In the alleyway there was the sudden sound of someone approaching. They made their way through the darkness as if they walked in the brightness of day, crunching upon discarded fish heads and broken glass. Mariah ducked behind the barrel, pulling his hand away from the smouldering stub he'd been about to put out. Sacha squashed in by his side, holding her breath as she listened in the shadows. Above their heads, Luger's boots thudded across the floor, and the door to the inn slammed shut as he stepped into the street. In the stark blackness of the alleyway, the sound of movement got closer to the open door, lit by the paltry glow filtering through the grate above.

From his hiding place, Mariah listened intently.

"Ást þú . . . ást þú . . ." Something stood in the doorway, its muffled speech filling the cellar.

Quickly realising that the voice was not Matthias's, Sacha edged closer to the side of the barrel. She peered warily from where she hid, keeping herself to the deepest darkness of the shadow and squinting out through the meagre gap between the barrel and a crate of empty brown bottles.

"Koma með mig . . . þú lykta af svínsleður . . . ," the person squawked in a high-pitched voice, like a parrot.

Then she saw the man. He stood in the half-light of the cellar, crossed with the shadows from the floor grates above and outlined in the amber lamplight. He was wrapped in a long coat, with black leather straps across his chest. He wore old seaboots that fit tightly, as if he had grown in them without taking them from his feet. His hair was pulled tightly to one side in long, thick strands. He reached out a large, gnarled hand as if to catch the falling dust that shimmered down through the fragmented beams of golden lamplight. His fingers shook with a gentle tremor, and Sacha could see that each was tipped with a long black nail.

The man turned his face and looked toward her, his red eyes caught by the smouldering cigar. He stooped as he walked, bobbing his skull as if his spindly neck could not bear the weight of his head.

She held her breath, hoping not to be seen as she froze to

the wall, unable to move as his eyes darted around the room, taking in everything.

In three steps the man had crossed the floor, stealthily tiptoeing around the barrels and crates until he reached the smouldering stub. He plucked it from the wood and sniffed the sulphurous, smoking tip. He flinched as the embers bit at his nose. He carefully held the cigar to his lips and tasted its skin with his long, snakelike tongue. In an instant the cigar was gone, snapped from the air in one bite. Then, turning quickly as though he were being called, the man left the cellar and was gone into the night.

"Who was it?" Mariah asked as the footsteps ran into the street.

"The kraken . . . It was the kraken."

CHAPTER

✴ 13 ✴

Hedonic Calculus

From somewhere deep in the night came a scream that pierced the heart. It hung like a crack of thunder, echoing in and out of the dark passageways, along the quayside and in through the open door of the Three Mariners Inn. For a moment it brought a hush that froze each voice midsong. Then as quickly as it came, it vanished into the night. The inn quickly emptied as men and women spilled into the alley to see where the call of distress had come from. They didn't need to travel far; there in the small, open square, bounded by four dark alleyways that led into the labyrinth of streets, a body lay slumped on the ground. In the swirling mist it looked as if it were but a mound of crumpled rags.

From the alley, Mariah and Sacha peered at the crowd that encircled the body like a rough-hewn fence of shabby coats and tattered trousers.

The dim lamplight shone through the mist upon their backs and heads, some topped with sea berets, others wrapped in rags to keep out the cold. They stared at the cadaver stretched out across the cobbles. Gashes pierced its neck and forehead.

"We need to get the copper," one said, prodding the corpse with his walking stick. "Can't have him left here like this . . . not right . . . second in a month and not a mile between 'em."

"We'll deal with it ourselves, can't have the law down here. Bottom End is the bottom end and the law has no place here, never has and never will," said Matthias sternly as he pushed his way to the front of the crowd. "Put him in the sea—no one'll know. They'll say the rocks did that to him."

"It's not what to *do* with him that bothers me. Been too many dead in these streets and we can't be blaming it on the kraken, not this time." The man prodded the body once more for any signs of life.

"I'll find the culprit," said a small, stubby man that Mariah had seen scurrying back and forth at the back of the crowd. "I am a detective, *private* of course, from London. You can trust me not to tell the police—they always get in the way, and my enquiries are very . . . *different*." Mister Grimm pushed himself to the front of the crowd, holding his silk top hat close to him. "Let me see."

Grimm stood before the body. He carefully examined the neat, broad scratches across the forehead and the three deep wounds to the neck. The face had frozen in a strange grimace. Grimm took a silver case from his coat pocket, quickly unlocked it and felt inside the velvet bag that lay within. He brought out a pair of fine gold spectacles, fitted with bright blue lenses that looked as if they had been cut from a single piece of precious stone. He carefully fitted them across the bridge of his nose and inspected the corpse.

"Don't know if we want an outsider doing this," Matthias said as he wiped his hands on his apron.

"It's either I or the police . . . Which do you prefer?"

There was no reply as the crowd huddled closer together, those on the outside pressing in for fear that the perpetrator of this hideous crime would grab them from the edge of the herd and drag them into the night.

"He was the one with Luger. I recognise the voice," Mariah whispered as he stepped from the alley and beckoned for Sacha to follow. "We have to see what he's doing."

Before she could protest, Mariah had taken her by the hand and pulled her into the street. Looking around, he saw that the fine black carriage had vanished, its thin tracks cutting through the sand that had blown across the cobbles.

"Luger got away . . . at the same time as the kraken," Sacha said, looking toward the warehouse by the quayside.

"Just before the scream," Mariah answered quickly, his mind racing. "Could be Luger," he said. "I heard a story once from Africa of a man who could turn himself into a lion and hunt people."

"Luger, the kraken?" Sacha asked quietly in disbelief as they stepped farther into the street and slinked closer to the crowd gathered outside the inn.

"Could be," he said. "Left the inn and was transformed to go hunting—that's why so many have disappeared from the Prince Regent."

"Luger ate them?" she asked sarcastically.

"And turned what was left into wax . . ."

Mariah edged around the crowd until he was close to Grimm. The street chilled with a fresh breeze that blustered in off the sea and carried with it a cloud of crystal sand that hissed as it blew across the cobbles. Grimm hunched over the bundle of rags that was the man, the thin hands sticking from the ample cloak in which the body was wrapped.

"We should take him inside," Grimm said as he prodded

the wound on the neck with what looked like a long red pencil. "I need more light if I am to make a proper examination. It's as if an animal has bitten him to death." He looked up at Mariah. "Take his wrists and drag him to the door."

"He goes nowhere," said Mathias as he pushed the boy away and stood between him and the body. "You're the detective. Tell us who did this and we can have done with the body. I'm not having a corpse taken into the inn. That's a place for the living, not the dead."

"Having eaten there, I could not tell the difference," Grimm replied under his breath as he adjusted the spectacles and stared at the street. "Whoever did this had one bare foot . . . the other wore an old seaboot." His spectacled eyes followed a trail of footprints that to the naked eye were invisible. He stooped to the sand-covered stones and peered at a shadowy outline set against the open drain that ran the length of the alley. "It's as if his foot were webbed . . . just like a large seabird . . . a pelican or albatross. The boot is well-worn, as if he had an impediment. We may not be looking—" He stopped short. He pulled up the collar of his coat and placed the spectacles safely back in the case. "Couldn't possibly be," he murmured, "quite impossible."

"I know what you're thinking," Matthias said as softly as he could for fear of being overheard. "Best not be said around here. There's already too much superstition, and it does a man no good at all to think such things on a dark night. Black thoughts are best for bright days. Best if we say nothing and leave it be. Don't think it would be a good thing for you to look any further." Matthias pulled back the ragged cloak that had covered the man's face. "Beggar," he said. "Won't be missed." Matthias nodded to a man nearby. "Get the cart. You know what's to be done. All of you up for a free drink, come inside and let me warm your hearts."

Sacha stepped back into the shadows as Matthias walked into the inn, followed by the crowd and Mister Grimm. The body lay in the street, arms outstretched, face covered. Mariah followed Sacha as the sound of cart wheels came across the stones.

"What will they do with him?" she asked.

"None of your concern, lass." A strong hand grabbed her by the arm and pulled her away from Mariah. "Should be tucked up at that fancy hotel of yours. Saw the American drinking in the inn, dressed like a lord," the man said in an Irish accent. "I'm not having my daughter spending the night out in the streets—you'll be coming home with me."

Sacha had not seen her father standing in the shadows of the inn, nor had she known how long he had been watching as she stood with the crowd, trying to peek at the body. He stank of gin; his face was smudged with snuff. She tried to smile as he held on to her arm, more to steady himself than to control her.

"We were just going back, came with a message for Mister Luger, but when we got here, he had gone," she said, thinking as fast as she could.

"So this is ya fancy boy, is it, Sacha?" the man asked as he squinted at Mariah. "This is young Felix, all the way from London with his fancy manners?"

"No, Father, Felix has gone away. This is Mariah."

"All the same," he said, slurring. "Best you be walking your father home to Paradise. The old lass will be locking me out and scolding me for drinking at the Mariners. Fancy that . . . have a pub meself and drink somewhere else."

"I said I'd be straight back. I have to get things ready for Bizmillah." Sacha pulled against him as he gripped her arm.

"It's a steep hill with many steps, and not a moon or lamp to guide my feet. You're coming with me and not another word'll be said," her father said sternly through his teeth, twisting her arm tightly. He looked at Mariah. "Family matter, boy. Not a word. Not if you know what's good for her."

Two men pushing a handcart turned into the alley. Sacha looked at Mariah, trying to smile. "I'll see the old lad home. I'll be back in the morning. The door by the steps is always open. Go now, go," she said briskly, waving him away. "Back you go, Mariah. Back you go to the Prince Regent.

"Ay . . . back to ya soft beds and feather pillows," her father growled.

Sacha took her father and turned him toward the dark street that led to Paradise. He swayed as he walked, letting go of her arm and reaching out to the wall to steady himself. Mariah watched, wondering what he would do alone. He kept an eye on the men who pulled the body from the cold, damp ground and tumbled it into the barrow. From its pockets jangled seven gold coins, which fell to the ground and clattered across the cobbles. Quickly the men plunged upon them. They scrambled to pick them up, and seeing Mariah, tossed one to him, as if to buy his silence.

Mariah caught the coin with one hand as the staggering footsteps of Sacha's father faded into the distance. He stepped back and leaned against the doorpost to the inn. A warm draught blew against the back of his neck. The smell of smoke and cheap beer billowed from a crack in the door. He tried to read the inscription on the coin, but he couldn't read the markings. He slipped it into his pocket and watched as the men folded the coat around the corpse and pushed the cart toward the door of the inn.

"Keep an eye on the cart, boy, and another coin'll come your way," one of the men said as he rubbed a golden penny against his chin. He smiled at Mariah, a grin filled with blackened teeth. "He shouldn't be any trouble. If he moves, give us a shout."

They pushed past Mariah and through the doors of the inn. He stood still, surrounded by the light of the gas lamp that hung above the peeling paint of the inn door. Mariah didn't want to move from its glow; an echoing inner thought told him he was only safe if he kept himself in the light. For several minutes he waited for the men to return, hoping he could follow the cart and walk with them through the alleyways until he could find the main street that ran from the harbour to the grand squares and fine parades of the town. All was quiet; he listened for Sacha's father as she led him to Paradise. Somehow he knew that they were already there, locked behind a strong door in the light of a cheerful fire and surrounded by her family.

He waited and waited, hoping that soon the men would leave their drinking and return to the task of taking away the stiffening body. The cart was pushed against the wall. It was as if he felt drawn to see the face of the dead man. He fought the desire to lift the old black coat and stare into the cadaver's eyes. Mariah knew that if he did so, he would have to step from the protection of the light and stand alone in the darkness next to the corpse.

Alone, his mind whirring, he tried to listen to the hushed conversation that crept through the door of the inn. He picked out the occasional phrase, talk of the kraken and sea creatures, murderous villains and the walking dead. Mister Grimm kept the conversation stoked like a raging fire. He filled the short silences with grunts of concern, adding to the pot any myth he could pick out of his imagination and how *he* had been responsible for its detection. All listened intently, as if in the presence of a great master. Grimm spoke ever louder of his toil and trouble, louder than the rest, in his finest Oxford accent. Mariah listened, clinging to the cold stone step outside.

On the hilltop, the clock on the church tower chimed once.

"One o'clock," Mariah said, knowing his companion in the

cart would not offer a reply. Tired of waiting for the men to return, Mariah slipped his cold fingers into the door crack and slowly pulled it open until he could see inside.

The inn was bright, and filled with pipe smoke, which hung like long blue strands. Grimm sat with his back to the door as Matthias filled his glass. The old candles had been replaced, oil lamps burned bright, and a full scuttle of coal had been thrown on the fire. They were set for the night as they drank the cup of conspiracy. Mariah's heart sank, knowing they would be there until first light and he would be left outside guarding the corpse. He looked at the cart and then at the street, which was now etched in silver moonlight.

Quickly, he strode from the steps and set off from the inn, burying his hands in his pockets and casting a last sharp look behind. His pace slowed as he reached the corner by the alley that had led them to the cellar. Mariah tried to remember what his mother used to say to him when he was afraid. He could see her in his mind, smiling, but the words had gone. Before him were the tracks of the carriage that had taken Luger back to the Prince Regent. He set himself to follow, walking in the centre of the narrowing road that led by the harbourside. He scurried past a crumbling old sandstone house, by stacks of twisted crab pots and houses strewn with hanging nets. He never looked back, always keeping his eyes on the fading tracks that crossed sand and cobbles, leaving only a teasing glimpse of where the carriage had travelled. His pace increased, keeping time with his deepening uneasiness.

From close by, he heard the patter of steps keeping pace with his. At first he thought they were but an echo of his own. But then, when he looked back again, he saw him.

Following Mariah and keeping himself to the shadows was a man. Mariah could see the trailing wisps of his long coat dragging against the shadows and stirring swirls of sand. He could make out the hunched shape that hid its face under a thick sea cap.

Mariah tried to convince himself that he was simply a fellow traveller making his way toward the bright streets. Just a coincidence, Mariah thought, a reveller on his way to a stacked garret, a fisherman fresh from the sea. But within several paces he knew this wasn't true. His wits told him not to stop, told him to run—because the follower was the kraken.

Mariah's gut twisted as he tried to hold back his growing sense of hopelessness. His mind flashed to the face of the corpse with its slashed forehead and neck. With every other step Mariah turned to glance at his nocturnal stalker.

A swirl of seabirds took flight from their resting place on the sharp-sloped rooftops above the quayside. Mariah looked up; the sky was filled with their cawing as they circled about the moon. He turned; the man still followed, slowing his pace as he jumped in and out of the long moon shadows and skirted the gutters.

With great compulsion Mariah burst into a trot, then a canter, his feet pounding against the mounds of sand blown by the wind. He cast back a glance; the man had begun to gallop, his uneven gait throwing his body from side to side, keeping him twenty paces behind. Ahead, the bright sign of the Golden Kipper lit the street. Mariah thought of Charity as he ran headlong toward the harbour. Again he cast a glance back; the kraken had fallen farther behind. It slowed, half-hobbling. Mariah pressed on, running faster as his antagonist disappeared back into the shadows, giving up the chase.

To Mariah's right was a long flight of steps that led to the customs house. With long strides he danced up the steps three at a time, smiling to himself, knowing the street to the Prince Regent was two corners away. He sighed heavily and happily. He looked up at the bright night sky and hopeful moon, and slowed to a walk.

A hand grabbed him by the collar and threw him to the ground. It had fired from the darkness, hid by an open doorway. Mariah rolled on the damp stone, twisted himself around and got up. Then came a blow hitting him with such force that it knocked him from his feet and down the first flight of steps. He looked up at the cloaked figure that hobbled toward him, its wide red eyes glowing in the shadows, its wet coat trailing salt water across the steps.

"*No!*" Mariah shouted. The creature took out a handful of golden pennies and scattered them upon him. It grimaced as it dragged its bootless foot across the stone. Mariah could see the webbed, gnarled toes that gripped the earth like bird claws. Upon each wrist was the broken band of an iron manacle, and above that a thin silver bangle etched with straw figures. From inside its coat it took a triple-bladed dagger. It grunted and coughed, spluttering seawater from its mouth as it stepped toward him.

"Trouble, boy?" came a calm voice from behind the kraken. The creature half turned as a staff crashed across its back. It fell toward Mariah, tripping over his feet and stumbling down the steps. Charity followed, hitting the creature again and again as golden coins spilled from the pocket of its long coat and clinked down the steps toward the sea. "Away with you," he shouted as the kraken turned and looked at him, shielding its head from yet another blow of his staff. "Back to the sea . . . your ship awaits you." Charity held out the staff toward the sea beast.

The kraken brushed the hair from its face and looked at Mariah, then at Charity, and nodded to him, seeming to understand. It turned, hobbling down the final steps as it disappeared into the darkness and the labyrinth of passages that ran to the harbour.

Charity turned to Mariah. "Not a place I would have expected to find you, Mariah Mundi."

CHAPTER

❧ 14 ❧

The Golden Kipper

M ariah sat at the end of a long table neatly set with drinking glasses and silver cutlery, all set on the finest, whitest linen. Behind him was a tall window that looked out over the harbour, the fishing boats bobbing back and forth and the lighthouse, which spun its beam out to the blackened sea. A large brass and wood telescope stood majestically upon an oak tripod in front of the window.

From his chair Mariah watched Charity sweat over the large black range that filled the entire wall of the open kitchen. A collection of curios decorated the dining room walls, framed by the bright white cornice that ran around the high ceilings and the polished skirting boards that edged the shining wooden floor. He had never seen anything so meticulously clean. Whilst Charity rushed back and forth, Mariah eyed the strange creatures that hung from the walls with their dull, lifeless eyes. Some he recognised, such as the bison and the moose; others he had no idea what they were or how they got there.

It was the large crocodile that caught his attention. The beast lay by the wall near the door, stretching several feet in length, its tail purposefully curled so it could fit the room. Mariah eyed it with fascination. The beast was so preserved that it gave Mariah a shy grin as it stared back through large brown eyes the size of saucers. Without thinking, Mariah smiled back, captivated by the creature's apparent under-standing, even though he knew the beast to be the work of a skilled taxidermist.

Charity untied the pleated blue apron from around his waist and rubbed it across his brow. He picked up a large oval plate from the counter and, using the apron to protect his fingers, carried it across the room toward Mariah.

"Bet you've never seen the likes of this, boy?" he asked ex-citedly, as if it were his latest invention. "Fish extraordinaire . . . from the deepest depths of the sea to your plate, and as fresh as the wind."

Mariah stared at a mountainous concoction of crisp, golden slices of fish surrounded by a ring of bright green mashed peas from which protruded slices of deep fried potato. The aroma leaped across the room, and his stomach growled with joyous anticipation. Gone were the thoughts of the night, the kraken and even of Sacha. The plate filled his mind with all the thoughts it could muster.

"Let's be thankful," Charity said, closing his eyes and speaking quietly. "Takes a life to bring this to us. Never for-get that."

Mariah clutched his knife and fork, and looked at Charity, waiting to be told when he could eat. The man smiled, raising an eyebrow and winking as if it were the start to a race. In the dim light of the tallow lamp, Mariah ate and ate, never lifting his eyes from the dish.

"Bread and tea," Charity said as he brought another tray to the table, this one laden with a loaf of brown bread that shimmered in its own heat haze. "Nearly there?" he asked Mariah, who gulped and nodded at the same time, knowing that his belly was practically full, yet wanting to eat more. "Then I better craft something for a sweet tooth," Charity said. He left the table and returned to the kitchen.

Mariah kept eating, following the bread in his mouth with a swallow of hot tea. He looked at the crocodile and smiled.

The creature smiled back and winked. Then it closed its eyes and appeared to sleep.

A sudden sense of dread filled Mariah. His stomach turned as he saw a short column of mist rise from the crocodile's nostrils and disappear into the air. At the far end of the restaurant, Captain Charity continued working, seemingly unaware that the stuffed crocodile was really alive.

"Captain Charity," Mariah whispered, not wanting to wake the creature. "I need to tell you something . . . urgently," he said, keeping his gaze fixed upon the crocodile as he picked up his feet from the floor and propped them as high as he could on the opposite chair.

"First we eat pricky pudding, and then you can tell me all about the kraken and Otto Luger," Charity said as the sound of cracked eggs echoed around the room. "Plenty of time to sort out the world before dawn. I'll have you back at the Prince Regent before they even know you're gone." He took a hot sponge cake from the oven. "Three minutes and then you'll be bathed in ecstasy," Charity shouted loudly. The crocodile opened one eye and looked from one end of the room to the other before it finally stopped and stared at Mariah.

"Is the bison from the Americas?" Mariah asked feebly. He got to his feet and hopped from the chair to the long window ledge that ran across the bay side of the room.

"You know well," Charity shouted. "Brought it back myself many years ago; liked it the moment I saw it."

"Was it hard to shoot?" Mariah asked. Now he stood on the window ledge, wondering if he could run the length of the restaurant, from table to table, before the crocodile could snap him from the air.

"Don't really know," Charity replied as he tipped the pricky pudding onto another large plate and covered it with steaming custard. "Bought it from a man at dock thirty-one in New York, just before I sailed home; never would want to kill something as beautiful as that. Everything you see I have picked up here and there. They are objects of art, things of fancy, keepsakes of my travels."

"Crocodiles?" Mariah whispered, his voice trembling, hoping the creature would stay where it lay.

"I wondered how long it would be before Cuba caught your attention," Charity said with a glint of mirth in his voice as he carried the pudding from the kitchen to the table. "'As the mournful crocodile / with sorrow snares relenting passengers . . .' Didn't take her long to snare you, did it, Mariah?"

"You knew it was alive?" he asked loudly, stepping down from the window as Charity beckoned him to sit back at the table.

"Alive . . . friendly . . . and full of fish. She's an old girl. Caught her myself." Charity picked up a leftover tail of monkfish and threw it to the beast. "Too big to keep her here, and yet whenever I take her for a walk, she always makes for where I found her."

"Africa?" asked Mariah hesitantly.

"The sands outside where the Prince Regent now stands,"

Charity replied. "Found her on the beach, just a tiny thing no bigger than your hand. Kept her in the cellar ever since. Floods with the tide, and she's good for eating any . . . left-overs." He laughed. "We were burgled once; two villains got into the cellar by the old coal hatch. They say you could hear the screams on Castle Hill. Never did find much, and for some reason the police didn't want to investigate the scene of the crime. Not like any crocodile I've seen before," he went on. "She has the legs of a lizard and only one webbed foot. More of a dragon than a crocodile."

Mariah didn't reply as he looked from Charity to the sleeping Cuba and back again.

"Have some pricky pudding," Charity said as he doled out two large scoops of thick sponge cake encrusted with wild brambles and syrup, covered in yellow custard. "Just the thing for an early breakfast."

A large golden clock hung above the door. It chimed a melancholy chime that jangled about the room. Cuba snapped at the air, brought to life by the two bitter notes. Her teeth snapped tightly shut as her large eyes gazed about.

"Hates sudden moves and loud noises . . . Never could train her to ignore them. Not best to be near her at midnight." Charity laughed as he dipped a spoon into the centre of the pudding.

"On the steps," Mariah asked quickly, "the creature . . . what was it?"

"That, Mariah, we will never really know. A kraken, a croquemitaine to frighten children. There are many things in this world that are beyond our understanding. One thing is certain: it wanted you."

"What of the money?" Mariah asked as he felt the coin in his pocket.

"Some say the kraken comes from a sunken ship filled with

Icelandic gold. A Viking treasure stolen from the grave of a king. That he carries the money to give as a gift for the death he leaves behind." Charity got up from the table and pulled a thick red velvet curtain across the large pane of glass. "Some things are best said in private," he said softly. He paused and looked about the room.

"There was a man killed by the Three Mariners, a cut across his head and three wounds in his neck, just like the kraken's knife would've made." Mariah thrust his hand into the air. "If you hadn't been there, it would have . . ." He stopped and thought for a moment. "Why were you there?" he asked. "How did you know?"

"Questions, questions. I have a great many for you. Here you are, not more than three days in town and already being rescued from murder. What of that man on the train? What became of him? Tell me, what of Otto Luger and Bizmillah? How do they treat you?"

"You were following me, Captain," Mariah insisted as he placed the knife and fork neatly side by side on his plate and folded the large white napkin.

"It was a coincidence," Charity said.

"You *were* following me."

"So, . . . what if I was? And a good job to boot. That thing would have had you in pieces. If you stand under the window of the Golden Kipper talking to your lady friend, then a man like me *will* be intrigued." Charity smiled and held out his hand. "Came along in friendship, remembered you from the train and wanted to make sure you were . . . . all right. I warned you then and I'll warn you now. There are events taking place that you would never understand, and you are caught in the middle of them."

Charity put his hand on Mariah's shoulder and looked him in the eye. In that brief moment Mariah could see every line of the man's battle-worn face. He wondered what sights that piercing blue gaze had looked upon, what wonders, marvels and misery they had beheld. In some hidden, half-thought way, he thought he saw his own future.

"Were you really in the Sudan?" Mariah asked.

"In the rebellion. Fought for two years."

"Did you ever . . . ?" Mariah asked, unable to finish.

"Your parents?" Charity replied, guessing Mariah's question. "I heard what you said on the train. Never give up hope. Search for truth until you find the answer."

"I would go there tomorrow," Mariah said, gritting his teeth, "search every inch of land for them. If I could just have some proof . . . " He paused. "Somehow, a scrap of paper telling me they're gone isn't enough. They're not dead, not in my mind, no matter what people say."

Charity listened, his eyes glistening with the flames from the lamp. "Sometimes things happen in war," he said, lost in thought, "things we never mean to happen. So cruel that our minds find them hard to remember, and our silence is looked upon as grim, heroic modesty when secretly we hate ourselves for what we have done." Charity looked at the few remains that lay scattered about the plate. "Filled and ready for the night," he said, a sudden change coming to his voice. "Time to have you back to the Prince Regent. Cuba needs a walk on the beach."

Charity stood and snapped his fingers. Cuba lifted herself to her feet, her long legs twice the length of a typical crocodile's and all but one ending in a clawed foot. She slinked quickly in and out of the tables, and sat by the door, her tail twitching excitedly as she waited for her master. Mariah followed at a distance as Captain Charity donned a heavy overcoat, took a long leather strap from his pocket and slipped it around the beast's neck.

"The locals get frightened if she's not on the leash. Only reason they tolerate Cuba is that they think she keeps the kraken away. It was an old fisherman gave her the name, said it was that of an angel that kept watch over children as they slept, and she's looked after this place whilst I've been away." The crocodile rose on its back feet and scratched the door. "Must be a rat somewhere. Loves the chase, and you never hear a squeak when she catches them." He laughed.

From the door of the Golden Kipper, Mariah could see the outline of the Prince Regent drawn against the fragmenting mist by the full moon. He stepped ahead of the crocodile and its keeper as the beast pulled against the leash and sniffed the air.

"Still can smell a rat," Charity said as he locked the front door and pulled up the collar of his coat. "The mist is bad again," he whispered. "They say that ever since they built the Regent, the sea's got warmer and the mists last longer."

They crossed the cobbled street and walked down the slipway and onto the sand. Cuba sprung back and forth like a young puppy, snapping at the air. Charity slipped the leash from her neck and watched her sprint across the sand and into the darkness. Mariah followed close by as he looked for the creature.

"Don't worry, lad," Charity said merrily. "Old Cuba will be chasing sea hawks. You're far too big a mouthful for her tonight, even though you are stuffed with the best fish and potato."

Mariah reached into his pocket and pulled out the ticket he had been given by Charity on the train.

"For my feast," he said as he tried to hand it to him.

"Not needed," Charity replied. "If I take the ticket, I may never see you again. This way I know you'll be back for a free meal—whenever you need one, of course." Charity held Mariah's arm as they walked. "Tell me one thing. Isambard Black, the man from the train—what became of him?"

Mariah paused, not wanting to say something out of turn. He looked at the houses and shops that littered the shore. Far to his right were three new bathing machines with candy-striped hoods. "I've seen him a couple of times," he said. "Bizmillah keeps us busy. He and Bizmillah keep company together. Last night, they were together in a room speaking and that."

"And what of the hotel? Have you had a chance to explore it yet?" Charity asked quietly as he guided Mariah across the sand toward the Prince Regent.

"Seen as much as I need. Sacha knows it better than any-one. Took me all round the place. From the highest towers into the dark depths. Hot as hell down there. Dark and steamy and smells of fish."

There was a cry of gulls far across the strand by the wa-ter's edge. The steady beat of Cuba's feet came across the soft sand, speaking of her coming. Like an obedient dog, she sat at Charity's feet, her long tail curled about her, its tip giving away the tiniest hint of excitement. In her mouth she gently held a fat, squawking gull, its bright white feathers pressed against her dark skin. Cuba growled to herself.

"Let it be, Cuba," Charity scolded the crocodile. "That's not for you." The crocodile obediently opened its mouth, and the frightened bird leaped from the jaws of death and took flight. Cuba danced on her back legs, swirling the warm sand beneath her with her long tail as the seabird circled and called out overhead.

"It's so warm for a winter's night," Mariah said as he picked up a piece of driftwood and threw it far away for the crocodile to chase.

"Touch the sand and feel the warmth underfoot," Charity

said, scooping a handful of steaming grains from the beach. "The sea is as hot as bathwater and the sand no better," he said as he tipped the sand into Mariah's palm. "Do me one thing, Mariah. Find me the reason for this and I think you will have some of the answers that you search for."

❋ 15 ❋

Reductio ad Absurdum

Mariah left Charity on the beach and climbed the long steps that ran the height of the cliff to the Prince Regent. Somewhere ahead he knew there would be a door; far behind he knew that Charity and Cuba would wait until he was out of sight and safe within the red brick walls of the hotel. Mariah gripped the cold iron railing as he climbed higher. Beads of sweat glistened on his forehead. Tall black gas lamps lit the steep stone staircase. Their amber light flickered in the swirls of mist that followed his every step. Set in the thick brick wall at the top was a dark wooden door, clearly marked in bright white paint with the word DELIVERIES.

Mariah turned to the sea and looked far below. There was Charity, as he said he would be, waiting and watching from the shore as Cuba scratched in the sand, swishing her tail back and forth as she chewed on driftwood. Mariah waved to his watcher and opened the door.

He looked back momentarily, a noise from the top step catching his ear. There, by the tiny parade of shops near the hotel, between the Italian Café and Gentleman's Hairdresser, was the lamplighter. He looked at Mariah and nodded as he hooked the gas handle under the wick and turned off the hissing supply.

Mariah smiled at him as he stepped inside the doorway of the Prince Regent, pulling the door firmly shut, waiting as the steps of the lamplighter clattered down the stone stairs.

Inside the hotel, he was greeted by the sound of the elevator. All was quiet at that early hour. As he strode down the dark corridors he mulled over the idea of doing his work before he went to sleep, hoping to please Sacha and to give himself time to understand what he had seen in the night. He couldn't shake the image of the kraken from his thoughts.

As he turned into the last corridor and up the final flight of steps to the stage door Mariah heard the sound of feet coming from far behind. He shuddered, stepped into a shadow out of the glare of the lamp and looked back. All was still. He brushed off the sound as a figment of his imagination, coughing to clear his throat, half out of fear and half worrying that he might have to run at any moment. The echo went on and on. He made a fist, digging the nails into his palm. "Who's there?" he asked, hoping there would be no reply.

Mariah waited and waited for whoever was in the darkness. No one came, no sound, just the gentle hum of the steam generator far below, rumbling as it always did.

In two steps he was through the door and into the theatre. He stood in the pitch black, knowing that to his right would be a small table with a brass candleholder and stout candle, and by the side would be the lucifer and striking plate. He fumbled blindly, sliding his hand across the table as he felt for the holder.

Outside, the footsteps came again. He pushed his back against the door and felt for the bolt, sliding it shut. He crouched in the blackness and listened. Again, all fell silent.

"Imagination," he whispered to himself as he at last found the candle and the lucifer. There was a bright spark. With a shaking hand he lit the candle.

Taking the candle, he went to the stage. There he lit the gas lamp in the wings and pulled out the saw box, checking the mechanical feet and all of the latches. He wanted nothing to go wrong; after all, he was the one who would be putting his life into Bizmillah's hands. Mariah swept the stage, set the backdrops on their long twisted ropes and fed the doves.

He had almost forgotten the fear of the kraken when the stage door rattled on its hinges. It was as if a sudden gust of wind had blasted against it. The curtains that hung from the high arch over the stage shook a little, and a myriad of tiny specks of dust fell from the ceiling to the floor. They would have been invisible had they not danced through the shaft of light that flooded the stage from the wings.

The shudder came again. Mariah quickly pushed the box back to its place, stacking the other tricks in order of use upon it and covering them all in Bizmillah's purple silk cloth.

"Very late to be doing your work, young Mariah," came a voice from the blackness of the vast auditorium.

Mariah stared out, unable to see anyone.

"Thought a Colonial boy would be tucked up in bed . . . in safety," said the voice sarcastically.

"Mister Bizmillah wants it to be perfect. Can't feed the doves in the daytime—they fly away." Then he realised whom he was speaking to.

"So you give away the secrets . . . You should be bound by oath never to divulge the secrets of the Order of Magicians. It would be on pain of death to give such vital knowledge to the uninitiated." Black walked through the darkness toward the stage. "Before you ask, like you, I couldn't sleep. It is something that has avoided me recently." He walked slowly down the dark aisle, clearing his throat as if he were about to make some majestic speech. "I have even taken to walking the streets by the harbour. Interesting place, especially at night. You meet the most remarkable class of fellow—don't you think?"

"I wouldn't know, Mister Black," Mariah replied.

"I forget, you are a Colonial boy, and as such would never venture away from where you are supposed to be." Black grinned as he stepped into the shaft of dust-filled light and looked up at Mariah. "But I'm intrigued. There is something about you that fascinates me. I was just saying to my good friend—" He stopped abruptly, seeming to worry he had said too much. "Pick a card," he exclaimed loudly as a deck of cards with bright red backs appeared in his hand as if from nowhere.

Mariah walked slowly across the stage, bent down and picked a card from the deck. He looked at the card and held it close to his chest.

"King of clubs," Black shouted, and Mariah nodded in agreement. "Pick another."

Mariah picked another card, and before he could even look, Black shouted, "King of diamonds.

"One more for luck," he said excitedly as he walked up the small wooden steps and onto the stage. "Just take one more card and then we will end this frivolity."

Mariah hesitated. He knew this was all a sleight of hand, that Black had memorised the cards or had presented them to him so he would pick certain ones from the deck. He eyed the cards one by one, feeling his hand forced in some way by Black. Purposefully, he plucked the card farthest from Black's fingers at the outer edge of the fan. The sight of the joker with its telltale cribbed edge and bright-coloured mantle flashed before him.

Mariah tried not to give away his surprise. He had held the card before. It had looked at him with its cross-eyes and magical wand in the train from London. Now it stared at him again.

"The joker," Black said. "It keeps coming into your life, Mariah. Perhaps the cards are trying to speak to you."

"I would prefer the language of men. If you don't mind, Mister Black, I have to work, and Bizmillah will be angry if things are not ready in time."

"Bizmillah . . . the friendly magician? He'll be well pleased, especially with *my* magic," Black said. He twisted his hand and from inside his coat took a triple-bladed dagger, like that which had been carried by the kraken. "Now, this is of interest, I am sure," he said as he held it out toward the boy. "Only three were ever made. They say they were forged in the burning volcanoes of Iceland from a type of metal ore that has never been found again. It has the sheen of gold and the strength of steel. I am searching for them all, and I will hopefully find them."

Mariah scrutinised the triple knife with its jagged tiger-tooth points; gleaming, sharp blades; whalebone handle; and golden hilt. The blades matched perfectly the marks he had seen on the murdered body outside the Three Mariners.

"Do you think you'll find them?" he asked as he stepped away from Black. He picked up the broom and then idly sauntered to the shelter of the wings.

"I search for many things: a pack of cards, a precious box and the daggers. I am a collector of trickery and mechanical conjuring," he said, and then the shudder came again, spilling more dust from the high ceiling.

Mariah turned to reply, but Black had vanished. He looked back and forth, feeling this was part of yet another trick and that Black would appear as quickly as he had vanished. "Mister Black," Mariah shouted as he walked across the stage and peered into the gloom of the auditorium. "Mister Black . . ."

With great reluctance Mariah turned the gas tap to extinguish the lamp. The stage vanished in the gloom that covered the falling sparkles of silver dust. He held the candleholder nervously in front of him as he slowly retraced his footsteps to the stage door. Slipping back the bolt, he looked into the passageway leading to the stairs that would take him to the tower. Far away he could hear the voice of the baker singing as he stacked the oven with the first loaves of the morning. Mariah was cheered that he was not alone, and that if he were to call out, then at least there was the faintest possibility that someone would hear him.

He leaned into the shadows and listened warily, then snuffed out the candle and placed the holder upon the table before striding out to the stairway. Mariah couldn't look back. He grabbed the door to the stairs and rushed through, keeping his eyes to the dimly lit floor for fear of seeing anything other than carpet and stone. Taking the steps two at a time, he ran as fast as he could until he reached the top landing and the door to his room. He pushed the door open and quickly stepped into the moonlit room, and taking the chair, propped it against the door handle so that it could not be opened from the outside. Mariah sighed as the moon beat in at the window, having scattered the clouds and sea mist.

The door to the elevator rattled open, and then came the footsteps that he had heard before. Slowly and stealthily, they took the three paces from the open elevator to his room. He waited, expecting to hear a knock or tap at the door. He could feel the presence of someone outside. *Black*, he thought as he stepped over to the bed and sat on the coarse blanket.

Then the door handle turned. Someone pushed against the door. Mariah saw the wood move in the frame. He jumped back farther on the bed as he grabbed the pillow and clutched it to his chest. The door moved again. The handle turned faster. He looked at the window, thinking of a way to escape. A gentle tap . . . tap . . . sounded against the door. He couldn't speak, his voice frozen.

"Mariah," came a whisper. "Mariah, let me in."

He didn't reply, unsure about the voice. There was a sudden kick against the door and the chair fell from its place, releasing the handle. The door was pushed open and the chair brushed to one side, scraping across the floor. Mariah clutched the privy pot that was by the bedside, holding it by its thin handle, ready to strike at whatever creature came upon him.

"Mariah," came the voice again. "I've been waiting for you to return."

A cloud crossed the moon like a thin, black blade as a figure stepped into the room. Mariah looked up as he drew back his arm, ready to strike.

"Sacha?" he asked as he stared at the dark shape before him. "Is it you?"

"'Tis I," she said as she struck a match and lit the lamp by the door. "Where have you been? I got rid of my father and came straight here. Waited by the back door for ages and you never came. I met Black and he told me he'd seen you in the theatre, so I came to your room. Surprised to see me?"

"Surprised?" he said quickly. "Sight for sore eyes. When you left, I was chased by the kraken . . . found by Captain Charity . . . met a crocodile . . . and then Black appeared and then vanished again. Not the most normal of evenings, I would say."

"So you met Cuba. She's nothing but a big lap dog. He found her on the beach, you know," Sacha said. "And the kraken, you say?"

"It's real, Sacha; I've seen it with my own eyes."

"So says many a man on a Friday night on the way home

from the Three Mariners," she said curtly, brushing the dark hair from her eyes.

Mariah told her every detail of the night. He showed her the coin in his pocket and told her how the kraken had attacked.

"The trouble is . . . the trouble is . . . ," he said slowly, reaching under the bed. "I almost feel more fearful of Black than the kraken. Black wants something," he said, looking nervously around the room. He reached for the box of cards that he had hidden. "I think he knows I have *these*." Mariah held out his hand. Resting on his palm and glowing in the moonlight was the pack of cards still neatly enclosed in the box. The joker stared out, his eyes glowing softly as if a hidden light inside the box were illuminating them.

"A fine and fancy deck of poker cards," Sacha replied as she stared at it, the golden braid that encircled the box shining boldly with an incandescent light.

CHAPTER

❋ 16 ❋

The Dancing Panjandrum

Two chairs were wedged against the door, their spindly legs pressed into the hard wood of the planked floor that ran seamlessly from wall to wall. Against them was wedged the small cupboard with its bowl and washpot, full of cold water. The last part of the barricade was the bed, which now spanned the narrow room. Sacha peered over Mariah's shoulder as he knelt in the firelight and unpacked the cards from the box. They were wrapped in a stiff piece of white paper. He slipped his finger beneath the red wax seal and slowly folded back the wrapper. It burst open with a sudden crack, giving out a shower of tiny blue sparks and filling the room with the musty odour of old books. Startled, Mariah looked at the inside of the paper. Beneath a heading reading THE PANJANDRUM was a fine-line drawing of a tower of cards. To one side was a list of instructions, giving the name of each card and how they were to be placed together.

Mariah looked up at Sacha; she nodded to tell him to go on, the flickering of the flames dancing across her face as she tried to read the words on the folded paper.

"Is it a game?" she asked quietly.

Mariah said nothing as one by one he placed the cards together, following the plan written out before him. Each card clicked firmly to the other as if they were waiting to be joined together and become one solid piece. King followed knave, wands linked with pentacles, each suit coming together, the tower growing quickly in the firelight. Finally Mariah held the last two cards in his hands and stared at the crossed-eyed jokers. One smiled back; the other grimaced with one eye closed and a hand placed over his mouth, as if he were refusing to speak.

Sacha tapped Mariah on the shoulder to bring him from his reverie and finish the tower. It was now twelve cards high. He placed the jokers on each side of the final span, their faces staring at opposite walls. He sat back and looked at the completed tower.

Then the tremor that had shaken the hotel earlier that night came again. It rattled the whole of the Prince Regent, sending a shower of dust cascading from the ceiling. The window rattled in its frame and cracked across the glass pane. The tower of cards didn't move.

Mariah looked at Sacha and then at the instructions. To his astonishment more words seemed to have appeared on the paper. He read them aloud. "Once the tower is complete — then amaze your audience with its magical fortuities. *Chi — Samekh — Digamma.*" His voice sounded like it came from another place.

Then came the faint sound of whispering. Sacha looked about her, sure that the voices came from outside the room and that the barricade would not hold against whoever came upon them. She looked at Mariah, hoping he could hear the whispers, too.

"Can you hear . . . ?" she said as the muttering grew louder.

"Chi — Samekh — Digamma," Mariah said again as if he hadn't heard her.

"Where is it coming from?" she shrieked as the clamour vibrated in her head.

"Don't say a word," Mariah said, his face fixed in concentration on the Panjandrum. Suddenly, they burst to life and began to hover above the floorboards. "Sacha, take my hand," he murmured, not taking his eyes off the cards. The tower started spinning, going faster and faster, each card blurring into the other as the manifestation whirled, sparking with every turn. "Can you see it?"

Sacha stared, unsure. "It's a trick," she said, not wanting to believe what she saw. "Just like what Bizmillah would have done."

"Not a trick," Mariah said, his stare fixed upon the spinning cards. "This is more like magic. Now I know why Albion gave them to me. Look," he gasped as the tower unfolded to frame a living depiction of jostling images. It glittered and sparked as the cards melted and transformed into a single image. There unfurled before them was a London street made up of tiny fragments of the Panjandrum. They swirled and changed with every second to form a moving picture in which dark figures walked back and forth. Striding boldly along the sidewalk was Albion, who pulled his collar up against the driving rain, his floppy hat tugged across his face. The bright sign of Claridges Hotel lit the scene as close by two men followed, trailed by a hansom cab, its horse decked in black plumes.

The Panjandrum raised itself higher into the air as the scene began to change. Inside the frame of spinning cards, Albion stepped toward the hotel entrance. In his hand they could see the postcard that Mariah had sent, the painting of the Prince

Regent visible. Without warning, the men that lurked behind grabbed Albion roughly by the arms and lifted him from his feet. Turning him to the road, they bundled him quickly into the waiting carriage. In the corner of the picture, lurking as if not wanting to be seen, was a grey-faced figure who brushed the steps with what appeared to be a long black broom. Then the man began to walk the pavement, and as he went along, he tapped some of the rain-soaked pedestrians gently upon their foreheads with the tip of a long, gnarled finger. With every touch he left behind a bloodred mark that set them apart from those passersby who went on their way unchosen.

"What is it?" Sacha asked, more intrigued at the spectacle than frightened by it.

"Whatever it is, it's wrong — I can feel it. This shouldn't be happening." Mariah edged farther away from the Panjandrum. "We have to stop it."

"Stop it?" Sacha replied. "This is amazing — moving pictures."

"But Albion, what happened to him?"

"Doesn't mean it was real; could be a trick of the cards," she argued.

"He had the postcard. I saw it in his hand."

Then three dark letters edged in bright gold appeared in the corner of the shimmering card frame. In the soft glow from the fire, they spoke the word together: "*ASK*."

"It wants us to ask something, Mariah . . . What shall we say?" Sacha said, her heart beating wildly.

"Say nothing. I don't like it. It's not good," Mariah cut back quickly, wishing he knew how to stop the cards.

"You're frightened of your own shadow. If it is a trick, it'll do us no harm. If it can see the future, then we have something that'll make us rich."

"Rather die poor than have this on my conscience. It can't be good — it's not right."

"Right or wrong, it's right before our eyes and it wants us to ask it a question." Sacha thought for a moment. "Is Felix alive?" she blurted before Mariah could stop her.

The Panjandrum shuddered. One by one, the cards fell from the air and landed in a neat pile on the floor. A final card hovered above the floorboards as if it were suspended by an invisible piece of string. Mariah wafted his hand above the card, hoping to snag whatever caused it to dance in the air.

The deck burst into life. Several cards leaped from the floor, chasing each other up to the ceiling, circling like a flock of geese. More and more began to dance this way and that before they too leaped into the air and flew to become one large mass that blanketed the ceiling.

Mariah looked up. It was as if the night sky had crept inside the room and pinned itself to the ceiling. Stars twinkled brightly as a glowing moon slowly crossed the vision. Then without any warning, all grew dark again. The far side of the ceiling began to glow with a bright red light. Steam billowed as far away a young boy took shape, one of many hunched in a dark hole, the floor strewn with milky pearls. From beneath a mantle of matted hair, two bleary, tired eyes stared out as blue, bloodless lips mouthed silent words.

"It's Felix!" Sacha shouted, leaping to her feet and jumping toward the apparition above her. "I can see you, Felix . . . You're alive." The boy didn't reply, his stare fixed, lips mumbling, deaf to her words. "Where are you?" she asked impatiently.

Her tone jarred Mariah. He saw in her eyes that she thought the boy was special, that he occupied a special place in her heart. "He's a million miles away from here, can't you see?" he shouted as he pushed her away from the vision. "I want this to stop. Felix is dead and this is a lie. Look at him — sitting on a bed of pearls and looking half-starved. If that isn't a wicked trick of these cards, then what is? I should never have taken them from Albion. I want them to stop . . . *now*."

"Tell me where he is," Sacha said urgently, ignoring Mariah. "*Please,*" she pleaded. "*Tell me.*"

"*No*, . . . stop it now," Mariah shouted above her. "We don't want to know. Felix is gone."

The cards twisted, imploding into the shape of a large golden orb that pressed closer and closer.

"It'll crush us," Sacha shouted as Mariah dived to the floor and scrambled to find the box of instructions.

"Stand back and say nothing more," he shouted as he rolled under the bed, one hand clutching the sheet of paper.

Sacha stood alone. The orb hovered in front of her, sparking blue and gold flecks of bright light that danced like the candles on a Christmas tree. Through the thin veneer of gold, she looked down upon the world as if she were a bird. Far below she could see the sunlit rooftops of the Prince Regent. As if cracked like a gigantic egg, the building was split open, revealed to her floor by floor. She was taken deeper and deeper. Spiralling down, she seemed to circle until the black rocks of the deep foundations opened up before her. There, nestling in the hollow earth, was a dark cavern, the floor littered in creamy pearls. In a sunken corner littered with oyster shells was a gathering of children, huddled together as a dark beast flicked its scaled tail back and forth.

Beneath the bed Mariah clung to the sheet of paper he had plucked from the floor. It twisted to free itself from his grip, as if it had a mind of its own. Mariah scanned the black etching that now appeared to smear itself into the paper, each word slowly smudging beyond recognition. Quickly he read the final three words before they faded. "*Za-yin* . . . za-yin . . . za-yin," he shouted as they melted out of sight.

A lightning bolt cut through the air to the heart of the orb. The vision exploded, throwing Sacha against the wall. The cards fell from the air and scattered like leaves across the floor.

Mariah heard Sacha's muffled scream and looked up from his hiding place. Sacha was struggling to breathe as the joker tried to smother her, clinging to the contours of her nose and mouth. Several cards held her tight against the wall, piercing her clothes and pinning her to the plaster as if they were daggers. Her arms were tethered tightly, a cluster of cards on each wrist as if the explosion had shackled them to her. He could see the life draining from her as she fought to breathe.

He jumped to his feet and pulled at the joker. It melted through his fingers, still sticking to her face, squeezing her mouth firmly shut. Mariah saw panic radiating from her eyes. She began to slump down, kept upright only by the suit of spades that held her to the wall. He pulled at the joker again and again. It stuck to his fingers, holding his hand fast against her skin.

"Za-yin . . . za-yin . . . za-yin," he shouted as he tugged at the card with his other hand. Her eyes rolled to the back of her head as she slumped forward, unable to breath. "Za-yin . . . za-yin . . . za-yin!" he screamed, pulling frantically against the liquefying card.

With a sudden and earsplitting squeal, Sacha gulped at the air. Mariah fell back toward the small fireplace, his hand clasping the now stiffened joker. It grinned at him, teeth clenched and eyebrow raised. One after the other, the suit of spades fell from their holding places.

"Quickly," Mariah shouted as he attempted to grab as many of the cards as he could. "Catch them before they can do more harm . . . The box is the only safe place for them." Sacha watched as Mariah scurried about picking up the cards. He wrapped them in the sheet of commands and pushed them into the case, then got to his feet and hid the box under the bed.

Sacha didn't move. She gripped the wall with her fingernails. "Old . . . Scratty," she said slowly, her eyes fixed on the wooden chair in the far corner of the room. "She's here . . ."

He looked at the chair. There in the shadows was Old Scratty. She sat bolt upright, a slight smile etched on her lips. Her hands were stuffed into the pockets of her smock, sleeves rolled back to expose the white, sea-washed wood.

"How did *she* get here?" Mariah asked.

"She wasn't there before. I looked at the chair and it was empty."

"She must have been, Sacha. Dolls don't just appear," Mariah said doubtfully. He looked at the doll. Then he saw the silver bangle upon her wrist, the metal tarnished to almost black. A sudden thought flashed across his mind. "That bracelet . . . I saw one just the same on the wrist of the kraken."

"Take it from her, then we can see," Sacha said, not wanting to move an inch nearer the smiling doll.

"You take it. I don't want to touch her."

"We can't leave her here. Bizmillah will wonder where she's gone."

"It's how she got here that bothers me. She wasn't in the room until the cards blasted everywhere. She just appeared, moved on her own, just like she did in the cellar," Mariah paused. "But dolls can't move on their own. Don't tell me she could have got here by herself."

"And don't tell *me* that cards can dance in the air and pin me to the wall," Sacha snapped. "We both saw it, and it was me that joker tried to kill." She paused for a moment, taking a deep breath to calm herself. "I know where Felix and the others are being kept. They're not dead. Just before the explosion I looked into the depths of the orb and Felix was in a cavern under the Prince Regent. That's what the cards showed me."

"And that's why they tried to kill you, so you couldn't find him," Mariah said as the thought suddenly crystallised in his mind. "If the cards are right, then Albion is in trouble."

"And Felix is trapped." Sacha looked hopelessly at Mariah. "We have to help him."

"Those men will know that the Panjandrum are here," Mariah went on, ignoring her. "He had the postcard of the hotel. They'll come looking here and find me. Black!" he said quickly. "I should have known. He said on the train he had been waiting for someone. He was waiting for Albion. He talked about tricks and magic and—"

Suddenly, Old Scratty's wooden arm clattered against the wall. Mariah saw that her fingers clasped a large metal key. He stepped to the manikin and slowly and carefully unravelled each of the stiff-jointed fingers, thinking that at any moment she would spring to life. The silver bracelet slipped across her wrist.

"It is the same as the kraken's," Mariah said. For the briefest of moments, he was sure that the smile had slipped from her face. A single tear rolled across her white china cheek, falling from her blind eyes as if he had spoken the name of someone long missed.

"You here to help us, lass?" Sacha asked Old Scratty as Mariah plucked the key from her fingers and held it to the light. "Is there a door for this key, Old Scratty?"

The doll's right hand suddenly fell from her lap, a finger pointing to the floors below.

"Let me see," Sacha said. She grabbed the key from Mariah and looked at the thick shavings of rust that flaked from its surface. She sniffed it. "Seawater," she said brightly. "This has been tide-washed many times."

"Deeper than the cellar?" Mariah asked.

"Deeper and more dangerous," Sacha replied.

CHAPTER

❧ 17 ☙

Pagurus

The call of the sea hawks heralded daybreak, and the sound of the crashing surf echoed around the four towers of the Prince Regent. Sacha huddled against Mariah, wrapped in a coarse blanket, not wanting to leave his side, fearing the shadows and the power of the Panjandrum. She held the rusty iron key in both hands, cradling it as if it were some great prize. Mariah opened his eyes and stared at the empty chair. Old Scratty had gone as silently and surreptitiously as she had appeared. In the cold grey light of morning, the events of the dark hours became a faded memory.

As the oil lamp had dimmed the night before, and its light had thinned to a whisper, he and Sacha had spoken of what to do next. Sacha had told him what she had seen as the golden orb had exploded. Mariah had hoped that it was but a fanciful dream.

"She's gone," he said softly as he tried to wake Sacha from her deep slumber. "Old Scratty has vanished again."

The chiming of a church bell announced the seventh hour. Sacha lifted her head and peered out of tired eyes.

"Morning?" she asked. She looked at the empty chair. "Gone?" she asked, not waiting for an answer. "Was any of it real?" Her thumbs rubbed the flaking metal of the old iron key.

"It happened, that's for sure," Mariah said as he rubbed the sleep from his face and tousled his hair. "But whether it was real . . ." What he had seen in the glow of the fire and on the steps to the customs house had somehow remained on the edges of reality. It tapped gently on his consciousness.

"Do you think she . . . ," Sacha asked, unable to finish the question as her thoughts raced. "Could she . . ."

"Better not ask. I know we'll see her again. She wants us to find something."

"Or someone," Sacha said quickly, wanting it to be Felix.

"One thing," he went on slowly. "The bracelet was the one the kraken had when he attacked me and Charity fought him off. Trouble is . . . The trouble is, Charity wouldn't tell me where he had been and why he was skulking around in the dark. Just came out of nowhere, said he'd followed us."

"Do you think he knows about the cards?" she asked.

"I'm afraid he does. I told him everything. And soon those men will come looking. If they have Albion, then they'll come for me. He's bound to crack and tell them who he gave them to. I'm going to have to move on. I can't stay here much longer."

"Throw them into the sea and lie."

"Better I just go back to London," Mariah said as he picked up the Panjandrum and stuffed them into his pocket.

"You'll do what you have to do," Sacha snapped as she got up from the bed, pushing it away from the door. "I'll be finding Felix myself . . . no problem in that. I have the key, and somewhere there'll be a door to fit it. If Old Scratty is right, then Felix won't be too far away."

"But you can't go on your own," Mariah said, reaching out to stop her. "You don't know who'll be waiting."

"Then come with me and don't run away." Sacha pulled her arm from his grip and opened the door. "This is bigger than us. We can't stop it now, don't you see? It's as if there were a wheel turning and you and me were on it, going around and around. You can't leave now, whatever happens." She held the key in front of his face. "This is our fate, Mariah, and there's nothing we can do to change that. Old Scratty knew; that's why she found us. Whatever is going on in this place has to stop. We can't go to the police; they'll never believe us."

"We could try; . . . tell them about the murder last night and the kraken."

"And they'd believe that?" Sacha asked mockingly. "I'm not going to run from this. If I stand alone, then I stand alone."

"What about Captain Charity?" Mariah asked impatiently.

"He's not here. It's just you, me and a cellar full of secrets. If you're in, Mariah, then we have to be gone." Sacha didn't wait for his reply, stepping into the corridor. She pressed the button to summon the elevator. Mariah followed sheepishly, his hands pushed deep into the pockets of his coat.

"What shall we do about Bizmillah?" he asked anxiously.

"It's Saturday. Besides, you prepared everything last night. That gives us until eight o'clock tonight. Should be enough time to see what's going on down in the cellars."

"What if we get caught?" he asked, his throat tight.

"Then we end up like Felix."

The elevator stopped. Sacha pulled the cage door open, stepped inside and waited for Mariah. Within a few seconds they were plummeting into the depths of the Prince Regent.

The smell of dank seaweed met them as the elevator slowed to a shuddering halt.

"That's as deep as we can go," Mariah said as he quietly slid the gate open and checked both ways along the dark corridor. As he peered from the elevator he listened to the swish of waves by a faraway portal.

"There's a storm and the tide is in," Sacha said. She sniffed the air. "Monica has been this way," she whispered.

Mariah listened even more intently than before. "How can you tell?" he asked. Sacha stepped out of the elevator and sniffed again, following the scent as if she were a bloodhound.

"The smell," Sacha replied just above a breath. "She and Luger went this way. Perfume and cigars."

Mariah sniffed the air. A sharp breeze rushed back and forth through the cellar from the sea. The faintest whiff of pungent tobacco hung momentarily in the air and then vanished. He followed Sacha, disappointed that he couldn't smell Monica's perfume. "Are you sure it's her?" he asked.

"Cheap perfume," she whispered back. "From a penny cart in the market, but strong."

The corridor led several turns to the left. It spiralled lower and lower, passing open doors and empty rooms, each lit by a single oil lamp set high upon the wall. The air grew thick with salt mist, which clung to their skin, drying upon the lashes of their eyes like crisp white icicles. With every step the heat grew more intense as the steam thickened and swirled in the fading light.

They turned a final corner, and there in front of them was a short flight of steps that led to a long, damp passageway. Far away in the darkness, they could hear the sea crashing through the doors and rushing into the cellars.

Mariah heard a scurrying sound and looked down the

stairs. The green-tiled floor appeared to move. Sharp shells clattered against each other. Black-tipped pincers snapped at the air, and red eyes on thin stalks stared back at him.

"Look," Mariah said, staring at the thousands of tiny red eyes that reflected the dim lamplight. "What are they?"

"*Cancer pagurus*," Sacha replied, incredulous. She went down a step to take a closer look. "Sea crabs, but twice the size of any I have seen before. We'll never get through that way; claws like that would snap through your ankle."

"How did Monica and Luger get through?" Mariah asked as a particularly large red crab, the size of a dinner tray, crawled on another's back and pulled itself up the step toward him, snapping its pincers.

"They must have gone in here," Sacha replied, pointing to a door alcoved into the wall and covered by dangling throngs of damp sea grass.

Mariah continued to stare at the pagurus that scraped its shell against the side of the step, beating its two large claws against the green tiles. "Where do they come from?" he asked quietly as he gazed at the creature. "It's amazing; look at the size of the beast."

"I've never been in this place before. Not even Bizmillah would come down here. Nothing but the wine cellars and—" She stopped speaking and pointed to the corridor.

In the misted half-light the crabs were quickly scurrying to the sides of the passageway. From beneath them emerged the gigantic back of an even greater crab. It shook the sand from its shell and slowly and silently lifted itself to the very tips of its spiked legs. It was the size of a grand piano.

The creature turned slowly, picking up a smaller crab from the floor. Crushing it in its pincers, it gorged itself on the red mucus that oozed from the broken shell.

Its black eyes, set on stubby stalks, scanned the passageway. It picked up a crab the size of a small dog and snapped it in two before pushing it ravenously into its mouth. Then it turned and stared at them.

Sacha and Mariah stood frozen.

The large pagurus took two long, slow steps toward them, picking its way through the scurrying masses that snapped at its feet. It stopped and snapped its pincers three times and then stepped even closer.

Mariah took hold of the large iron ring that formed the handle to the door closest to them and turned it as quickly as he could.

"The door's locked," he shouted as the creature came toward them. "There has to be a key somewhere."

Sacha took Old Scratty's key from her pocket and tried it in the lock. It twisted part way and then stuck tight and would move no farther. She tried to turn it as Mariah pulled on the handle.

The pagurus ambled toward them sideways, too big to turn to face them, squeezing itself along the narrow passageway. The chafing of its shell squealed into the distance like chalk on a board. It snapped its claws at them with every step.

Sacha pulled on the rusted key, and it finally pulled free from the lock. She looked crestfallen as she panted and glanced back toward the creature. It edged its way closer.

"Just run," Mariah said. "We can go back up."

"What about Felix?" Sacha asked. She held the key like a knife.

The pagurus quickened its gait. "There must be another way . . . quickly . . . run." Mariah pulled Sacha by the arm. "This way."

Together they set off at a fearful pace, running back the way they had come, up two flights of the spiralling corridor and then onto a long landing. Far behind they could hear the clattering of the pagurus as it chased them, its mandibles echoing like chattering teeth.

"Which way?" Mariah screamed in a panic.

"Straight on, I think," Sacha said, knowing in her heart that she was lost in the labyrinth of passageways that honeycombed the cellars of the Prince Regent. "It all looks the same. Have we been here before?"

The sound of the crab was getting closer.

In the distance, lit by a lamp, was a small door. It was set two feet from the floor, as if it were a hatch into a lower room, and was held tightly shut by a rusted metal latch. As they drew near, Mariah could see that the corridor turned to the right and then suddenly stopped. They could go no farther.

The sound of the steam generator shook the walls of the corridor. A vast cloud of white steam billowed from a ceiling vent, smelling of the sea. It curled along the dripping tiles as hissing drops of boiling water splattered to the floor. By accident they had discovered the heart of the Prince Regent.

Mariah waded through the cloud of steam, which hung at waist height, until he found the latch to the door. It held fast, thickly crusted with salt.

"No way out," Sacha said. She looked back and saw a gigantic claw edge its way slowly around the corner of the passageway.

"Give me the key," Mariah insisted. His voice twisted with fear.

He snatched the key from her and began to hammer at the door catch. The salt cracked open, following the line of the rusted metal. Mariah turned as the pagurus scuttled closer, stopping every few feet to wipe the swirling mist from its eyes with its mandibles. It clashed its claws as if they were cavalry sabres. Suddenly, it darted forward, lashing out with a claw that caught Sacha by the hair, pulling her from her feet. She vanished beneath the pall of steam that blew from the grating above them.

"Mariah!" she screamed as she was dragged backward toward the creature's mouth. "Mariah!"

Mariah hit the lock a final time and watched the door spring open. He turned to the pagurus. The great crustacean lurched, unable to turn the bulk of its carapace in the narrow passageway. Sacha screamed again.

Seeing his chance, Mariah stepped toward the pagurus, and slashing at its eye with the key, cut it off with one blow. The crab flinched and stepped back.

Mariah screamed in terror as he hit the half-blind creature again and again. It instinctively flicked Sacha from its grasp, hurling her across the floor toward the open doorway. She pulled herself inside.

"Come on, Mariah," she shouted.

The crab twisted itself to one side and then suddenly freed both claws, seized Mariah and pulled the boy toward its mouth.

"Shut the door!" he shouted as he vanished in the churning steam.

The pagurus saw Sacha and staggered toward her.

"MARIAH!" she screamed, hoping to see him through the thick fog.

Then she heard a sudden thud pounding again and again on the back of the creature. A shadow veiled in steam leaped from its back and to the floor.

"The door," Mariah shouted as the crab attempted to see its attacker. Mariah ran toward the entrance.

Sacha fell backward as he landed on her. The pagurus was at the entrance, reaching for them. Mariah got to his feet as the heavy claw pushed its way deeper into the room, snapping wildly in the air. With all his might Mariah pushed against the door.

In the dark room Sacha struck a lucifer. It burst into life and the pagurus suddenly recoiled. Mariah, seizing the advantage, slammed the oak door against the creature and slid the bolt shut. He sighed with relief and looked at Sacha.

"Do you have many left?" he asked as the match began to fade.

"Enough to light this," she said as she took a thick stubby candle from her pocket and lit it with the dying flames of the lucifer. "I don't like the dark," she said softly. "Father used to lock me in a cupboard and say the Boggat would come for me if I got out. So now I always carry matches and a candle. Never feared the Boggat or anything since."

"Does that include vanishing dolls, krakens and giant crabs?" Mariah said breathlessly as he leaned against the oak door, smiling at her in the soft light of the candle flame, the steam generator humming and hissing somewhere close by.

"*And* a London boy who brings pandemonium with him . . ."

CHAPTER

⋆18⋆

Moon Sand

They sat for several minutes in the shimmering candlelight and listened to the pagurus.

It tried to force its claw into the edge of the door and pry it open, but soon gave up and clattered away down the passageway.

Mariah peered through a crack in the door, watching the creature. It slowly crawled out of sight, but he knew it would be waiting in the darkness, ready to pounce and snap them in two with its claws. Sacha sat quietly, playing with the candle wax as it dribbled down her fingers and into the palm of her hand. From all around them came the hissing of the steam generator as it pumped boiling water to the farthest corners of the Prince Regent.

"How long can we stay here?" Sacha asked Mariah as he sat down and looked about him.

"The pagurus is still there," he said, motioning to the passageway outside the room. "Doubtless it'll just wait. There must be another way of getting out."

Sacha raised the candle above her head, lighting the high ceiling and a far stone wall. "Do you think that these are the foundations?" she asked as she stared at the large, thick stones cut neatly into blocks the size of a carriage. "They say there used to be a hot spring here and people would come to swim in the water. There's still a faucet in the refectory. A golden tap that the guests can drink from at a shilling a time."

"That's why Black said he was coming here . . . to taste the waters." Mariah got to his feet and ran his hand along the rough blocks. "These are old stones," he said. "Look at the marks . . . Cut by hand. Do you think we're below sea level?"

"Far below," Sacha replied thoughtfully. "The theatre storeroom is on level with the beach. How much farther down we are, I don't know."

"And the steam generator . . . who looks after it?" Mariah asked.

Sacha paused and thought. It was something she had never considered. She had seen the waiters in their fine coats, an army of maids, chefs and cooks, but she had never seen anyone come up from below the ground.

"Takes care of itself," she said after a while. "It must; I don't know anyone who works down here."

"Then it'll be the first steam engine that runs on its own," Mariah exclaimed as he walked farther into the shadows, following the contours of the wall as if he were looking for something. "Here," he shouted from the blackness. "Bring the candle and see what I've found."

Sacha followed his voice. The tiled floor soon became broken stone and then turned to small boulders of rubble, which littered the floor. It was as if she had walked into the ruins of an old castle. She thought the hissing of the generator sounded like the breathing of a sleeping dragon. She could not believe that she was still inside the Prince Regent, far below the level of the sea. All around were remnants of the building of the hotel. Discarded shovels, picks, broken bottles and empty mugs were strewn by the wall in a makeshift rubbish dump.

"Look at this," Mariah said excitedly as he stood in a sealed-up doorway. "It looks like the entrance to whatever stood here before the hotel."

Sacha went over to him and held up the candle. It cast long shadows across the room. She could clearly see the old door-way that had been cut into the thick stones and then sealed in the same fine red brick that clad the Prince Regent. Looking up, she could see that the lintel above the door was made of stone, and running through the centre was a crack a finger's width across.

Mariah pointed at a place in the wall where some mortar was missing. "I can smell the sea and feel a breeze coming through." Sacha stepped forward, the candle suddenly blustering in the whistling draught that seethed through the narrow slit. "A way out," he boasted. "Maybe we can knock our way through and see what is on the other side."

Sacha handed him the candle and took a pick from the rubble-covered floor. "Never give a boy a man's work." She smiled as she swung the pick and, with a sharp blow, smashed it into a loose brick. "There," she said in a satisfied voice as rubble and mortar fell to the floor. "That'll be your first one out of the way."

Mariah looked through the small hole that had appeared at waist height in the brick wall. In the light of the candle, he could see several stone columns supporting the floor above. He could hear the sound of the generator close by.

Sacha pulled him clear and in two swift strokes had forged a hole big enough for them to enter. She dropped the pick, wiped the dust from her hands and struck another match for herself.

Mariah walked ahead on the hot, dry sand that covered the floor. From the meagre light he could only see a few feet, but it looked as if the ruins went on into the distance. Following some instinct, he allowed himself to be taken the way of the generator. He looked to see if Sacha followed. There she was, an arm's length behind.

They threaded their way through the stone columns, the hiss of the steam calling them on and the heat reddening their faces and wetting their brows. Mariah held the melting candle above his head, hoping that the light would claw its way farther and that he would see some other light in the distance.

After a short while, he looked behind him and realised that he was alone. Sacha was gone. Panic rushed through his body. He turned suddenly as a shadow startled him. His mind raced as the sound of the generator quickly turned into the breath of a beast. Shadows danced from the flickering candle, and his eyes invented strange creatures in the gloom. His lip began to quiver.

"Sacha," he called. "Sacha . . ."

There was complete silence. Mariah pressed himself to the wall, hoping it would consume him. Fearfully, he looked this way and that. Then he saw a glow many yards away. By the base of a stone column was a small fire. Hunched over the glow was a dark figure.

"Sacha?" he asked.

She turned and waved him to her. As he drew closer, he saw that what at first he had thought to be a fire was an old glass lamp. It gave a warm light and lit Sacha's face. She sat quietly looking into the gloom.

"Why did you go?" he asked.

"When I struck the match, I saw something glinting. You had gone ahead, and I just had to come and see." She held a black leather wallet encrusted in salt. It was stuffed with crisp five-pound notes, all neatly folded. "I found this," she said. "And something else."

Sacha pointed to the wall that stood four paces behind them. Mariah saw the outline of a man lying in the sand, a top hat placed next to him. He raised the candle and cast the light upon the body. It shone against the white skull and glistened upon the skeletal fingers.

"He's dead," Mariah said.

"He's certainly not well," Sacha said. "And beyond that, he's supposed to be running this hotel."

Mariah didn't ask what she meant. Sacha had already held out an envelope and a calling card in a neat silver case.

"Otto Luger," she said as she gave the card to Mariah. "I glanced at the letter — it's to him. I think he was murdered."

Mariah looked again at the skeleton. It was picked perfectly clean. A suit of fine clothes lay in a tattered pile upon the bones. The jaw of the skull had fallen open, as the once proud head had tilted to the side. There were three small round holes neatly placed in the temple.

"The knife again?" Mariah mumbled to himself. Then he turned to Sacha. "Who could have done something like this?" he asked her. "And how can it be Luger?"

"The hat's inscribed with his name and the letter was inside. It has to be him." Sacha looked at the crisp piece of white paper in her hand. "It's to Luger and it's not signed." The note was scrawled in an unsteady hand. The paper was embossed with a crown and two lions, and she could make out the words "Claridges Hotel." "Listen. 'Dear Otto, Something has brought dissatisfaction to my door. I need to see you urgently. If we are to continue in our venture, then you must meet me tonight.'" Sacha held out the note. "If this is the real Otto Luger, . . . who's running the hotel?"

Mariah went to the carcass and lifted its hand. He carefully slipped a gold ring from its third finger and held it to the oil lamp.

"It's the same as Luger's . . . a ring with a swan crest." Mariah put the ring into his pocket.

"Leave it, Mariah, you shouldn't take from the dead."

"I'm sure he'd want us to find out who did this to him. When all this is over, we can do what is right and give him a proper send-off. Captain Charity would see to that, I'm sure." Mariah looked at the glistening bones and wondered what the man would have looked like. From the cut of the fine suit, he could see that he would have been the same size as the Luger he had met and had dressed in the same elegant style. Even the shoes bore a remarkable similarity to those that had squeaked along the corridor when Mariah had hidden away behind the aspidistra. Whoever was running the Prince Regent, he had a strong resemblance in height and frame to the skeleton that now rested against its foundations. "We had better search him for anything else," Mariah said as he got to his knees and rifled the pockets of the suit.

"Done that," Sacha replied guiltily.

"And?"

"Found this." She opened her hand and there, glowing like a bright full moon, was a pearl the size of a chestnut. "It's a sea pearl."

"You shouldn't take from the dead, Sacha," Mariah scoffed.

"It must be worth a hundred pounds. With that and the money in the wallet, I'd have more than I would earn in a lifetime."

He took the pearl and held it to the light. "But it wouldn't be come by honestly. Better to starve than to steal your bread."

"If I sell it," Sacha mumbled, "I could leave this place and never work again."

"And forever have the image of that corpse dancing in your dreams to remind you where it came from," Mariah said as he gave the pearl back to her. "Take it, change your life and see what good it does you."

Sacha held the pearl and felt its warmth.

Mariah searched the floor where the body lay. "There must be something to tell us what happened here."

"He was murdered," Sacha replied.

"Well not for his money . . . or the pearl."

"For the Prince Regent?" she asked.

"And whatever secret this place keeps locked within its walls," Mariah said as the candle finally melted away in his hand. "If this really is Luger, then the man who masquerades as him is the one who did this. Do you think we could find this place again?" He bent to examine the body once more.

"We could try. But for what reason?"

"So we can show Charity. He'll know what to do, find someone who can sort the whole thing out." Mariah opened the coat and looked at the crisp white shirt that lay beneath. There, just above the heart, were three small puncture wounds cut into the fabric; around each was the slightest smear of faded blood. "Not much blood." Mariah pulled the shirt to one side. There, tucked into the trouser belt, was a pearl-handled pistol. "He carried a gun," Mariah said as he carefully picked up the pistol and checked the chamber. "And he never used it. So he was either surprised by or knew the person who killed him."

"So why did they leave him here?" Sacha asked.

"Thought he would never be found. If it hadn't been for the pagurus, we would never have come this way. There must be another way out," Mariah said.

He turned and walked on, holding the lamp, this time checking that Sacha was still nearby. Sacha quickly stuffed the wallet into her deepest pocket. She gripped the pearl in her hand.

Soon, they had reached the far wall of the ruin. Here there were just two granite columns holding up the roof. A thick covering of hot sand swathed the floor. It was just how Mariah had imagined the surface of the moon.

"There has to be another way out," he muttered. "Check by the wall; I can feel a breeze, but can't tell which way it comes from."

Sacha searched the shadows by the wall and moved her hands across the stone along each line of mortar. Somewhere nearby she could feel the breeze.

"Here." Mariah fell to his knees and held the lamp above a small pile of sand that shifted in the draft. "Come and dig."

They scooped handfuls of sand away from the hot air that blew in through the floor. Quickly they found a lattice of small stones that whispered as the air gushed between them.

"It must be a way to the floor below this one," Mariah said as he picked up larger rocks from the ever-widening hole. "Listen — I can hear the generator."

The sound coming from the hole was louder and more urgent than they had heard before. It was as if they were sitting within the boiling tank of a large steamship that pushed its way against a high sea. The churning of the engine sent a short, sharp jet of air gusting through the rocks. Mariah dug even quicker, moving the hot rocks with his reddening fingertips.

Then his hand struck against a strip of hot black metal. Perching upon a lintel of thick stone, he pushed away the rocks from each side of a thick grate. "Must be an air vent to the generator," he said as Sacha piled the stones from the hole behind her. "If I can get my fingers around the bar and pull, then we should be able to—"

Mariah had no time to finish. Without warning, the vent gave way and the hole quickly began to deepen. He scrabbled for a footing as Sacha was sucked by the cascading stones deeper into the hole, slipping by him and into the darkness without a chance to scream. She vanished from his sight. With both hands he grabbed at the rocks, hoping to pull himself from the avalanche, but the torrent of shingle and sand dragged him deeper. Mariah could hear the stones clattering far below as they pelted through the opened vent. Then the lamp spilled its oil upon the rocks, bursting into bright flame all around him, his sleeve catching on fire as his feet slipped from their perch.

Mariah reached out away from the flames, his footing lost in the streaming rock. Falling, he grabbed the stone lintel, which was now buried deep in the sand. He dangled from his fingers as stones pounded his head. The rock burned against his palm as he clung to it. One by one his fingers lost their grasp.

From above his head he heard the sound of shifting stone as the whole floor began to move. The lintel slowly tilted toward him. He gripped it tighter, finding a firm hold against a piece of jagged rock that fitted his hand. He looked down. The darkness went on forever, clouded by billowing spouts of hot dust.

"Mariah!" came a shout from below. "I'm trapped!"

He could hold on no longer. The heat loosened his grip, his sweaty fingers slipping from the rock. He tried to scream, but fell silently into the black hole.

CHAPTER

✴ 19 ✴

Camarilla

The wheezing of the steam generator seemed to come from somewhere nearby. Mariah sat in complete blackness, unable to see his hand in front of his face. He rubbed his palm over his eyes, hoping he could push away the dark veil and see the world again. It was no use; all was covered in smothering gloom.

The chamber into which he had tumbled was much cooler, and the subterranean breeze stronger. He sat on a pile of sand and shingle, slowly breathing and listening to the echo as he wondered what he should do. The trickle of shingle finally stopped as the hole above his head filled itself, the lintel holding back yet another fall of rock. A slow dribble of sticky blood seeped across his forehead, and his fingers were raw. He coughed loudly, the dust from the rockfall filling his nostrils and swirling about him. "Sacha!" he shouted, the walls whispering back to him. "Are you here?" There was no reply.

Wiping his mouth with his coat sleeve, he slid from the pile of stones, knowing he would have to fumble blindly to find an escape. His hands felt their way in the darkness, painfully touching each stone as he crawled sideways across the skree. His mind spun dizzily as he stared wide-eyed into blackness.

Something touched his chin. At first it brushed against him like a cobweb floating by. Then it came again, bolder, firm, grasping his face.

He suddenly realised that it was Sacha's hand, and she was buried in the rocks. He pulled at the stone and shingle, the rough edges ripping at his raw fingers. The rocks spilled downward as Mariah dug to set her free. In the sand and grit he could feel the contours of her face as he pushed away the small boulders that were piled on top of her like an ancient tomb.

"Sacha!" he shouted as he lifted her with bleeding fingers. "Can you hear me?"

She coughed, spitting sand, and pulled him close. "I was drowning in the shingle," she said, squeezing him as if she'd thought she would never feel another living person. "I could hear you shouting, but couldn't speak." Sacha coughed in the darkness as they sat holding each other. "How far did we fall?"

"Too dark to tell," Mariah said as he looked up. "Do you have a match?"

Sacha reached into her pocket and, sitting back, opened the thin box and struck a match. In the sudden glare Mariah could see the far wall of the room and glimpsed the rusted grate hanging from the ceiling on a broken hinge. To their right was a large, stone-vaulted entrance and a short flight of steps that ran down and turned sharply to the left. In the brief moment of illumination, it looked as if it were the entrance to an old church, etched in carved ivy leaves, a gargoyle's head looking down from the high arch.

"Again," Mariah insisted as the match failed. "Light another."

Sacha lit one and held it tightly in her fingertips. "I haven't many left," she said quickly. "We'll have to find something else for light or we'll be walking blind."

"At least we're alive," Mariah replied. "I was beginning to think that this place was trying to kill us both."

He pulled a handkerchief from his pocket and wrapped and knotted it against itself to form a long wick. He lit the end closest to the match and watched as it slowly started to smoulder, then burn. "Should last an hour," he said, seeing the surprised look on Sacha's face. "We learn many things at the Colonial School." He smiled.

"I didn't get the chance to go to school," she said curtly as the shadows crisscrossed her face. "Taught myself to read and write. Cleaned for the cleric and pinched his paper and pens. Silly man. Spent more time writing than he did on his knees. The Reverend H. F. Cataxian . . . He wrote *The Incredible Adventures of Doblin the Goblin.*" Sacha seemed thankful to talk of something other than their plight. "My house is across the road from his. We lived crowded together in the rooms above the inn; he lived all alone in a house so big, you could lose yourself in it for a week."

"I have that book, brought it with me from London," Mariah said. "I've read it several times."

"Then when we get out of this place," she said slowly, looking at the ground, "perhaps we could visit him."

"That we'll do, and sooner rather than later," Mariah replied uneasily. He helped her up and walked toward the stairway. "I have this," he said, showing her the gun. "Never thought there would come a day when I would think of using one of these. But if they were prepared to murder Luger, the same could come to us."

"Then it's a chance I'll take. Rather die for something than live for nothing. Felix knew there was treachery in this place. He told me he wasn't safe, and then he was gone."

"And we will find him, Sacha. He must be here somewhere. Him and all the secrets that this place contains." They took the first steps down and then turned, spiralling down the sand-covered treads.

Soon, they had reached the floor below. It looked as if it had been cut from the solid rock on which the Prince Regent had been built. The sound of the generator grew louder with each step they took along the narrow passageway. It was just wide enough for them to walk arm in arm, linked against the darkness.

Mariah held the pistol in his hand, and Sacha held the light above them, its smouldering wick illuminating the damp sandstone walls that oozed with tendrils of hot salt water. Coming from an opening ahead of them was a shaft of bright amber light that sliced through the darkness. Sacha moved quickly forward, then waited for Mariah as she peered around the edge of the opening.

Inside the large vaulted room was the steam generator. It was unlike anything Mariah had ever seen. A large, green polished pipe was screwed into the rock face with thick brass bolts. To one side was the steel piston that juddered back and forth along a bright rod that was fixed to the far wall. Behind this was an engine the size of a small house, which chugged away like a slowly beating heart. Every so often soft jets of steam spurted from its ventilating valve as the rush of burning air was sucked through a labyrinth of pipes around the room and then into the high ceiling. All was lit by a stand of blue lamps fixed to the high ceiling.

"The steam engine," Sacha exclaimed.

"Not like one that I have ever seen. There's no stoker, no firebox and no water. It's as if it were sucking the steam from the earth itself."

"Listen," Sacha said. "Can you hear the crying?"

Mariah listened. All he could hear was the chugging of the generator and the whistling of the steam through the miles of piping that circled above him like the coils of some vast snake. The clanging pipes echoed through the cavernous chamber. He shrugged his shoulders.

"There it is again . . . Can't you hear it?" she asked.

Mariah bent forward and cupped a hand against his ear. The noise of the generator filled his head. "Nothing," he said.

Sacha groaned, frustrated. "I'm sure I could—," she said as she heard the faint cry yet again. "There . . . you *must* have heard that."

Mariah shook his head as Sacha walked toward a doorway half hidden behind the generator.

"This way," she said, walking quickly.

Mariah followed, taking a last look at the generator, which grew up from the solid rock floor into the high ceiling. The lamplight glistened on the glimmering paint and polished brass bolts. "Amazing," he whispered to himself. "Perfectly amazing."

Sacha followed the sound of the whimpering into a long, brightly lit passage. Running far into the distance were a thousand tiny lamps that had neither wick nor flame. She looked at the clear glass spheres. Each covered a thin wire and glowed brightly, dazzling her eyes. Mariah followed, pistol in hand.

Soon they passed into yet another vast chamber. On a high metal gantry suspended from the ceiling by long, thick-linked chains, they crossed a steaming pool of fermenting blue water. They swung gently back and forth with every step until they reached another archway. It howled with a stiff gale, which pushed them back with its ferocity. The wind rippled the water and spiralled mist into the heights.

The sound of crying seemed to be as far away from Sacha as ever. It was as if she were chasing a rainbow and no sooner had she stepped nearer than it moved another pace away. It came again and again, but she was still the only one who could hear it. Each time, she turned to Mariah and he just shrugged his shoulders in reply.

Mariah pulled the collar of his coat over his face to protect it from the wind. He helped Sacha forward as she struggled to keep upright in the air rushing through the narrow tunnel.

"It must cool the generator," Mariah shouted, his voice carrying just above the howl of the gale. "Sucked down from above. If we find where it comes from, we'll be able to get out."

Sacha got to her hands and knees and crawled the last few feet of the corridor, the wind beating against her and peppering her with blistering specks of golden sand. Mariah staggered on behind, cupping the pistol in his hand, holding it close to him.

"VENTS," a voice shouted. "CLOSE THE VENTS." There was a sudden tremor in the passageway and the sound of metal grating against stone. The gale squealed its final breath, and then all was silent. From far behind, the tremor came again as a strong metal door clanked firmly shut.

Sacha looked up at Mariah. She was covered in a thin layer of sand. They crept forward, not knowing who was ahead of them.

From just beyond yet another archway, they could see the light of a glistening crystal chandelier. When they had crept through the archway, they saw that it hung majestically from the vaulted ceiling of the chamber, at the same height as the gantry on which they now crouched, just out of sight of the people below.

Mariah peeked carefully over the metal rim of the elevated pathway that crossed the room. There below was Luger, smartly dressed and very much alive. He wore the same crisp white shirt and neatly pressed jacket. His monocle was squeezed against his nose; his hair was greased back from his face. Monica fussed about a stone table, wiping the piles of sand from its surface with a horsehair brush as she stood on a long stone bench that looked as if it were hewn from the floor.

Standing together by the large wooden doors were two men. Mariah recognised the ruddy face of Mister Grimm. He waited impatiently with his companion, his hand rubbing the golden lion's head that topped his mahogany cane. The other man was tall and thin, with a white face, pinched cheeks, thin lips and a small black beard, which tipped the end of a long, pointed chin.

"Grendel," Mariah whispered to himself.

Mister Grimm fiddled with his blue lens spectacles. He took a silver timepiece from his pocket and checked it several times with agitated fingers. Grendel twitched, the muscles in his face shivering beneath his thin white skin.

"Mystery, mystery, so much mystery. Why we can't meet in an upper room instead of below the sea, I'll never know," Mister Grimm said.

"Is he ready to perform for us?" Luger asked as he sat at the head of the stone table and nodded for them to join him. Monica brushed the last of the sand to the floor. "This dreaming he does better find out who was in my room last night. I've a feeling they will be back, and I have far too much riding on this caper."

"Have we ever let you down?" Mister Grimm asked as he took Grendel by the hand and led him to the seat opposite Luger. "Best he sits here, and then he can see you face-to-face, Mister Luger."

179

"All I ask is he sees the one who is messing with my head."

"You are an impatient man, Mister Luger," Grendel said as he sat on the cold stone. "Projection is something that can take time. It isn't stumbled upon or bought; it is a gift."

"Thought it came in a little green bottle and smelled of laudanum," Luger said, looking at his watch.

Mister Grendel laughed to himself. "That substance just takes me from this world and allows me to wander where I please. And it is *not* laudanum . . . nothing so crude or so vile and corrupting. Just three drops of this linctus and I am free of worldly passions and desires. There is nothing greater. Just three drops, Mister Luger, and you could come with me."

"Drink and have done with it," Luger barked, his words echoing around the vault. "Have your dream and be paid well. Tell him, Mister Grimm. I *have* to find the one who was in that room."

"Then I shall, I shall. Nothing would give me greater pleasure than to leave this present company. But first, tell me, is there anything that you don't want me to see — for once I am projected, then there is no door that is closed to me and no wall that can keep me out. Secrets will be a thing of the past. Do you understand?"

Luger looked at Monica, seeming unsure. She smiled at him and shrugged her shoulders, tilting her head to one side.

"There . . . there are many things that I would not like the world to know and hope you would keep secret, and I am sure we can come to some sort of . . . *agreement*?" Luger rambled, aware he had unleashed a creature that could cost him more than he'd planned.

"Shall I see what I find and then discuss a price?" Grendel asked, unscrewing the top of a small glass bottle that he had quietly removed from his hip pocket. "I assure you that we can keep secrets, and our prices are very reasonable."

"It's insurance, Mister Luger," Grimm chimed in, casting a sly look at Mister Grendel to say no more. "Consider it an investment. We would become *guardians* of whatever we found, with the promise that the secrets would die with us."

"I would prefer if you kept your wanderings to the rooms above the ground," Luger replied as he again looked to the silent Monica for help. "I have a business venture in which I am cultivating . . . *things*."

"Of value?" Grendel asked. He sniffed the contents of the bottle.

"Significant and beautiful," Monica interrupted. "Tell 'em, Otto. If he's gonna see through the walls, then he'll see the kids and the pearls — so have done with it."

"*Monica!*" Luger bristled.

"We'll cut you in on the deal," she said briskly, avoiding Luger's gaze. "Otto is cultivating pearls. Far below this room is a cavern stuffed with giant oysters. He feeds them on . . ." She paused and looked at Luger. His face reddened.

"Steam and ordure," Luger mumbled as if he were about to explode with embarrassment.

"*Or-* what?" Grimm asked.

"Excrement . . . or whatever else you would like to call it," he groaned.

"You feed it to the oysters?" Grimm asked, amazed. "Now I know why my mother told me never to eat shellfish."

"They adore it," Monica said, chortling to herself.

"It's taken from the town sewer — steam heated, filtered and then fed into the cavern. The oysters are kept at twice the heat they would live in, in the sea, and tended by kind, loving hands. Just think . . . giant pearls," Luger said, offended by the tone of Grimm's voice.

"You get people to work down there?" Grimm said as he loosened his tie.

"They have no choice. How can I say this in the kindest way?" he asked Monica.

"Slaves," she said, cutting to the chase. "Mister Luger gets a particular type of brood to work in the hotel. Ones where the family has no care or concern for them. They have been well paid for, and they come here. The strongest are selected and disappear from upstairs to go and work . . . downstairs." She giggled and pointed downward with a glove-clad finger, giving a little shiver of delight.

"And the pearls?" Grimm asked, his voice falling to a whisper. "They are disposed of . . . locally?"

"Let us just say that the *ladies* of Paris are adorned with the finest pearls hot, steaming sewage can grow," Luger said as he smiled at Monica, raising a thick eyebrow.

"Smu . . . smuggled?" said Grimm cautiously as Mister Grendel put the green bottle to his lips and sipped the linctus.

"In a way that you would never expect." Monica chuckled.

Grendel quietly convulsed in his chair as the linctus seared through his body. He coughed gently, closed his reddened eyes and slept.

A sudden swirl of sand spiralled up from the floor beneath the table as if it were disturbed by someone's passing. Monica shivered, pulling her feather boa high around her neck as her eyes searched the room.

"Is he sleeping well?" Luger asked sarcastically. "This is the most expensive sleep I've ever paid for."

"But it'll be worth it, Mister Luger. We will find your tormentor, *and* I have had news from London. Associates of mine have found the man you were looking for and are bringing him here right now. He was located on the steps of the Claridges Hotel and is now enclosed in a carriage that travels to this very place."

"What of the Panjandrum," Luger enquired cautiously.

"The telegram was obviously vague. We cannot have our secrets displayed for the world," Grimm said, pulling a crumpled piece of paper from his pocket. "It says, 'ALL IS WELL. BRINGING OUR FRIEND FROM CLARIDGES. SURPRISED TO FIND A POSTCARD OF THE PRINCE REGENT IN HIS POCKET.'"

"So someone *is* here; it's all beginning to fit into place. Sleep on, Mister Grendel, and find the thief and the Panjandrum," Luger commanded wistfully. "If he is found, perhaps my suspicions will be confirmed."

"I tell you, Otto, it's Bizmillah; he's the one Grendel should be scoping out," Monica insisted.

"Leave it to the master and he will soon have the answer," said Grimm. "Mister Grendel is not dreaming; he has left his body and walks in another realm. He can see that which we cannot with our veiled eyes, and there are those who also walk in that world who can show him the way to tread to find your answer."

Monica blushed and shuddered at the same time. She looked uncomfortable and stared around the room as if looking for the invisible Mister Grendel.

"You say he can see things from the other side, things that ain't human?" she asked nervously.

"Indubitably. If there is a single ghost, then he will see it, and, not only that, tell us where it has been. You see, all creatures leave behind them a trail," Grimm said. He held up his spectacles. "With humans it takes the form of heat. See, I have these spectacles that when tuned correctly can see the footsteps of someone long gone. All I need is to have the smallest piece of the suspect, a hair or fragment of clothing, and I can find their tracks days after they have walked that way."

"And when will he wake from his sleep?" Monica asked feebly as she stood up and walked to the doorway.

"Not long, he never takes long. Time is not time where

he walks. It is compressed, shortened and of a spiral nature. Today and tomorrow are of the same place, linked sideways and not in a continuum. A lifetime here can be moments there. Wherever there is, of course." Grimm spoke quickly, as if hoping his words would cover his own confusion.

Grendel suddenly lurched from his dreaming, sitting bolt upright and staring at Luger. "All is not as it appears, Mister Luger. Bizmillah argued with one of your guests as your room was invaded by *children*."

"What?" asked Luger urgently.

"Two of them, a boy and a girl. They know more of this place than you would think. They are near, Mister Luger, very near. And that is not all, is it, Miss Monica?" Grendel said shakily as he stared at her.

"Where are they now?" Luger asked.

"There," Grendel said calmly as he pointed his cane toward the gantry above their heads. "They are hiding and have listened to everything you have said."

Luger spun around and looked up, not noticing Monica slowly slipping from the room. "I can't see them. Are they ghosts?"

"For the moment they are alive, Mister Luger, very much alive."

Mariah had heard enough. He grabbed Sacha and ran across the gantry to the doorway on the other side.

"Quickly," shouted Luger. He bolted from his seat and ran as fast as he could, urging Grimm and Grendel to follow. "There are stairs to the left. We must stop the children."

"They will not go far, Mister Luger, not from London's finest detectives."

CHAPTER

✳ 20 ✸

Ixion

Mariah and Sacha scuttled along the gantry like chased rats, swiftly moving on all fours. From below they heard the slamming of the chamber door as Luger and the detectives rushed into the corridor in an attempt to cut off their escape.

"They have Felix and the others . . . It's true," Sacha said. "We have to get them out."

"They have Albion as well. Did you hear them? That's what we saw in the Panjandrum," Mariah said as they stopped at a junction of four narrow tunnels only wide enough for one person to pass at a time.

Sacha rested against the wall to regain her breath. "Which way shall we go?"

Mariah looked into the tunnels. Far away he could hear clanging metal doors and footsteps beating against the stone. It seemed to come from three directions at once.

"That way," he said, pointing to the narrowest tunnel, which dropped steeply away, and pushing Sacha ahead. "Grimm's so fat, he'll never get down this way."

As they ran, the walls pressed in on them, eventually narrowing to the width of their shoulders.

"I don't think this goes anywhere," Sacha said, feeling suffocated as the walls closed in. "If we go much farther, we'll be trapped."

"Look at the floor, Sacha . . . Footprints, all leading away. Something has to be ahead of us."

Sacha felt the key twitch in her hand. It leaped forward, pulling her, seeming to sense the lock it was made to fit was close by.

"The key," Sacha said as it began to twist free from her fingers. "It's come to life."

Mariah looked as the key twitched back and forth trying to break free of Sacha's grip. "Every key must find its lock,'" he said, the words coming to him suddenly. "Follow it. Let it lead you."

Sacha hooked her finger into the large, rusted ring and let her grip loosen. It pulled strongly against her hand like a divining rod. They followed, the sound of Luger and the detectives coming nearer. The lights of the passage began to flicker and dim as they went deeper. The key pulled her like a wild horse in full flight, lifting her to the tips of her toes.

Mariah looked to see if they were being pursued. The noise of the chase had fallen away into a far whisper. The slope on which they now ran steepened, the rocks breaking up under their feet into loose gravel. They were far away from the generator, and yet the throbbing of the machine reverberated through the solid rock. Every few paces, chunks of stone crashed to the floor, smashing into tiny splinters about them.

Sacha ran on, the key taking her deeper into the darkening tunnel. It shuddered frantically, vibrating in her fingers and singing like a tuning fork. Bit by bit, the fragments of rust fell from the key as the note grew louder and louder. Far ahead they heard the same pitch an octave lower, rumbling like a double bass.

"We must be nearly there," Mariah said as he chased behind her, clutching the pistol and wondering if he could ever use it against Grimm and Grendel.

Forty feet away a turn in the narrow passage opened into a wider hallway. It was as if a fault in the rock had split open into a small cave. In front of them was a metal door with a large iron lock.

The key knew it was home. It sung merrily to itself, altering its pitch to that of an excited song thrush. In return, the mortise hummed loudly. Sacha was dragged across the vault, and the key slipped itself into the lock. It clunked home and turned itself several times.

The door slowly opened, creaking as if it were pushed by an unseen hand. The smell of sewage billowed into the cave as a sea green mist leached across the floor.

"Do you think this is the only way out of here?" Sacha asked as she tried to pull the key from the lock, to no avail.

"It's a chance we'll have to take, but I can't see Luger being able to fit through that tunnel to get in here."

Sacha went through the doorway as Mariah carefully examined the lock. He twisted the key back and forth, and with one sudden shift it sheared in half, giving out a feeble twitter. He held it in his hand and looked at the mortise. The keyhole melted into the metal plate as if it had never existed. Then to his surprise, the key grew another head, the iron glittering with a blossom of sparks as if it were fresh from the foundry.

"Look," he said as he held out the key to Sacha. "It's just snapped off in the lock and now look at it."

The key looked new. It warbled a higher note. Sacha took it and pressed it into her pocket.

"It changed to fit another lock?" she asked as she felt the shape. "It's different than before, and a solid piece again." The key warbled as if in agreement, then fell silent again.

"Whatever it's doing, once we close this door, it will never be opened from the outside," Mariah said. He slammed it closed, sealing them into the tunnel beyond. Gone was the lanyard of bright lights, and now the gloom was dimly lit by blustering tallows that smouldered on bone plates stuck into the wall like a hundred teeth. Each plate was smeared in thick wax from the remnants of a thousand candles. They were placed just above the floor, so as Mariah and Sacha walked by, their flickering shadows were cast against the ceiling of the tunnel.

Here, there was no breeze. The heat was intense, and a soft, glowing mist threaded between their feet. Mariah took off his jacket and slung it over his shoulder. He held the pistol, the metal cool and smooth against his blistered fingers.

"So we go to find Felix?" Sacha asked as she led the way. "He's been a prisoner all this time."

"Taken by Luger because he found out what was going on," Mariah replied.

"Then it'll be the same for us if we're caught," Sacha said. "Wouldn't be surprised if there are two wax manikins already, one for me and one for you. We'll end up as slaves. Shovelling poop and up to our knees in oysters."

"Then at least you'll be with your Felix," Mariah said cuttingly.

"So why the manikins? What do you think Luger could be doing with them?" Sacha asked, ignoring his remark.

Mariah was silent for several paces, mulling over the image of the manikin. It had been fashioned to look like a boy. He looked down and saw a pool of tallow melting on the hard, white bone of a candleholder. It seeped across its surface in long, thin dribbles of wax. Suddenly, he realised the secret.

"Luger's smuggling the pearls out of England inside the manikins," he exclaimed. "That has to be it. Just think, here we are in a seaport. Ships come in and out every day. Luger sends the pearls to France by boat, disguised in the waxworks and hidden in the coffins. Who'd want to look in one of those to check if something had been hidden inside?"

"My father," Sacha said softly. "It's his job to check the cargo of everything that comes and goes from the harbour."

"But I thought he was a coastguard," Mariah said.

"That and a customs officer. It's all part of the same job. Defending the coast and stopping the smugglers," she said. "Sometimes he's been known to turn a . . . blind eye . . ."

"To the smugglers?" Mariah asked.

"To everyone. It's a small place, and we have ways of doing things you wouldn't understand. Doesn't make him a crook," she said indignantly. "How do you think I really got the job here? It wasn't because of my hard work. Luger knows my father; they drink together and play cards. They've been pally ever since he came to town. Only stopped drinking together when Miss Monica turned up."

The passage soon opened up into a large cavern, criss-crossed by metal gantries that ran across the high, vaulted ceiling. It looked like the inside of an idle factory built into the side of an immense cliff. Sacha and Mariah stood on a high metal platform overlooking a brown lagoon of steaming water. By the side of the pool was a discarded pile of opened shells that shimmered in the light. All was quiet except for the gentle lapping of small waves that spilled from a faucet in the rock wall. They looked about them; there was no sign of Luger or the detectives.

On the far side of the cavern was a small wooden door

with an even smaller metal grate cut into its centre. Mariah could make out a shadowy face pressed against the bars as if to get at the stagnant air that filled the chamber. Two white hands gripped the bars as the face peered out.

"Felix," Mariah whispered to Sacha. "Over there, behind the door."

"FELIX!" Sacha shouted, her words vibrating around the cavern. "We can get you out!"

"No," came the reply. "Not safe!"

Sacha looked frantically for a way down from the gantry. To her right was a narrow flight of metal stairs that fell steeply to a shingle path leading to the door. She ran quickly and scurried down the steps, clattering against the treads.

"NO!" shouted Felix as he rattled the grate, pulling against the door. "Go back . . . go back!"

Sacha pressed on, ignoring his shouts, taking the metal steps two at a time. In the muddy water a single eye, woken from its sleep, peered up at her. It squinted, just above the surface of the water, and with a swish of a long tail moved silently closer.

"Stay back," Felix shouted again in desperation. "Ixion will find you . . . A crocodile . . . in the water . . ." His words echoed around the vault.

Mariah stared into the thick brown pool, looking for a sign of the beast. The water was still but for two ripples that shimmered for a moment and then were gone.

"Sacha, stop," Mariah shouted. "Come back!"

A sudden, sharp blow knocked Sacha from her feet. The beast slid back into the water in a swirl of mud, preparing to strike again.

"Ixion!" shouted Felix as he rattled helplessly on the door.

Sacha got to her feet, and Mariah aimed the pistol at the churning water. Ixion launched itself again from the pool, pushing higher from the water this time, teeth-filled mouth gaping and hopeful. There was a dull thud as the pistol fired. It cracked around the cave like a crash of thunder, stilling the moment and the beast that fell across the shingle path and stared at Sacha. It panted, seeming unperturbed by the blood that trickled from the wound across its cheek. Then it raised itself to the tips of its toes and stood as if it were a racing hound ready to give chase.

"Stay still," Felix said softly. "It can only see with one eye. Luger cut out the other with a sword when it attacked him."

Mariah turned the chamber of the pistol and pulled the hammer to fire again. There was a dull click as the hammer struck a spent cap. He aimed the gun and pulled the trigger four more times. Each one clicked the sound of its emptiness, its shell spent and fire gone. "No more bullets, Sacha. I can't help you . . ."

She stood motionless, staring eye to eye with the crocodile. It grinned, then paced slowly toward her.

Sacha stepped back toward the staircase of the gantry, holding out her hand to grasp for the rail. The crocodile walked faster. It grunted to itself, barking like a dog and dribbling spit from its multitude of razor teeth. It crunched along the path, coming closer and closer.

Mariah crept down toward Sacha as silently as he could.

Ixion drew closer, hunching his long, scaled back as he prepared to strike. He shivered, bristling his sharp scales and stiffening his tail. Sacha screamed, sensing the creature's anger as it stared at her and flared its nostrils.

There was a scrabble of shingle as Ixion leaped at Sacha, jumping its own length in a single stride. It twisted its skull as its long jaws opened, ready to snap at her neck. Sacha fell backward as it soared toward her.

With one hand Mariah suddenly pulled her up onto the

staircase. Ixion fell short, his jaws clamping shut and just barely catching the hem of her dress before tearing free and landing heavily on the shingle. Sacha started running up the stairs as the creature snapped at the air, but she froze in panic when it gripped the bottom rung of the metal staircase, twisting and shaking it as it writhed back and forth.

Mariah dragged her higher, shouting and screaming for her to run. She was stiffened with fear, her body refusing to obey her mind as her heart raced faster. The crocodile spat muddy water from its jaws, appearing to smile at her.

"Go back," Felix shouted. "Come again tonight; he's always tethered at night—Monica sees to that. Find Luger's magic box."

Sacha finally made it to the gantry and looked at the pitiful face that stared at her. Felix pushed his starved hand through the bars to wave farewell, and then it slipped back into the darkness, like the hand of a drowning man.

"Go . . . find the box."

"We can't leave him," she said as Mariah dragged her away.

"Nor can we stay; the creature would kill us if we tried to help Felix escape," he said as they ran along the platform, jumping from gantry to gantry as they quickly made their way toward an exit high up in the cavern wall.

Far below, a door clunked open. The sound of voices flooded the lagoon. Ixion slithered out of the pool and grunted hungrily across the cave floor.

"Come to Daddy," Luger shouted, holding out a mutton joint whilst wafting a sabre in the other hand. "Can't be *too* careful," he said to Grimm and Grendel, who cowered behind him. "I didn't buy this beast for its timidity."

Mariah looked down through the lattice of metal braced thickly with crisscrossing cables. He could see Luger feeding Ixion as the two detectives huddled against the wall. The sound of crunching bone skimmed like a bouncing stone from the water and rose up to where he was hiding in the dim light near the ceiling.

"Doesn't look like they are here," Grimm said as the crocodile snapped greedily at another piece of meat.

"Doesn't mean they weren't," Luger retorted cynically, his voice tense and dry. "We checked every other passage. They had to have come here."

"But they're not here now," Grendel snapped, looking uneasy in the presence of the crocodile.

"I am not fond of crocodiles, Mister Luger, not fond at all," Grimm said nervously.

"Crocodile?" Luger asked as if Grimm had made some tedious mistake. "This is no crocodile, but a crocogon, a combination of two strange creatures—*Varanus komodoensis*, from a small island in the Ocean of Sumbawa. A real dragon and a crocodile, brought together by selective breeding."

"It is like a creature I once saw in one of my dreams, and not something I would like to pass the time of day feeding," Grendel said.

"From that fragment of cloth, it would appear that it has already eaten," Grimm said slyly, pointing to a ripped piece of black calico on the shingle path by the side of the lagoon.

Luger threw the meat into the pool and watched as Ixion slithered away. He picked up the ripped cloth and looked intently at it, searching for the identity of the wearer. Mariah and Sacha listened from high above, and Sacha looked at the torn hem of her dress.

"Can I help you?" Grimm asked, taking the spectacles from his pocket and putting them on.

Luger handed him the torn cloth and said nothing. He looked about him and listened. Sabre in hand, he walked to the door of the cell and peered in through the grating. "All is well," he muttered, seeing the huddled group of bodies in the dark corner of the cell. "None of you been seeing things? Not even you, Felix?" No one answered.

"It's very straightforward, Mister Luger," said Grimm. "For a price Grendel and I could follow them and have them done away with. Obviously, whoever left this behind had a close call with your *pet* . . . I would think they have not gone far yet, and with these spectacles they should be easily found. Now that we have this piece of their garment, I can track them for days and they will never escape."

Luger thought as he rummaged in his pockets for a trinket to bargain with. "I would give you seven of my finest pearls."

"It would be twenty, Mister Luger. I can see eleven at least in the shingle about my feet. Payment strictly on completion of the task?"

"Done," said Luger as his pocket watch chimed. "I have to sleep now and sleep here. It is something I must do." He climbed the steps of the gantry and, propping himself up, fell into a deep, yet fitful sleep.

"Come, Mister Grendel, we have feet to follow and pearls to collect," Grimm said. He pushed the cloth into a small pouch that hung around his neck. Taking the spectacles from his nose, he twisted a small tuning knob on the side and placed them back on his face. He stared about him. "There," he said quickly, "and there . . . and there." He pointed to different places along the path. "Quick, Grendel, they are not long gone. I think they are just ahead of us."

"What shall we do with Mister Luger?" Grendel enquired, stepping over the comatose body that blocked the gantry.

"Feed him to the crocodile?" Grimm replied.

CHAPTER

❧ 21 ❧

The Waxworks

Mariah tried to quiet Sacha as she sobbed, holding the torn edge of her dress, the realisation that she had almost been bitten by the creature overwhelming her with fear.

"Grimm has a device that can track our footsteps," Mariah whispered. "We have to get ahead of them."

Far below, Mister Grimm sauntered along a narrow gantry, his head bowed low as he looked at the footprints only he could see. Grendel followed, looking back at the snoring Luger, who lay against the metal bars.

Mariah peered over the balustrade as his pursuers went from platform to platform. He looked into the long, dark tunnel that lay ahead of them, pulled Sacha to her feet and dragged her into the darkness.

"What of Felix?" she asked as they were engulfed in the muffling black of the passage.

"If we can escape the Prince Regent, we will get help and come back for him," Mariah replied.

"But who can we ask for help?" Sacha said as they stumbled up a stairway in pitch darkness.

"Captain Charity, anyone," he said, feeling quite alone. "I wish my father were here; he'd know what to do."

She spoke without thinking. "The one who left you at the Colonial School to pursue his own ends."

"He had to go," he blurted back. "It's not that easy. Choices have to be made all the time. They would have come back . . . they would." Mariah hit the wall with his fist.

"At least my father brought us with him."

"At least my father wasn't a drunk and a thief," he parried.

They went on in a seething silence, unable to get away from each other.

"Who would do all these things?" he muttered to himself. "I'll go for Charity, and you can stay here."

"Not on your life—I'm coming with you," Sacha said. "Leave me with Luger and Monica?"

"You'd be in good company." They turned a corner and saw an elevator door. To one side a red button glowed brightly against the black-painted rock in which it was set. Instinctively, Sacha pressed the button.

"I thought there was only one in the building," Mariah said.

"This is no ordinary one," she said. "Look at the button, and listen—you can't hear any steam."

The elevator approached at high speed. It forced the air down the tunnel like wind through a whistle. Then it suddenly stopped and the metal cage opened by itself, a green light illuminating their feet.

Mariah stepped inside, followed by Sacha. There were two buttons set in a brass plate. The upper was etched with the word LABORATORY—the lower with OFFICE.

Sacha reached out to press the lower button. Mariah stubbornly pushed her hand to one side and, with a satisfied look upon his face, pressed the button for the laboratory. The door slammed shut, and two steel bolts shot from a hidden enclosure like sharp bayonets and held it fast. The elevator trembled and then shot upward at such a speed that they both fell to the floor. Within a few seconds they had arrived. The door opened and they rolled out into the laboratory.

The room was furnished with a large wooden desk and a vast copper kettle covered in cold wax, and was filled with Bizmillah's discarded magic tricks and scientific devices. It had two levels, with what looked like a stage taking up one side. A thick velvet curtain divided the room, and leading up to it was a small flight of wooden steps.

Mariah sniffed the pungent smell of cooling wax. Splatters and drips hung from the walls. Hanging from drying rails were various outfits. Dresses and smocks, trousers with patches to cover torn knees. In the corner, draped over a manikin, was a long black dress covered in sequins and a pair of fine opera gloves, which glinted as if studded with diamonds.

Sacha had seen these before. They were the same as those worn by Monica. She walked across the room and slid a glove onto her hand. It was soft and warm, glinting in the glow from the lights that adorned the ceiling.

"Do you think he's made a waxwork of Monica and will have her in the cavern for knowing too much?" she joked. Mariah still sulked as he walked about, head downcast.

"And one of you for being so cheerful?" he replied as he walked up the wooden steps and peeped behind the curtain. "That's if there's not one already," he said in a muffled voice before pulling his head quickly from behind the bloodred drape and calling her over. "You're in for a surprise, Sacha . . . Look."

Sacha went behind the curtain and reappeared clutching a wax head in her arms, its hair tied back in a bun.

"Does this really look like me?" she asked. "And that's not all." She pulled back the curtain. "You're there as well, and it looks as if you've been hung for your troubles."

Mariah looked behind the drapes. There above him, filling the entire ceiling, were wax manikins hanging from long steel hooks. In the corner was a boy of his age with deep brown hair that stuck out this way and that. Beneath was a thin face and wide eyes. A label hung from the sleeve of its black jacket. He walked to the manikin and read the label . . .

Mariah Mundi—*next week.*

"He planned to have me gone by next week?" Mariah said angrily. "We'll see who'll be gone by then."

Sacha laughed grimly as she turned the label and showed him the date. "It was done on the day you arrived. *Tomorrow* is next week."

"Then he'll have to catch me. I'll not work for him in his oyster lagoon. What happens if you get too old? Does he feed you to that crocodile?" He snapped the hand off his waxwork. "He shan't have the joy of packing *me* off to France."

Mariah pulled the manikin off its hook and let it smash to the floor. He kicked the head as hard as he could, sending it through the air and smashing against the wall. He shouted triumphantly as his wax head splintered into tiny pieces, a cascade of pearls scattering across the floor.

"Look, Mariah . . . Pearls!" Sacha shouted. "You *were* right."

"And this hand is all we need to prove his guilt," he said as he put the hand in his coat and looked for the door.

198

Suddenly, the elevator burst into life and the door shut. It was sucked far below in a single breath.

"Luger?" Sacha asked. She threw her wax head to the floor and stamped on it several times to reveal a cache of fine, round pearls. "These are for my sisters," she said as she grasped the pearls, putting them into her pockets. "If he's in the business of killin'—then I'm in the business of takin'."

"And not a moment too soon," Mariah said at the sound of the approaching elevator. "We have to get back to the Prince Regent."

Sacha spotted a door hidden behind a small drape at the side of the room, a key fitted into the lock. The door opened into the tunnel by the entrance to the beach. She knew this place well. To the right was the theatrical storeroom, where Old Scratty lived; farther along was the staircase that led to the elevator and the Prince Regent.

The elevator ground to a sudden halt, the sound of the sliding door echoing about the room. The voice of Grimm shouting to Grendel and Luger was the last thing they heard as they slammed the door and turned the key to lock the door from the outside.

In two minutes they had sneaked through the corridors and summoned the main elevator. Now they stood holding the brass rail, feet fixed into the safety rings as they hurtled toward the hotel dining room.

The gate slid open and they were bathed in sunlight. The room was decorated with tall silk screens, and large parlour palms in red earthen pots lined the windows along one side. A waiter pushed quickly by, carrying a silver tray stacked with dirty dishes from the tables.

"Eating?" shouted the steward, pulling a cloth from a window table, scattering crumbs into the air. "We serve theatre staff," he said joyfully. "Bizmillah has left the building with a guest, so he won't be here to chide you for being lazy."

Sacha shook her head, smiled and turned away, pulling Mariah by the sleeve.

One of the waiters seemed to be strangely interested in Mariah. He stared at him through deep, murky eyes. Mariah looked away, and then moments later looked again. The waiter, who still had his eyes fixed upon him, smiled and looked away.

Sacha had noticed him, too. "He was Felix's friend," she whispered. "He was with him on the night he disappeared. Spends a lot of time talking to Luger."

The waiter smiled again, and then gave a genteel wave to Sacha before disappearing into the kitchen.

"Let's go," said Mariah, moving toward the exit.

"Going?" said a voice from the other side of a silk screen. "And so soon." Grimm peered around the dragon prints and smiled.

"Indeed, Grimm, . . . indeed." Grendel peered down at them from above the screen.

"So, . . . as long as we are all are here, I would like you to come with us," Grimm said as if he were inviting them for tea.

Suddenly, the chef burst out of the kitchen, knife in hand, a scowl to sour milk across his face. "*You!*" he screamed as Grimm turned to look at him. "Yes, you." Grimm opened his mouth but could not say a word as the chef grabbed him by the throat and dragged him across the room to the door, followed meekly by Grendel. "Out of my restaurant, now!"

"But we're here on Luger's business . . . we have to . . . take boy . . . to him," Grimm sputtered as the chef's large hand squeezed his throat.

"They are my guests," the chef replied, lifting Grimm from the floor with one hand and summoning Grendel to leave with the other. "They will stay as long as there is food on the table." He looked at Mariah and signalled with his eyes for them to run.

Mariah grabbed Sacha and pulled her through the kitchen door. They tumbled to the floor at the feet of the waiter. He grabbed Sacha by the arm, dragging her to her feet.

"This way," he said as he pulled them both through the kitchen. "It'll take you through the cellar and into the street. Go—Felix was my friend . . ." He smiled as he pointed them down a short flight of steps into a basement packed with fruit and cases of wine. Ahead they could see two open doors that led into the square. They ran through the dark room and into the bright light of day, the sound of the chef haranguing Grimm and Grendel fading into the distance.

Peachtree

CHAPTER

✶ 22 ✶

The Emporium Vaults

T he streets were full of people milling around the large market taking place outside the Prince Regent. Mariah and Sacha ran, weaving in and out amongst the brightly coloured stalls.

There was a sudden shout from the crowd for Mariah to stop, and a large, burly man lashed out and tried to grab his coat. Mariah ducked, managing to dodge the man. Sacha hid behind a stall.

"Here!" she shouted in a panic as Mariah ran farther away. "This way!" Mariah turned. "If we go through here, we'll get away," she said quickly. Mariah ran to her, stumbling.

A carriage stopped abruptly outside the Prince Regent. Mariah looked back and saw Albion dragged from the coach and into the square. Two men dressed in black suits and long coats held him by the arms. He turned and saw Mariah. He nodded at him, then quickly looked away as he was hauled up the hotel's marble steps.

Grimm and Grendel stepped from the revolving door of the Prince Regent. They greeted Albion with a slap to his face, then looked up and down the marketplace, holding their black walking canes. Grendel adjusted his spectacles as he squinted in the bright morning light. They looked at each other, then stepped into the courtyard. Mariah and Sacha saw them and ran.

Together they proceeded through the market, Grendel sniffing the air as if he could track Mariah and Sacha's scent. Grimm looked at the ground, examining each footprint. He placed his spectacles on his stubby nose and gazed intensely at the mud, pointing.

"This way," he said, his voice echoing against the brick wall of the Prince Regent. "I can see their footmarks. The spectacles work well, even in daylight." He adjusted the gold frames and turned a small dial on the side of the glass. "Even better," he said, walking quickly.

"I can smell them!" Grendel said. "Fear dripping from their bodies like dew. There's nothing better than a chase, especially on market day." He plunged his cane firmly into the mud, following his fat friend.

Grimm pushed his way through the revellers, knocking a stand of fine ale to the ground, ignoring the swearing of the man who stood close by.

"Leave him be. This isn't your matter," Grendel said to the man, who glared at Grimm. "We are *detecting*, and nothing can stand in the way of that!" He pushed the man, who fell onto his backside, landing in the mud with deep indignation.

"This way!" said Grimm happily, as he strutted through the market. "Their footsteps are still hot. I can see them through the spectacles. They are not long ahead of us. They are running, running, but they will never escape."

"A good investment, good investment," Grendel replied as he scurried on behind.

Ahead of them, Mariah and Sacha beat their way through the market. Sacha turned and caught a glimpse of a fine black top hat, and realised that Grimm and Grendel weren't far behind.

"They're coming, Mariah. We'll have to go this way," she said as she pointed to a side street that led away from the market. Crossing the street, they went through an archway into a narrow lane that led into the centre of the town.

To each side were arcades of the strangest shops that Mariah had ever seen. In the window of a fishmonger was a large black skate hanging from a hook by its tail. Its mouth was open, seawater dripping from its face, doleful, glazed eyes staring at Mariah.

"We can't stay!" Sacha said, pulling his coat sleeve, trying to get him to walk faster to get away from the marketplace. "I know someone who we can go and see. He's a collector. He works at the Emporium. If we go there, I *know* we'll get away. I know he can help us." There was desperation in her voice—she seemed to be speaking to convince herself. As they clattered across the bright stone cobbles into another crowded street, she looked back. Far behind them two silk hats followed, one squat, the other tall and thin, to match their wearers.

Together Mariah and Sacha ran along Bar Street, its narrow buildings reaching high above them.

Sacha stopped suddenly and pulled Mariah into the doorway of an old snuff shop, the windows displaying the words EBENEZER BARTHOLOMEW'S. MAGICAL SNUFF. GUARANTEED TO BLOW THE COBWEBS FROM EVEN THE MOST STIFLED OF BRAINS.

Mariah read the fading words and wondered what Sacha thought Ebenezer's goods could do for him. Sacha turned to the door but didn't go in. She pressed her face upon the glass, as if to enquire who was inside. She grabbed Mariah and turned him toward her.

"Look inside!" she said. "Look inside!" They hid their faces against the glass. Then in the reflection of the window, Mariah saw a constable in a helmet and long black cape amble by. He seemed to be searching for someone or something. Sacha waited.

"It's safe," she said finally. "He's gone."

"Why were you hiding from him?" Mariah asked as he turned and looked into the street, to see the constable walking away, hands firmly clasped behind his back.

"It's Jack Teal. He's a friend of my father's. If he sees me here, he'll know I'm up to something. You don't understand, Mariah. This place has got eyes and ears, and whatever we do, someone's going to see us."

Sacha looked back along the street and saw Jack Teal talking to Grimm and Grendel. They engaged him in polite conversation, bowing and nodding as they exchanged pleasantries. Grimm took the spectacles from his nose and folded them neatly, placing them in a black bag and slipping them into his inside jacket pocket. He gave them a reassuring pat.

"He knows them!" Mariah said as he saw the discourse taking place. "What are we going to do?"

Sacha grabbed his hand. "This way," she said. "If we keep on going, we can outrun them."

They left the narrow lane of shops and turned. Sacha led the way down the hill toward the harbour, the fresh smell of the sea blowing in the breeze. In front of them, they could see the pinnacle of the Emporium decked with a large Jack that flew in the wind.

"Not far," Sacha gasped, smiling at Mariah, the confidence returning to her face.

In five minutes they stood beneath the tower of the Emporium. By the door to the market vault inside was a pillar of bright yellow sandstone that reached high above their heads. Beside it were blackened windows, etched with news of the latest sale of remnant goods and all that had survived the most recent wreck upon the rocks.

The door was shut. A gargoyle of a coiled lizard looked down upon them. Sacha pushed at the large metal handle that ran across the door. It opened suddenly, and they fell inward with a jolt, down four worn steps onto the stone floor below.

The vault opened up before them. It was a large, ornate bazaar, candlelit and yet still dark. It seemed as if there were no shadows but those created by a soft light in the distance. At the end of the corridor of shops, all with their windows tightly shuttered, Mariah could see a faint light coming through the thick glass of one shop window.

Cautiously, they went farther inside, Sacha leading the way. To each side of them were arched doorways covered with beaded curtains and symbols of their trade hanging above.

A large hand etched in gold swung silently above one shop door: The Great Plagiarus—palmist and phrenologist—May the bumps on your head speak great voices of the future—no credit. Stuck to the window was a small note, quickly etched in a child's crayon: *Closed—due to unforeseen circumstances.*

Mariah felt he was a lad of unforeseen circumstances.

"It would be nice if we could see the future," he said to Sacha as they gazed into the shop windows they passed by. "Should have asked the Panjandrum what would happen. All we did was watch it like a circus—a waste, really." He sounded downcast, his voice fading.

Sacha tried to smile, but in her heart she knew that somewhere not too far behind, Grimm and Grendel were coming. Grimm would wear his spectacles and see their hidden footsteps, following like a faithful hound.

At the far end of the covered arcade was the brightly

painted front of Quadlibett's Fine Vendorium. It appeared to glow, every inch richly ornate. Every tin, bottle and bag that filled the window begged to be purchased. Mariah found himself mesmerised by the sight of jar upon jar of luscious delights. His mouth welled with anticipation and his stomach stirred.

Suddenly, a man appeared in front of him, a small, tasselled hat upon his head, a pair of cobalt spectacles stuck firmly upon his nose. He was dressed in a crisp black suit, a cravat of the finest gold etched with purple dragons and a white shirt with a stiff collar. What caught Mariah's eye the most was his shining emerald ring.

The man gave a polite cough. Startled, Sacha turned, not having realised he stood there. The man laughed.

"Hello, Sacha," he said. "I take it you came here on your own?" He held out his hand in a gesture of friendship. "And who is this?"

"Oh, this is Mariah. From London. The Colonial School. Works with me at the Prince Regent."

"Like young Mister Felix," Quadlibett said. "I am Quadlibett, owner and patron of this arcade. Sadly, not all my tenants have lived up to expectation, but you can buy things here from around the known world. Headbands from the Native Indians of the Americas, the finest herbs from Tibet and any article of clothing you would ever wish to wear. And . . . in my very own vendorium, the best chocolate known to man."

"We're in trouble, Mister Quadlibett," Sacha blurted out.

"Sacha, you're always in trouble!" Mister Quadlibett said. He led them to the door of his shop and opened it. Mariah gasped. It was the most amazing tabernacle of delight that the eye could perceive. There before him were shelves and shelves of tinned biscuits, boxes of sweets and packets of the finest delicacies that he'd ever seen. His stomach twisted with hunger. He laughed as if he had entered paradise. Mister Quadlibett tapped the side of his nose and gave him a knowing wink.

"I take it, Mariah, you're like everybody else that comes into this shop. You can see in their eyes that they want to devour everything!"

"It's true. I've never seen anything like this before!"

"Then you will be my guest," the man said. "Pick anything you want."

Mariah's eyes searched every tin. There was a myriad of colours: greens, blues, black, turquoise, the deepest of reds and a scarlet that almost burned the eye to gaze upon it. He read the labels. GALLACTO'S BUBBLE MINTS, CARUSO'S CHOCOLATE — they were all there, all the favourites, waiting for him to eat them. He thought long and hard as his hand wafted backward and forward along the line of tins, and then he decided.

"I'll have one of those!"

He pointed to a tin box neatly crafted into the shape of a row of books. He read the label: MADISON'S MAGICAL WONDERS.

Mariah had only ever seen one before in his life, an expensive gift sent by a parent to a boy at the Colonial School.

Now it was Mariah's chance. Mister Quadlibett reached for the tin.

"You choose well, lad. You choose very well. The most expensive thing that I have. Yet let this be a gift from me to you."

He took the box from the shelf. He opened it and held it toward Mariah, whose hand darted inside, taking a piece. Then quickly, without speaking, he ripped the chocolate from its golden skin, pushed it into his mouth and sighed. He sat at the small table in the corner of the shop, content. He smiled in thanks to Quadlibett.

As Mariah ate and gazed about the Vendorium, Quadlibett took Sacha to one side and whispered to her, "You said you were in trouble, Sacha? Real trouble that you cannot fix yourself?"

Sacha looked at him, then looked back along the dark arcade.

"Being followed," she said nervously. "Something happened at the Prince Regent."

"And where does young Mariah fit into this trouble?" Mister Quadlibett asked.

"There's something else. It's to do with Felix."

"Felix? I remember him well!"

"He disappeared. We thought he was dead or had run away, but we found him. He's being kept prisoner in a cavern beneath the hotel."

Mister Quadlibett looked out to the street. "I think conversations such as this should be kept behind closed doors."

He pulled the door shut and locked it. He turned to the oil lamp behind him and lowered the wick.

"Now," he said, "let's talk about what you have seen, and maybe Mister Quadlibett will be able to pour some oil on your troubled water."

Quickly, impatiently, Sacha told him all that had happened.

CHAPTER

✺ 23 ✺

The Shovel Hat

Mister Quadlibett looked at Mariah. "I can tell you're a lad of secrets," the vendor said, offering him another chocolate.

Mariah picked one from the box and placed it quickly in his pocket.

"For later," he replied.

"Later is always worth preparing for," Quadlibett said. He pressed another piece into the lad's hand. "Take plenty."

"How much do I owe you for these?" Mariah asked.

"For you, lad? Nothing. Now tell me—your eyes speak of secrets. There's no room for those between the three of us, so tell me what troubles you."

"Since I arrived from London things have been happening. There was a man on the train, Isambard Black. Said he'd been booked into the hotel for three months."

Mister Quadlibett looked at him. "People come to the hotel all the time. What makes him so different?"

"It was what he did. He was in the same compartment of the train. He shared secrets with me, told me things. And there was a man I met at Kings Cross, Perfidious Albion. He gave me a pack of cards, told me I had to keep them safe, then send him a postcard to the Claridges Hotel. So I did, and this morning, some men turned up at the hotel, dragging him from a carriage." Mariah stared at Quadlibett as if he were part of some game that had spun out of control. "There are also two others who say they're detectives. They followed us through the streets before we came here. Is this just some other coincidence?" Mariah asked.

"One tall, the other short and fat?" Quadlibett asked. Sacha nodded. "Grimm and Grendel."

"You know them?" Sacha asked.

"Know of them. They have a reputation in town already. Things are not kept a secret here for too long. Like the body that was discovered outside the Three Mariners. Strange how it was found again this morning under the bridge; it was said there had been a fall—a lost vagrant. But I have never known dead men to throw themselves from bridges. Kraken's back, or so they say, and the beach steams." He thought for a moment. "Best we see Mister Charity; he will know what to do . . . A strange adventure for you both."

There was a sharp rattle on the shop door.

"Best go in the back," Quadlibett said to Sacha. "You know the way out should our guest be unwelcome. Barrels and stairs . . . barrels and stairs," he muttered.

The door was rattled again, this time more urgently, and was quickly followed by frantic banging.

"Grimm and Grendel?" Mariah asked as he stepped from the brightly lit shop into the dark storeroom hidden behind a blue curtain.

"Whoever it is wants to see us," Quadlibett said sprightly, as if it didn't matter that the detectives could be at the door. "Go and hide; keep listening. If it's them, there is a way of escape that may intrigue you."

Sacha pulled Mariah farther into the darkness and slid the curtain across the doorway, blocking it with a wooden stand decked in jars so the entrance would look like nothing more than another display of sweets.

The door was rattled again, this time followed by a raucous voice that sounded as if a gull had taken human form.

"Quadlipet . . . Mister Quadlipet. I need *string*, Mister Quadlipet, and you are the only man I know with a large enough ball."

"Mrs. Sachavell, with all this shouting and ranting, I thought the world had caught fire, and all you require is *string*?" he said as he opened the door.

"Yes, Mister Quadlidot, and without a good length I shall be unable to work. There are customers afoot and money to be made, and how can I wrap my cod ends without a decent yard of string?"

She stepped into the shop, pushing Quadlibett to one side as she ogled the shelves.

"How much string can I have?"

"As much as your conscience allows you to take without payment, my dear Mrs. Sachavell," Quadlibett said patiently as he closed the door, went behind the counter and then handed her a ball of rough string as big as an ostrich egg.

"Without payment, Mister Kudlipet? Such a gent, and I know I can return the favour. My fish is so fresh and dainty that it will please a man's heart. I'll bring some when I close up and see you taken care of," she said fondly.

The thought of sampling any delight of Mrs. Sachavell's chilled him to the bone as the smell of her "fresh" fish filled the shop. Mrs. Sachavell took a yardstick and began to measure what her conscience would allow her to take.

Sacha watched, her eye pressed to the gap between the wall and the curtain as Mariah searched the storeroom for a way of escape. As he looked around in the dim light he noticed that the shelves were not stacked with sweets but with cases of wine, tobacco and gin. He crept back to Sacha.

"Smuggler . . . gallons of gin hidden," he said loudly enough to be heard in the Vendorium.

"Did you hear that?" Mrs. Sachavell asked anxiously, her eyes twitching from side to side.

"What?" replied Quadlibett, biting the smile from his lips. "I heard only the sound of your conscience stripping the ball of string."

"Voices," she said earnestly. "Someone called me a smuggler. I heard it as well as if they were standing behind me. They know about my . . ." Mrs. Sachavell stopped, as if afraid whoever had spoken could hear her.

"What would they know about?" Quadlibett asked.

"Nothing." She paused. He watched her empty the ball completely of string.

"Has your conscience taken enough?" he asked.

Without warning, the door was shoved open and in stepped Mister Grimm.

"What shop is this?" he asked.

"Quadlibott's Fine Vendorium," Mrs. Sachavell replied.

"Are you Quadlibott?" Grimm asked the woman as he took the divining spectacles from his face and put them into his pocket. "And what do you do?" he asked Quadlibett, without giving Mrs. Sachavell a chance to answer.

"I am measuring the length of a woman's conscience," he said as he took the yardstick from Mrs. Sachavell and held it like a school cane in front of Mister Grimm's face. "And at the moment it measures twenty-five yards."

"Thankfully, a conscience is not something from which I have to suffer. Tell me, both of you. Have you seen a lad and lass nearby? Could be said to be in a hurry?" Grimm asked.

Before they could answer, Grendel stepped into the shop, lowering his head to ease himself through the door. He sniffed as he squeezed by Mrs. Sachavell, doffing his hat and smiling to reveal a row of perfectly formed gold teeth.

"Can't smell them here, Mister Grimm. Are you sure they came this way?"

Grimm snorted. "To this very door and no mistaking."

"Then they must be here somewhere," he said nonchalantly.

"They *are* here Mister Grendel; I know it to be true. Don't be deceived."

"Be assured we will not delay your search, but this is not the place for it to continue," Quadlibett said. "There were two children here, but they've gone. Mentioned a train to London and a hotel . . . if I heard them correctly." Quadlibett looked at Mrs. Sachavell. "Now you have exceeded the limits of your conscience, Mrs. Sachavell, and I am sure there will be a queue at your stall awaiting a ready supply of fresh fish."

"Best be off," she said. "But will be back with some nice cod end; can't beat a bit of cod. Fish gone scarce since the kraken came." She rolled the string around her hand and left the shop with it trailing behind her.

Grendel closed the door and turned the key as Grimm put on the divining spectacles.

"You don't tarry with us, do you, Mister Quadlibett?" Grimm said, looking up at him.

"I tell you what I heard."

Grimm looked at the shop floor and studied each plank. "Certainly been here at some point—I can see the footprints. Still very warm; I think they're close."

"Then you have eyes better than a man of your age should possess. I can see no footprints," Quadlibett grumbled.

"But not everyone has what my eyes have," Grimm said as he pushed the divining spectacles closer to his face. "And not everyone can see what I can see."

Quadlibett didn't reply, but turned briskly, climbed up a small ladder and took a large tin from the highest shelf. "I have something for your journey, gentlemen." As he turned he gasped and pretended to slip, opening the lid as he fell to the floor.

He showered a cascade of the whitest of powders across the room. It dowsed Grimm and Grendel, and billowed in bright clouds. Grimm spat with dissatisfaction as it covered the glowing footprints. Quadlibett quickly got to his feet and purposefully tipped even more of the powder across the floor and down the front of Grimm's trousers.

"FOOL . . . NINCOMPOOP . . . MISCREANT . . . IMBECILE!" screamed Grimm. "How can I see where they have gone?"

"Gentlemen, . . . what a travesty of my complete inebriation. How can I apologise?" Quadlibett said remorsefully as he turned the key, opened the door and in one movement managed to usher them both from the shop.

"Which train to London?" Grendel asked as the door was shut and locked in his face.

"We are deceived: there is no train, and he knows more than he's telling," Grimm said.

"And we are on the wrong side of the door," Grendel replied, shaking the powder from his coat and wiping it from his nose.

"Then we will wait—there can't be any other way out of this place. It is built like a fortress, with a high tower for us to keep our watch."

Quadlibett smiled to himself. He closed the blinds on the windows, and as he did he watched Grimm and Grendel head into the darkness of the arcade.

Turning around, he crossed the shop. He smiled and rubbed his hands together. "A job well-done . . . well-done," he said. "You can come out—the way is clear. Mrs. Sachavell has stolen all of my string, and Grimm and Grendel are showered in powder."

All was quiet. Lifting the curtain to one side, he pushed the false shelves back into place and looked into the storeroom. He walked three paces and slid the cases of gin back across the open escape hatch. Reaching up to the shelf above, he took an old silver condiment jar and sprinkled the floor with a thick grey dust. With one breath he blew the dust into the corner of the room.

"There . . . ," he said to himself with great satisfaction. "It's as if they had never been here."

CHAPTER

✳ 24 ✳

Caladrius

The sewer smelled like a charnel house on a hot summer's day. It twisted and turned as it descended steeply to the harbour. Sacha carried the small lamp that she had taken from the shelf in Mister Quadlibett's storeroom. It lit her feet, so she could see the large brown rats that scattered this way and that as she squelched through the drain. Mariah trailed behind, holding his nose and trying not to touch the walls of the culvert. They dripped with a green slime, which also hung from the roof in small clusters. Every few yards he could see a shadowy opening cut into the side of the culvert and packed with boxes and barrels. Each carried the symbol of a small bird against a full moon. Some were covered in thick horse blankets; others had tipped over and been left to bob in the pools of cess that formed against the brick dams.

Sacha walked on, ignoring everything around her. She was bold, sure-footed. She pointed up to a string of metal grates that allowed the fleeting daylight to shine momentarily upon Mariah's face.

"Princess Street, corner of Tuthill," she whispered. "Soon be at the harbour."

"And then?" Mariah asked as they continued walking.

"Then we can find Charity and get Felix," she said.

"You say Felix's name like he's your beau," Mariah replied.

"*Friend*," she said. "There's more to life than beaus." Sacha smiled for the first time in many hours. The lamplight added an extra radiance, abundant in joy and hope. She looked at Mariah. "Do you believe in yourself?"

"If I knew what you meant, maybe I could say yes," he replied.

"Do you believe we'll get out of this?" she pressed.

Mariah couldn't reply. His mind raced. He thought of Luger, the waxworks, Grimm and Grendel. Everything flooded in, taking his thoughts uncontrollably from mayhem to misery.

Sacha butted into his thoughts. "You have to believe. It's a state of mind. Think we're done for and we are. Drop your head to the ground and we'll end up in the dirt."

"If it were that easy," he muttered as he looked at a shaft of bright sunlight streaming through the drain overhead, "I would be able to get rid of this sack of despair that I carry."

"Then we go on?" Sacha asked, prodding him in the arm. "Take this to the end and rescue Felix and the others?"

"I don't have anything else to do," Mariah replied miserably.

"My grandfather said that if people don't have a vision, then they will perish. If we don't have a dream, then we fritter away our lives with nothing. Our days are like grass—one day green and fresh, the next dry and ready to be burned in the fire. I don't want to live a life like that." Sacha stood in front

218

of him, her faced flushed. "We can make a difference: set them free—put an end to Luger . . ."

"Get caught by Grendel and Grimm and end up in the oyster prison, or have Black catch us?" Mariah replied.

"You can change the way you think, Mariah. It's here and now, no past, no future. *This* is where we live."

"In a sewer, running from two madmen?" he asked.

A heavy thud resounded through the tunnel from far away. The earth seemed to shiver. The thud came again as another iron drain cover was picked up and then dropped back into its place. One by one came long, loud thuds that sent billows of dust into the sewer.

"Here, Grendel, . . . here," came Grimm's voice. "I can see it clearly. This way . . . They must be in the sewer."

Two streets away, Grendel pulled on another iron sewer grate. Grimm adjusted his spectacles, turning the dial until the lenses glowed bright blue. He stared at something only he could see. Rising from the drain was a red mist telling him of their presence far below. He looked into the distance to a small square of houses, where the vapour rose from the ground. "Leave it, Grendel," he shouted. "They are ahead, far ahead, down beyond the square."

Grendel looked up, hoping to see what Grimm perceived. "Where?" he asked.

"I can see them, and that is all that matters. By the beerhouse . . . quickly."

Their voices carried far below, as an echo spoken from another world.

"They're still tracking us," Mariah said.

Sacha stepped from the light of the drain back into the shadows. "They have to use the street. We can get to the harbour before them, and across the beach to the Golden Kipper. They won't take on Captain Charity, not if we tell him what they've done." She made off along the thin ledge of bricks that flanked the pools of dirty water and then down a flight of steps.

"I'll show him the hand," Mariah said, dragging behind in the blackness as Sacha and the lamp strode on ahead.

"Not far," Sacha said as the sound of lapping water filled the sewer. "One more flight and—" All she could see was the sewer tunnel disappearing into black water. "High tide. We won't get out for hours," she said, holding the lamp above her head to light as far as she could.

"There's another way," Mariah said, seeing a tunnel at the far side of the sewer vault.

"We never go up there—nothing's ever hidden in that tunnel."

"We have to get out of here before Grimm comes and gets us," Mariah insisted.

"But not that way, not now."

"Don't tell me you're scared?" he asked.

"I'd go anyway, but up there . . . please . . ."

"A ghost or demon, or just another story to keep the nosy away from your father's smuggling?" Mariah asked. "Don't want me to see what's hidden so I can't tell?"

"Let's just wait for the tide, and then we'll get out."

"And don't you think they'll be waiting for us by then with some story of how we've robbed Luger? They'd have us in irons and in jail before you could call your father. And me with a pistol in my pocket and you with an enormous roll of notes."

"We could go back," she said. "Sneak back to the Emporium."

"You know what, Sacha, I had a vision . . . back there in the dark with Grimm shouting above my head. A thousand feet busying themselves with life, running back and forth for bread and fish. But in a stinking sewer amongst the filth and the rats, I realised that it doesn't matter. All these years I've been thinking only about myself, but I know now that my life could be snapped away in an instant. Life . . . life is more than running after bread and fish. My parents are gone, and I'll find out why before I leave this earth." Mariah took her face in his hands. "I'm going into that tunnel and I'll take whatever comes my way."

"Then I'll come too," Sacha said.

As they climbed the steps inside the tunnel Mariah could hear the distant chiming of a music box. It came again and again, and as they drew closer, a whispered song followed each note.

"It's coming from in there," Mariah said cautiously as they saw a gap in the wall where the bricks had been pulled away. "Smugglers?" he asked warily.

"Not here, not now," she whispered back as she shaded the lamp with her hand. "Hasn't been a boat in this last week—not another one until tomorrow."

"Then who?" he asked in a murmur as he crept slowly to the side of the entrance and tried to look beyond the shadows.

Sitting by a small fire and holding his head in his hands was the kraken. He wailed as he wound the handle of the music box time and again. He sang a tedious refrain over and over in words they couldn't understand as he pressed his eyes into his palms.

Mariah edged closer, Sacha pulling against his coattails and wanting to run. He suddenly knew he had to see the creature again, that it wasn't to be feared. He stepped into the dark shadow and climbed the rubble.

The midden on which he walked collapsed beneath his feet. He fell into the room and the kraken leaped up, drawing a three-bladed knife.

"No!" Mariah shouted, holding out his hand. "We won't do you harm."

The creature lowered the knife and looked at Mariah, not speaking. He stepped back and sniffed the air, pointing to the light in the sewer beyond.

"He knows you're there," Mariah said as Sacha hid. "It's safe. Come in."

Sacha stepped into the chamber. It was warm and dry, and lined with Persian carpets and swathes of fine cloth. Hanging from the ceiling was a silver cage holding a pure white bird the size of a sea hawk. A flickering silver candelabra rested upon a walnut table by the figurehead of a ship. The figurehead was cut into the shape of a smiling sea-maiden, her hands outstretched in welcome.

"Elvira . . . the figurehead is Elvira . . . She went missing from the Three Mariners." Sacha stepped toward it. "He had it all along, and he's nothing but a sad old man."

She looked scornfully at the kraken, with his bent neck and frail old bones. He seemed to try a half smile as he coughed and held his chest.

"He's sick," Mariah said.

"That's what we were frightened of?" Sacha said as she looked at the kraken, his old eyes bulging in his head, hair hanging in loose patches scattered between psoric lumps of flesh. "Just a legend—when you see the real thing, it couldn't harm you."

The kraken slumped into the small leather chair on which he had sat. He rubbed his face with his blistered hands, and flakes of salt-dried skin fell to the floor. He pulled his coat closed, snuggling in the folds to keep warm.

"He needs a doctor," Mariah said. He went to the creature, and picking up a stretch of sailcloth from the floor wrapped it across his back.

"They say he slaughtered people," Sacha said.

"I don't think it *was* him. Thief . . . yes, . . . but no murderer."

The kraken looked at him and tried to speak. "Scratty . . . ," he said in a scratchy voice. "Scratty?"

"He can speak," Mariah said, backing away from the beast. "He talks of Old Scratty; he wants the doll."

"From the look of this place, he wants everything," Sacha replied. "Kraken's been a-stealing. This is from a ship that set sail to France a month ago," she said, pointing at the Persian rugs strewn across the floor. "So is the music box—saw 'em go on myself. It sank on Brigg Rocks, not a soul saved."

"Caladrius . . ." The kraken spoke again in a feeble voice. He showed Mariah his parched hands, then held them to his blue and blistered lips. He stood up and fumbled with the minute lock of the silver cage, his fingers too swollen to turn the key. The white bird sat perfectly still, its head folded under its wing. "Caladrius . . . ," the kraken said again as he slumped back into his chair and held his head in his hands. He looked to the bird, pointing with a long, leprous finger. "Caladrius . . ."

"He wants to free the bird," Sacha said. "He can't turn the key."

Mariah turned the key. The door opened by itself as the kraken wound the music box, bringing the notes to life and letting the tune dance. He slumped back against the worn leather, resting his head against the high chairback. He swayed his hand back and forth with the chimes of the music, as if hoping that the bird would fly from the cage. It sat motionless, and then in time to the music, as if it too were part of the machine, slowly unfurled its long neck.

It looked like a pure white swan with eagle's wings and the claws of some great auk. It shimmered in the firelight, and opened its golden eyes. Staring at Mariah, it slowly edged to the door of the cage and stuck out its long neck. The feathers shimmered bright white and in an instant turned to silver, as if they were liquid mercury. It looked at the kraken, turned its face away and glared at the roof of the vault. With one wing-beat it took flight, flying round and round above their heads, cawing and whooping. It then landed between the kraken and the fire, rustling every feather. It stared at the creature as it shook its great silver wings. The kraken looked back, the skin peeling from his face, his hands blistering and breaking open as his fingernails fell to the floor.

"Caladrius . . . ," the kraken said as new skin began to cover his old bones and hair sprouted upon his head.

"He's healing," Mariah said quietly. The silver wings of the caladrius began to tarnish and age as feather after feather dropped from the bird, piling about its feet. "But the bird's dying."

"It's dead," Sacha said as the caladrius dropped to the floor by the fire.

"No death . . . ," the kraken mumbled. "It brings life."

"I didn't hear you speak until tonight," Mariah said.

"I can also laugh and eat and do many things now that new life has come to me." The kraken smiled at them. "Am I sad and old?" he asked Sacha.

Mariah stepped toward the kraken. "They say you're a murderer, that you steal children and leave money behind. And you attacked me last night."

"It was not my intent to harm you. I look for Scratty. I search for her everywhere, but I kill no one. I have seen who does these things, always at night, always with a three-bladed knife. I am a kraken, and the one you seek is human, like you. He carries a cane with a silver tip." He got to his feet, opening his webbed hands as he looked at the covering of fresh skin. "The caladrius was on a ship; I saved it from the sea and kept it for Scratty, to bring her to life. Now I can't find her." The kraken picked up the bird and placed it in the silver cage.

"We've seen her; we know where she is. She's in the Prince Regent," Sacha said, trying to smile at him. "Bizmillah uses her in his act—he's a magician."

"And a woman with him?" the kraken asked. "Tall, thin, elegant, with a painted face?"

"Monica," Mariah blurted out.

"Monecka Carpova . . . more than a magician—a sorcerer, temple master, witch of the sea." Mariah and Sacha gasped.

"It was she who took Scratty from me," the kraken continued. "Turned her from flesh to wood and gave her the face of a puppet."

"Then we will find her for you and bring her back," Sacha said, holding out her hand. Then she hesitated. "We've a *slight* problem . . . We can't go back yet, as we are being pursued by a man who can see through the ground and follow us even though we are in the sewer."

"We need to find a man called Captain Charity," Mariah said. "Last night when you followed us, I saw you in the window of his restaurant by the quayside. We have to find him."

"I am from the sea; I cannot go out in the light of day. Look how I was before; the sun melted my flesh as if it were wax. I looked for Scratty at sunrise, and it took my skin from me." The kraken thought for a moment, looking around the room. "But I remember the place. There is another way, a dark way."

CHAPTER

✳ 25 ✳

Lex non Scripta

They waited out the hour. The caladrius lay in the cage, its long, limp neck wrapped around its body. The kraken had left the pile of discarded silver feathers by the fire. As they talked he picked them up one by one and dropped them into the flames. Each time a feather touched the blaze, it sparkled and glowed. The deep black that had sullied it upon the healing of the kraken was banished, and it turned pure white.

Mariah was eager to hear the story of where the kraken had come from. The kraken looked at his hands, got to his feet, crossed the room and stared at himself in a looking glass, which hung lopsided from the wall.

"Am I not beautiful?" he asked, half-laughing. "If I were born this way, it could be understood; strange what life does to you."

"You haven't always been like that?" Sacha asked.

"If you but knew of what I have endured," the kraken said. "If you but knew . . ."

"And this place," she said as she looked at the finery that decked the room. "Do you wreck the ships from which you steal?"

"I salvage what I can, but the wrecking I leave to wind and storm, and the deceitful hearts of men with their false lamps strung from cliff tops."

"Who would wreck a ship?" Mariah asked.

"You'd be surprised what man would do if there was a shekel to be made, isn't that so, Sacha?" the kraken asked.

She shrugged and looked at the ground.

"What does he mean?" Mariah asked her.

"Expect he's been spying and listening to conversations he shouldn't," Sacha replied.

"I came here to search for someone," the kraken said. "Listening to drunkards plotting was not my plan. I am glad my life is in the sea—there is too much death in this harbour."

"How many people have been murdered, Sacha?" Mariah asked.

"Eleven, could be twelve . . . They say it was him. Started when he turned up, and he was seen running away into the sea."

"I saw the one who did it; I would recognise him," the kraken protested. "Would you stay, looking like me, if twenty men with burning torches and swords came a-chasing you?" Sacha was silent. "Very well . . . I will live in this place until I can find her, and then we will go back to the sea."

"So why do they think you're the murderer?" Mariah asked.

"Blame that which is different, the outsider, the ghoul. It is easier for them to look for me than to believe it could be one of their own," he replied quietly.

"And what *are* you?" Sacha asked, looking him up and down.

"I am whatever you want me to be. A sea monster, a phantom, a vampyre, a ghost seen with the corner of your eye. Take your pick and make stories of it. Isn't that what they all do? I am a kraken now, and that is all I know." The creature stopped and looked at the flames. Sacha saw the reflection of the fire burn in his eyes. "There is something far away, a thought, a dream that often comes to me, and then it's gone. It is as if I should remember, but cannot. Perhaps if I could recall what it was, I would know more." The kraken looked at Mariah. "When did you find Scratty?" he asked.

"She found us, turned up in my room at the top of the hotel. She just appeared from nowhere—and brought us a key."

"Then there is still life left in her," the kraken said as he stood up and started pacing. He looked up at the ceiling and bade them to be silent. "This is the time; they are nearby," he said as he took the caladrius from its cage and tucked it under his arm, its head hanging by his side.

Without saying another word, he set off from the vault. Sacha picked up the lamp and followed. Mariah plucked a tall candle from the stand and shielded it from the draught as they snaked through the tunnel back to the entrance. The kraken went on ahead in the blackness; each time he looked back, his eyes burned as if they were on fire. He turned sideways and slipped through a small entrance that they had not noticed as they had fled the Emporium. He waited for them on the other side.

"Your *friends* wait for you at the harbour mouth. They make enough noise to wake the dead. Soon there will be just a foot of water and they will come looking for you. Come this way and they will never find you."

"They can see where we've been," Mariah said. "It's as if we leave our footprints in ink across the land."

"Even if they can track you, they can never come this way, not unless the fat one cuts off his stomach and big rump. When I have seen you to the one you seek, I will come back and wait for them." The kraken grinned, running his long green tongue over his sharp, fishlike teeth.

After a quarter of an hour, they had walked through a maze of passages that grew narrower and narrower. Finally they reached a long metal ladder, which was loosely cemented into the intricate brickwork that spiralled upward. The kraken put the caladrius inside his jacket and climbed quickly. Sacha left the lamp behind and followed. Soon they sat just beneath the surface of the street, the sound of seagulls cawing above.

"This will take you to your friend. It is near where I first met you," the kraken said to Mariah as he took a golden coin from his pocket and gave it to him. "Take this, give it to the man. I have been stealing his fish, and this should cover all that I have taken. Now go. Push on the grate and it will give way."

"What about Old Scratty?" Sacha asked as the kraken slipped down the ladder.

"I will go for her tonight, and then we shall be gone. When the caladrius sees the moon, it will live and Scratty will be well."

"Will we see you again?" Mariah asked.

"You would want to be in the presence of a sea monster again?"

"Only if he is like you," he said, smiling as the creature slipped away into the darkness of the tunnels.

Mariah and Sacha sat together in the narrow shaft of light that slipped through the grate above their heads. "You stink," Mariah said to Sacha.

"And you're no rose. Bizmillah will want to know where you've been in those shoes," Sacha replied, looking at his muddy feet.

"I'm not going back to work for him. It's over for me, Sacha. After we set Felix free, I'm going back to London."

"And leave me here?" she asked.

"You'll not be alone for long; there'll be some fool to take over this friendship."

"Felix said that once, and look what happened—you turned up on a stormy night and stood the world on its head."

Mariah pushed on the metal grate above him. It slipped easily from its mounting, and he peered out into an alleyway. All he could see were the white walls of the Golden Kipper and the back door with its brass knocking plate.

"Come," he said as he pulled himself from the sewer, stood and then helped Sacha up. He looked around and knocked briskly on the door.

Sacha slid the metal grate back into place and jumped toward him as a slat on the door opened and a large eye peered out at them.

"Yes?" came a weary voice.

"Come to see Captain Charity," Mariah said as the eye looked him up and down.

"Not here," the voice replied, sounding irritated.

"But he must be," Mariah insisted, feeling a growing sense of unease.

"Gone away . . . business . . . Left me in charge, and even though I have only one leg, I still know what to do. You're not the physic, are you? I may be eighty, but I know today is Wednesday and Napoleon is the king of France."

"It's Saturday and Napoleon's dead," Sacha interrupted as the clatter of feet came from far away down the street.

"Died on Saturday? Napoleon? What will the duke do now?" the man asked as if his world had come to an end. "You *are* the physic, aren't you? Come to take me to Saint Mary's workhouse? Well, I'll tell you this . . . I'm not going." The man closed the slat, leaving Mariah and Sacha to listen to several bolts being slid quickly across the entrance as he fortified it for the invasion.

Mariah led Sacha to the front of the alley that led to the street on the quayside. Far away he could see Grimm and Grendel standing by the mouth of the sewer, waiting for the tide to subside. Grimm fiddled impatiently with his divining spectacles as Grendel looked around, seeming nervous about the cawing gulls that swooped above his head.

"This way," Mariah said as he opened the front door. "He has to be here — said he'd be in all Saturday."

The Golden Kipper was empty. All the tables were neatly dressed in white tablecloths and silver cutlery. The wooden floor had been freshly swept, and the steps to the upper tables had been freshly waxed. Mariah could hear a fumbling of the lock at the back door. He took Sacha by the hand, and they sneaked through a long corridor and watched as a small man with one leg, curly hair and a bushy white beard slid a bolt back and forth.

"Open or closed, open or closed?" he asked himself as he tried to recall what he was doing and where he was. "Can never remember how these newfangled things work."

"Captain Charity, where is he?" Mariah asked, startling the old man.

The man jumped back, his wooden leg slipping on the waxed boards, and fell to the floor in a crumpled heap. "Who . . . who wants him?" he asked.

"Mariah Mundi — an old friend," Mariah replied, holding out his hand to help up the man from the floor.

"Old friend? Codswallop . . . never heard such rubbish in all my life. Captain's friends are all young — he doesn't have any old friends — except me, and I'm not that old . . ." His eyes flickered quickly from side to side, spying the room as if he were looking at it for the first time. "Monday did you say?"

"Mariah Mundi," Sacha chipped in.

"He mentioned something was happening on Monday — but never said what it was." The old man went back to sliding

231

the brass bolt in and out as if they weren't there. His wooden leg scraped against the floor. It was carved with several small mice that appeared to run back and forth, their long tails entwined in sprigs of holly.

"You don't mind if we take a seat?" Mariah asked him.

"Take what you want. I've counted the cutlery, so no pinching the spoons . . . It's always the spoons . . ."

"Cuba about?" Mariah asked.

"That's it, that's it . . . He's taken that beast for a walk. Bit my leg clean off, it did. Had to carve a new one. Fancy keeping such a thing as a pet—and it's me who gets to look after it when he goes jaunting about the world fighting for Queen and country." He spoke as if he were almost in his right mind, his eyes fixed on Mariah. "Go on then, up you go. Better get seated before the rush."

The old man ushered them to the staircase that ran from the windowed salon overlooking the harbour to the ornate dining room above. Sacha rushed ahead and darted to the window seat, pulling the curtain closed so that she was hidden from the room below.

It was low tide, and the street on the quayside was packed with people in their finest coats, taking the air. Fishermen scraped upturned boats and mended torn nets. Grimm and Grendel could be seen looking into the emptying harbour, waiting for the water to recede before taking it upon themselves to brave the mud and search the sewer.

Mariah pulled up a chair next to Sacha and sat in the window as they waited for Captain Charity to return. The smell of cooking fish and the slosh of fresh batter being mixed came from the kitchen. Looking along the narrow promenade that led to the Prince Regent, Mariah could make out the form of Captain Charity walking in the roadway, leash in hand. Cuba strutted proudly at his side, snapping at passersby. Charity paid no attention to this, his eyes fixed upon the sea and the shimmering mist that filtered from the wet sand. By the harbour wall a small brig was beached and a caravan of small donkeys pulled carts of coal up to the road.

Soon, the door to the Golden Kipper slammed and heavy boots and scampering claws were heard upon the stairs. Mariah and Sacha heard the old man shout that Monday waited for him and he had never been visited by a madman who thought he was a day of the week. Charity laughed as he held on to Cuba, who tried to race ahead, sniffing the steps as if she could smell the sewage upon their feet.

"Aha," Charity said when he saw them, a broad smile upon his wind-reddened face. "Both of you villains stinking up my restaurant, eh?" He gave another laugh as he loosened Cuba's leash and let her run free.

The crocodile leaped toward them, fussing their shoes and biting at their leather soles.

"Thinks you're supper." Charity grinned. "And so you could be, about the size of a good meal, the pair of you put together." Charity stopped and looked at Sacha. "My dear girl, haven't seen you in ages. My how you have grown. Father still up to his usual tricks?"

Sacha nodded and gave a shy grunt.

"He'll learn; they all get caught one day—can't go on forever. So what's new in the land of misadventure?"

"I have this coin for you and we're being followed and—," Mariah blurted.

"One thing at a time," he said, looking at the gold coin that Mariah held toward him.

"The kraken gave me this for you—he stole fish and said you should take the money to cover the cost."

"Kraken? Fish? Where did you hear such a tale?" Charity asked as he took off his large overcoat and threw it onto a horned stand.

"He lives in —," Mariah began.

"He lives in the sewer and has done so for a while. His room is decked like a fine lodging house, and he has the caladrius," the captain said as if it were common knowledge.

"You knew?" Sacha asked.

"I have visited the room on several occasions—left him some bread. I thought it was the kraken that was taking the fish. The heat of the water has driven all the cod away; the beast would starve in an empty sea."

Mariah handed Charity the golden coin and quickly told him all that had happened since he last visited the Golden Kipper. The captain strutted up and down as Cuba curled herself tightly in the corner of the room and went to sleep, leaving one large eye open.

"You have done something of great worth," Charity said as he pulled back the curtain and peered down to the harbour. "What I would have given to see that bird in flight. I have heard so much of its power and dreamed to stand in its presence — and *you* two get there before me." Charity shrugged, watching Grimm and Grendel as they cautiously climbed down the ladder to the sewer mouth. "Your two friends are about to come searching for you," he said.

Mariah watched as Grimm disappeared over the harbour wall, his silk hat slowly bobbing out of view. "What if they find the kraken?" Mariah asked Charity.

"I have a good mind to take Cuba for a walk . . . into the sewer. He hasn't had sport for such a long time." Charity laughed, musing on the sight of Grimm and Grendel scurrying like frightened rats from the chomping jaws of the crocodile. "But first tell me about Otto Luger and all you have learned."

"I found this," Mariah said as he pulled the wax hand from his jacket. "It was on a manikin; it was made to look like me in every way. There was one of Felix, too. Luger has them hanging from the ceiling."

Charity took the hand and held it to the light. "Wax," he said, sniffing the fingers. "Looks like there is something inside."

With that, he put the wax hand on the table and went to the kitchen. Moments later he returned, a metal bowl of bubbling water in his hands and a soup ladle wedged in his pocket. He placed the bowl on the floor and then dropped the hand into the water. They all stared into the water as if looking into a cauldron.

"What's it doing?" asked Sacha, tapping her fingers nervously on the table.

"Melting," replied Charity as the wax liquefied before them. "Look," he said as the fingers began to break from the hand and float to the surface.

Within the hand they could see small, pea-sized droplets. As the wax melted they all began falling to the bottom of the pan.

"I knew he was up to something," Charity said with a smile. "Pearls . . ."

CHAPTER
✻ 26 ✻

Smutch

The light had faded. The lamplighter made his way along the empty seafront, tipping the flame to each lantern. He pulled his coat tightly against the wind and rattled the gas tap of the lights as they slowly burst into life. Mariah watched from the window of the Golden Kipper, standing by the large brass telescope that Charity had brought up from the main dining room. As the man walked by, he looked up at Mariah and smiled, touching the tip of his grubby oilskin hat and then walking on.

Sacha sat with Captain Charity, engrossed in conversation. She had chattered through the afternoon hours until dusk began to fall and Charity lit the table candles. He had pulled a red velvet rope across the stairs, keeping away the customers that had trickled in from the cold wind.

Sacha had told him everything she knew,

feeling no reason to doubt him, trusting what she saw in his eyes. He listened intently to all she had to say. Sacha enjoyed talking, but she enjoyed his listening even more. Mariah had chipped in here and there, filling in missing details, but Sacha dismissed him with a wave of her hand, as if this were her story.

Mariah had finished his fourth mug of chocolate and left them to talk, going to gaze out the window toward the darkening mass of the Prince Regent.

"How far will this look out to sea?" he asked, looking into the eyepiece of the telescope and seeing the distant summit of grey, mountainous waves.

"To the very limits," Charity replied, turning momentarily. "You can see a ship on the horizon as if it were in the harbour."

Mariah scanned the murky water for the starboard light of a ship. The ocean looked cold and empty, the white crests of the swells glowing in the moonlight. He thought of the kraken scavenging from the wrecks on distant Brigg Rocks. He searched the distant cliffs for lamplighters hanging lanterns to lure ships upon Cornelian Rocks. He followed the line of the coast, peeking into the windows of the large houses of the esplanade that overlooked the bay until he finally spied the Prince Regent. It was as if he could reach out and touch each pane of glass. A shiver of excitement ran through him as he looked into a lit room and spied a man adjusting a ginger rug of curls upon his head to cover a bald pate.

Mariah giggled to himself as he went from window to window, peeping inside and looking at the guests. He tried to make out what the guests were saying as he viewed them from afar.

Everything was exposed to the view of the telescope. From his vantage point he could see the hotel chef barking orders as the service began for early supper. His tall white hat flashed by the open window of the fourth-floor restaurant as he ran through the parlour palms and into the kitchen. A floor below, Mariah could see the windows of the water spa, and swinging the telescope higher, he tried to pick out the casement of his tower room. He searched the slate roof of the first tower, looking for the porthole that overlooked the town.

It was as he alighted on the high tower that he saw the face of Albion. He was pale and drawn, pinched at the cheeks, with a dark bruise around one eye. The man stared down upon the harbour from a high window lit by a single candle, which flickered against his face. He appeared to be speaking to someone in the room with him, someone listening from the shadows. He lifted his manacled hands and touched his forehead, lowered them and touched his heart and then each shoulder. He mouthed one final word, as if saying the name of someone he loved.

"Captain, Captain!" Mariah shouted. "I see Albion; he's in the east tower, and his hands are chained."

Captain Charity pushed him from the telescope and stared into it. "You're right, my lad; I can see the man and another behind him. Looks like . . . looks like . . . *Bizmillah*, the old scoundrel. Then we have a chase. We will not only rescue Felix but will have Albion as well."

"We'll go alone," Sacha said as she stood from the table, her biting tone stirring Cuba from her dreams.

"You'll not go at all if you speak to me like that, will they, Cuba?" Charity said, his voice sabre-sharp as the crocodile got to her feet and snapped at the air.

"But this is our business," she replied stubbornly. "We got into this, and we'll get out of it."

"You've always been too proud for your own good," Charity said. "This hasn't been your business since my foot stepped from the train the night Mariah arrived. Do you think I have wasted all my time frying fish and listening to old wives' tales since I've been back? I was called home, got a letter from the Prince Regent a year ago begging me to return. It was signed by Otto Luger." Charity pulled a crumpled note from the pocket of his trousers and laid it on the table in front of them. "On my very first morning, I went to the hotel and saw Luger. The man denied ever writing it to me or even knowing who I was. I showed him the note and he nearly choked on his cigar. He had me thrown from the building and told me never to return." Charity banged the table with his fist. "You, my friends, have started the job for me, and now we will complete it together. Luger is dead, and an impostor is in his place. As an officer of the Crown, I will have the murderer, you shall have your friend and Mariah . . . Mariah will have that which is rightfully his."

"What do you mean?" Mariah asked, but Charity ignored him.

"Smutch," Charity shouted. "Smutch, come hither—I have a plan of merit in which you will play your part."

The hobbling sound of the old man came from below. He slowly climbed the stairs, singing to himself.

"Captain?" he asked when he reached the landing.

"Going hunting, Smutch. You and young Sacha have the task of keeping watch."

"Keeping watch?" Sacha protested. "You're taking Mariah and leaving me behind? Why do I have to keep watch with some old codger?"

"Only for this part of the game, my dear," Charity said quietly, leaning toward her to take her into his confidence. "Come tonight, we all shall have our tasks as we storm the Prince Regent."

"Storm? Prince Regent?" muttered Smutch. "Sea looks fair to me, just a few whitecaps." He sat at the table and looked at Charity.

"I want you to keep watch on the sewer entrance. Mariah

and I will take Cuba and see what we can find. Should be less than an hour. Stay here until we return, and then we shall take on Luger . . . whoever he may be."

Sacha attempted a faint smile as Smutch snuggled into the window seat and stared out at the quayside.

"Keeping watch," he said to Sacha as Charity and Mariah slipped from the room, taking the crocodile on its long leash.

Sacha heard the door slam. Mariah looked up to the window and smiled at her. Smutch waved a white handkerchief, bobbing his head back and forth in time to the marching music that danced in his head.

"Frightened?" Charity asked Mariah as they walked down the slipway.

"Should I be?" Mariah replied as Cuba dived into the slowly filling harbour. "I've nothing to lose, Captain. Anyway, we've got Cuba; surely nothing will harm her?" Mariah said, gleaning a sense of danger from Charity's voice.

"And I have this," Charity replied. He brushed his cape to one side and pulled a three-bladed knife from his belt.

A sudden chill blew through Mariah's coat, slithering up his back and making the hairs on his neck stand on end. This was the third knife he had seen with a triple blade.

"Why does it have three blades?" he asked. "I have seen the likes of that before. The kraken has one just the same, and—"

"So he should, so he should," Charity said as he walked along the causeway, which was slowly being overwhelmed by the rising tide. "A triple blade for a triple death. Kills not only the body but the mind and soul, a blade for each, and will keep even the most fearful ghoul in its tomb for eternity."

"That's how they killed the *real* Luger. The body in the foundations had the mark of that knife on it."

"Not *this* knife," the captain said, half-smiling, the moon shadowing his face. "Surely not *this* knife? That would implicate me in a murder."

"The kraken said —"

"Krakens tell tales. They are the storytellers of the sea. Krakens sink ships, eat whales and turn into giant squid when the sea covers their heads. It's only when they appear on land that they look like *he* does now. If you saw him in the midst of the ocean, you'd never listen to any of his tales again." Charity paused and looked him in the eye. "And if he saw you, he would pick the flesh from your bones and think nothing of it."

"So he's not a man after all?" Mariah asked as they reached the entrance to the sewer.

"Not in the slightest. The kraken is a changeling."

Mariah said nothing. He thought of what the kraken had said of Monica. Suddenly, everything was starting to make sense.

He stopped for a moment and remembered the Colonial School. Gone was the eating of hot toast by the fire. Gone was the servant who had polished his shoes and cleaned his room. Now Mariah was alone in a world that had changed beyond all recognition. It was as if this town were in another dimension, that somehow the laws of nature had been suspended. The track on which the train had travelled had crossed the boundaries of the mundane and brought him to a land filled with magic and murder.

The crocodile slithered from the harbour into the sewer. Charity climbed along a short, rusted iron gantry that led under the long pier into the darkness. Mariah followed him, his trust of the captain fading with each step. He felt like a child of Abraham being led up the mountain.

They listened as they waited in the tunnel entrance. Far away they could hear the fumbling of footsteps and voices moaning in the darkness.

"Lost," the captain whispered. "I had been waiting to see if they would come out of the tunnel. If you don't know the sewer, you could stay in here forever."

"We found our way to the harbour easily," Mariah said.

"But you had Sacha to show the way; she grew up in here, scurrying like a rat and hiding contraband." Charity brought out a silver tube from his coat. It was tipped with a glass lens in the shape of an eye. He opened a small rivet on the top and unscrewed the cap. With a pair of tweezers, he dropped in three pieces of what looked to be lumps of white bread from a silver tin. He then stooped to the water, submerged the tube and quickly screwed on the cap. There was a loud hissing sound as the chemical and the water mixed together. Slowly the lens began to glow with a bright phosphorescent light, so powerful that Mariah turned away his eyes. There was an explosion of brilliant white, which lit the entrance to the sewer from wall to wall.

"Lasts a half hour," Charity explained as he took a leather hood from his pocket and cupped it over the lens. "Can't be having them see we're about; in battle you always have to have the edge. Now we'll find Grimm and Grendel and have some sport."

Mariah hesitated, a bone-numbing dread creeping through his body and stopping him from following. Soon, Charity had disappeared ahead and all the lad could see was a faint outline lit by the escaping glow of the torch. He listened to the gulping water of the returning tide and the drip, drip, drip from the crumbling bricks of the sewer ceiling.

Cuba swam beside him, her eyes visible, as if charged with an internal fire. They glowed like two red jewels floating upon the black velvet that filled the tunnel from wall to wall. The creature moved effortlessly in the thick soupy water, a mist of stench dancing in wisps upon its surface. Mariah walked slowly, the crocodile keeping pace as if it were luring him to a quiet place and the end of his life. Mariah bit his lip nervously as he left the night behind and entered fully into the dripping, festering world of the tunnel. Cuba swam on, churning the turbid water.

Ahead, Charity had hidden in a small alcove cut into the sewer wall. He shone his torch back toward the entrance. A pinpoint of light burst through a minute hole cut in the leather hood, shining like a white lance, illuminating Mariah's coat pocket. He walked on as if being dragged closer by the beam. He quickened his pace. Charity shone the torch on the water, looking for Cuba; all he could see was a trace of bubbles that slowly burst through the surface.

They could hear Grimm barking at Grendel. The echoes rushing back and forth distorted their words. Charity stood deathly still as he holstered the torch in the bottom of his coat pocket and with the other hand pulled Mariah toward him. There was a glint from the three-bladed dagger as if it were sparkling from within, and a churning of the water by their feet spoke to the nearness of the crocodile.

A dim light came from the lair in the tunnel ahead of them. Grimm's voice was brash and clear. It was easy to hear that they were neither lost nor uneasy. Grimm scolded Grendel for being so stupid as to have not had the foresight to bring a lamp; now all they would have to show them the way through the tide was the candlestick from the table.

Grendel muttered in disdain, and they heard him dragging something across the floor.

"Do you think he'll speak?" Grendel said.

"He'd better tell us where he took them, or he'll never put to sea again," Grimm replied.

"We could sell him to the *London Chronicle*," Grendel said. "I once saw a picture of a man covered in hair who had been brought up by wolves. Surely a living kraken is worth more than that?"

"If we find the lad, Luger will pay us more than for any

photograph. Anyhow, I have been thinking that it would be more profitable for us to take over Mister Luger's enterprises and have him done away with."

"Again? But I thought you'd already—" He stopped as the kraken moaned loudly, the bonds cutting into his wrists. "Lucky we fell on him when he slept—he'd been out killing swans. I've a good mind to have that one plucked and roasted before the night is out."

"It's not a swan, Mister Grendel, not with the feet of an eagle," Grimm said, kicking the body of the caladrius out of the way.

"Shame to leave this dead thing just to rot," said Grendel. "Once we've finished with Mister Kraken, we could take it with us."

"For one so thin, Mister Grendel, your mind is constantly filled with thoughts of food," Grimm barked as Charity and Mariah listened from the passageway.

"And look at you, Mister Grimm, never eating more than a mouse and growing wider by the day. What justice is that?" Grendel snorted in false concern. "Well, he's trussed and ready to be transported back to Luger's dungeons. The tide should be topping out, and we need to be away. Don't want to spend the night staring into this creature's eyes."

Grendel tied the last knot around the kraken's wrist and lifted him to his feet. He dragged him to the doorway and into the dark tunnel. Grimm followed, candle in hand to light the way.

"Slowly, Mister Grendel, slowly... My gait is not the length of yours, and we may need to stay together."

Grendel didn't reply. He clutched the kraken with one hand and stood motionless, staring down the long chamber at the lapping water. In the distance he could see the red glow of two large eyes coming toward him.

In the dark the crocodile took on an even larger, wilder appearance. Grendel sunk back, pulling the kraken with him.

"FIEND . . . OGRE . . . BEAST!" Grendel screeched as the crocodile pulled itself from the water and began to walk toward him.

"Beast? Mister Grendel, we have the beast, and we will take it to the Prince Regent for *interrogation*—"

"Beast, Mister Grimm, a sewer beast, there before us, a red-eyed sewer beast."

"Nonsense," Grimm said, lifting the candlestick into the air to light the way.

Cuba scurried by Charity and Mariah as they pressed themselves against the wall, covered by the shadows. The crocodile flicked its tail back and forth, almost dancing with excitement, breaking into a trot as it lumbered its black shimmering mass toward them.

"Use your cane, Mister Grendel, USE YOUR CANE!" Grimm shouted at the top of his lungs, turning and running back up the steep incline of the tunnel.

CHAPTER

❋ 27 ❋

Calando

The last they saw of Grimm and Grendel was their shadows dodging in and out of the torchlight. Cuba had been called to heel as Charity laughed at the sight of the two detectives scurrying into the darkness, believing themselves to be chased by the crocodile.

Charity pulled several pieces of sausage from his pocket and fed the creature one piece at a time. Cuba sat upon her hind legs with her tail wrapped around herself and snapped up each piece.

"Job well-done," Charity said. He untied the bindings that cut into the kraken's wrists.

The kraken attempted to smile, seeming worried about what Charity would do next. Mariah saw the look on his face and gently took him by the arm.

"I fell asleep," the kraken said. "It had been so

long since I last rested; every night I have searched the streets for Scratty."

"You will not search much longer, for tonight she shall be found and all will be well," Charity said.

"This is Captain Jack Charity," Mariah said. "It was his fish that you stole, but don't fret . . . I gave him the money."

"I know," the kraken said earnestly. "I saw you bring the bread. I was hiding from you. No one was supposed to come into this place. It is—"

"Haunted?" Charity asked. "Never been one to be afraid of ghosts. It's only the living that can do you harm."

"Believe me, Captain Charity, I have met others who can work in realms that you would not believe existed."

"And turn a kraken into a China doll?" he asked.

"Even that," the kraken replied. "If you had not come, I don't know what they would have done to me."

Charity laughed wryly. "Where they go, they shall not find comfort. What will you do this night?"

"I think we are united in the same task and our fate lies entangled in the Prince Regent," the kraken replied.

"Whatever we do, we should not pass through the entrance to the harbour. And we have but a quarter of an hour within this lamp, so we must depart. Can you show us the way?" he asked.

The kraken led them to the mouth of the tunnel. Charity clicked his fingers and Cuba obediently leaped back into the dark water and vanished.

"Do you walk the way of men or krakens?" Charity asked as they stood beside the deep pool.

"I go the only way I know," the kraken replied, stepping into the water.

"Then bid us safe passage?" Charity asked.

"I may be a monster, but I would never eat my friends," the creature replied as it sank farther into the depths.

As it did so, it began to transform.

The long tentacles of a sea beast slowly replaced the shape of the man, as if he were being absorbed by a squidlike creature, turning him inside out into something hideous. The water bubbled and boiled as the kraken grew. Long, spiked tentacles thrashed about in the black foam as the kraken opened its horrendous beak and sucked a draught of stagnant air from the sewer.

Suddenly, it lashed out toward them. Charity jumped away, but Mariah was grabbed around his neck by a thousand minute cups that gripped him tightly and sucked at his skin. More tentacles took hold of his arms and legs, lifting him to the ceiling. The creature dragged itself from the water, filling the sewer entrance. It rose, standing on what seemed to be a hundred thick, bloodred tentacles strong enough to pull any ship to the depths. It stared at Mariah through two gigantic eyes and opened its blue beak, hissing. Then as if obeying some faraway command, it put Mariah down with the gentleness of a father's hand, sank into the water and disappeared.

"I thought you would meet your end," Charity said, checking Mariah over to make sure he was unhurt. "Knew it wouldn't keep its word. Never trust a changeling; what they say to you in the flesh is not the word they will keep when they change forms."

Mariah pulled a small spike from his neck and held it in the torchlight. "But I don't think it wanted to hurt me. The kraken only kills in the minds of those frightened of the tales you tell."

"I have seen many things, and nothing will ever surprise me again." Charity turned and walked toward the tunnels that led to the street above.

"In the restaurant you said I would have what is rightfully mine. What did you mean?" Mariah called out after him.

Charity hesitated. "My words ran away with me. I didn't

mean to say anything, and I can't remember what I meant," he mumbled, scanning the sewer with the fading light. "Best be making haste — the torch fades, and soon all we will be left with are the memories of this place."

"But I remember clearly, Captain Charity: 'As an officer of the Crown, I will have the murderer, you shall have your friend and Mariah will have that which is rightfully his' — that's what you said. Word for word. What belongs to me that I don't know about?"

"If you could have anything in the world, what would it be? A new life . . . a certain future . . . an inheritance? What would you choose?" Charity spoke quickly, giving him no time to answer. "See, . . . you don't know. So why should I tell you now? It's all about patience, Mariah . . . Mulciber . . . Mundi."

"How did you know that? I have never told my full name to anyone. How did you know?"

"A guess, a stab in the dark?" Charity replied, weaving through the passageway. "Mulciber? Doesn't that mean someone who can bend metal?"

"It was my grandfather's name," Mariah snapped, feeling like Charity amused himself at his expense. "You seem to know me well, Captain. So what of my future?"

"It'll come to pass, . . . but for now, we must keep to the task at hand." They walked in silence and soon reached the ladder that led up to the street.

Mariah wondered what would become of them all. He felt as if he were about to climb a high mountain. His mouth dried with fear; his eyes stung with the stench of the sewer. His heart beat loudly in his ears. He realised now that Charity was a bigger part of his life than just a coincidental meeting on a train. It was as if Mariah were an actor given only his lines, waiting for some unknown voice to speak the other part. He knew the journey to his future would start with the first foot he placed on the ladder. It would be a step that would take him not only to the street above but also to the unknown.

"Climb quickly," Charity said. "Now that Grimm and Grendel are out of the way for a while, we are free to attack the Prince Regent. You up to it, lad?" He pushed slowly on the metal grate that covered the sewer entrance.

"If the kraken isn't killing people, who is?" Mariah asked as Charity peered through the narrow gap between the cobbles and the grate.

"That remains to be found out," Charity whispered. "The streets will never be safe until they are stopped."

"The kraken said that he's seen the same man appear every time someone is killed."

"Krakens say many things." He stopped for a moment and looked at Mariah, who clung to the metal with white fingers. "Look beyond what you can see; understand that there is a veil cast upon your eyes."

Charity opened the grate and let in the cool of the night. It brought with it the smell of the sea and the sweet fragrance of fried fish.

"Good to be home," Charity said, licking his lips and pulling himself up into the alleyway behind the restaurant.

The streets were empty; the mist from the beach hugged the sand and the cobbled road that led along the quayside. Mariah stayed a pace behind the captain; he was uncertain how Charity knew so much about his life. He had seen the captain look sideways at him on several occasions during the afternoon's conversation, weighing him up. It seemed like Charity had heard about him from someone and was trying to see if it was all true. Mariah couldn't get that thought out of his head as they entered the Golden Kipper—someone had told Charity all about him. The only other person who knew Mariah's full name was Professor Bilton, but why would he have told Charity?

"Smutch!" Charity shouted with surprise when they reached the landing at the top of the stairs.

Smutch was still in the window seat overlooking the harbour, but he was gagged, and his hands were tied with several knotted napkins.

"Who did this? Where's Sacha?" Charity insisted.

Mariah covered his face. Smutch's wooden leg was hanging from an elk antler on the wall. Mariah instantly knew this was Sacha's doing.

"Only playing a game," Smutch muttered. "She'll be back soon. Tied me up, took off me leg and gagged me gob. Said she would go away and then come back, and I had to guess . . . who . . . she . . . was . . ." In a momentary flash of lucidity, he realised he had been fooled. "Knew I shouldn't, Captain, but she had such a smile and the voice of an angel and—"

"Enough, Smutch. How long has she been gone?" Charity asked, helping the old man strap on his wooden leg.

"Just after she saw you disappear under the quay, she invented the game. Did you see where I've put me powder?" the old man asked, his brain slipping from the mundane back into his own world.

"Prince Regent?" Mariah asked, scanning the beach through the telescope.

"She'd be a fool to go alone, and yet that lad, Felix, has a power over the girl."

Mariah continued to peer through the lens and search the promenade and the beach. It was only a few minutes' walk from the Golden Kipper to the Prince Regent, but he hoped that Sacha had dawdled along the way.

Funnels of steam broke through the beach, held down to a foot above the sand by the cold night air, billowing out as if from a fissure of a gigantic volcano about to erupt. At the water's edge, the water bubbled and spat as the gases from below percolated and simmered to the surface.

Mariah caught sight of the kraken striding through the mist, his long hair trailing over his shoulders. He stepped boldly toward the Prince Regent.

"What do you see, lad?" Charity asked, putting an arm around his shoulder.

"The kraken . . . going to the Regent."

"Sacha'll be there already . . . up to some trick or other. This has taken so long to put together, and for it to be spoiled when we were so close—" He stopped, knowing he had said too much.

Mariah looked at him. "I suddenly feel that I am just a pawn in your game," he said accusingly.

Charity sighed, thought for a moment and then pointed to a small picture above Mariah's head. "It's surprising how we never see the obvious, lad. Do you recognise the place?"

Mariah scanned the faded painting. The yellows and greens had blurred together, but it was obvious that this was a house set at the end of a long drive lined with trees. In the distance he could see the banks of a river, and beyond that the far hills of the south. In the foreground was a young boy with fine blond hair. The child smiled out from ages past, but in an instant, Mariah had recognised the eyes.

"It's you!" he said. "And the Colonial School?" he asked slowly.

Charity said nothing. He left the room and went to the kitchen, appearing a short time later clutching a folded piece of parchment. He cleared the table by the window and, with great ceremony, unfolded the parchment and laid it out before Mariah.

"Recognise this?" he asked as he smoothed the paper with the back of his hand.

"A writ of worthiness," Mariah said as he read the charge at the top of the page.

I, Professor Jecomiah Bilton, in this, the first year of my incumbency as head of the Colonial School, do hereby discharge from duty John Mariah Charity into the company of Her Majesty's army for Colonial Service—Student First Class—23rd December 1866.

It was twenty years ago today. You're a Colonial boy. You have my name. You . . . you . . ." He paused, blinking back tears. "You knew my father."

"How did you not know who I was? I was your father's best friend. We shared everything, closer than brothers. When you were born, he gave you *my* name. I was in India at the time and never saw the young lad that he wrote so much about." Charity pulled a packet of letters from his pocket and placed it on the table. "You can see for yourself—they're all in your father's hand."

Mariah untied the letters and carefully opened the first one. It was written in purple ink on white velum. He eagerly scanned each line and followed each curl and scrawl. In the bottom corner of the note was a drawing of a small boy with wiry hair, wrapped in a blanket. A line underneath read, *Mariah . . . the only time he's quiet is when he sleeps.*

"See," Charity said, smiling. "All I have said is true."

"Why didn't you tell me sooner?"

"Bilton wrote to me and told me of your discharge. I had been in the Sudan searching for your father and mother. The professor was concerned that so many boys had left the Prince Regent, and having also had the letter from Otto Luger, I took the fastest ship I could find. The train was a coincidence—I never expected a Colonial boy to travel first-class. I'd planned to wait and keep watch, only making myself known when the moment was right." Charity looked at Smutch, who had fallen asleep in the window seat. "There is more to tell, but tonight we must end what has begun. I know you have it in you. Just like your father. I can see a lot of him in your eyes."

"What was he like?" Mariah asked. "He left so long ago, sometimes it's hard to remember."

"A fine man, Mariah, a fine man, kept from you by circumstances."

"Are my parents really dead?" Mariah asked nervously.

"That I do not know, but I will continue searching for them. I cannot rest until I have found proof."

"And what of tonight?" Mariah asked, stacking the letters on top of each other and tying them again into a tight bundle.

"We will find Sacha, Felix and Albion, and who knows what will become of us?"

CHAPTER

❧ 28 ❧

The Sea Witch

eside the steaming beach, in the darkness
of the entrance to the Prince Regent, Sacha
felt she was being watched. She had slipped
quietly from the moonlit sand into the cover of
the brick portico. To her right was a large storeroom filled with bathing carriages. The wooden
lattice door that led into the labyrinth of tunnels
was unlocked, the chain hanging limply, so she
slid back the bolt and sneaked inside. She turned
to see if she was being followed, but saw no one
in the murky shadows.

The sound of the steam generator came as a
reassurance to her, its hiss echoing through the
passageways like a whisper inviting her farther
inside.

She was gladdened to see the oil lamp by the
door of Luger's workshop was still lit. She retraced her steps in her mind; she knew she would

have to find Felix alone. She couldn't sit around waiting for Captain Charity to make a plan. She had to go now; *she* had to be the one who set Felix free, she thought as she walked, trying to justify to herself why she'd had to tie up Smutch.

She reached the door at the end of the passageway. It was wedged slightly open by a small dune of sand, which had been washed there by the last high tide. She pulled against the thick iron handle, the door opening with a low moan. She shuddered, the urge to look back overwhelming her. For a moment she thought she could hear footsteps. She quickly pulled the door shut and slid the bolt on the inside, breathing heavily, fighting the urge to run. She began to regret leaving Mariah behind and coming alone as she thought about what could be following her.

She turned a corner and began spiralling deeper beneath the Prince Regent. To her left was the long dark tunnel that led to the oyster lagoon; ahead was the passage that would guide her to the giant pagurus. She stopped and looked about, sure that the sound of footsteps echoed somewhere beyond. It was a tap, tap, tap of metal clattering against the stone floor. Occasionally, it came through the tunnel as a muffled thud, then returned to the crisp click of metal on stone. She looked down each tunnel, unsure where the echoing was coming from.

Far away a door slammed shut, sending a sudden, chilled draught toward her. She set off into the narrow tunnel toward the oyster lagoon, hoping she was running away from whomever she was hearing.

The sharp sound of clicking heels grew nearer. Just ahead was another wooden door, strapped with iron braces. Sacha pulled on the metal ring and the door edged slowly open, grinding against the stone floor. She could feel panic slowly rising from the pit of her stomach. With much haste she rushed through the opening and pulled the door closed, bolting it and turning the key that was in the rusty mortise.

Sacha looked down the tunnel. To one side was a cutting in the rock, as if a burrow had been commenced, then abandoned. It was dark and deep enough for her to hide in without being seen. Quietly, she tucked herself inside, holding her breath to stop the panic from breaking out. From beyond the door she could hear the clatter of footsteps coming along the corridor. For a moment they stopped, and the door was suddenly rattled against the lock. Sacha saw the iron ring of the door handle move.

Then all was silent. The rumbling of the generator seemed far away. Sacha knew that someone stood on the other side of the door. She listened intently; all she could hear was the thump of her own heart. The door handle rattled again. Instinctively, Sacha slipped a little farther into the darkness, peering out just far enough to see the door, pressing her cheek against the warm stone.

Suddenly, a black-gloved hand slid through the door as if the door weren't there. Its fingernails pierced the gloves like red talons.

Sacha cowered down, making herself as small as she could in the darkness, covering her face with her hands. Her stomach twisted. She looked again, hoping the hand had retreated back to the other side of the door. To her terror, a shoulder pushed through the solid wood, then a foot, a white ankle and finally half of a body.

It was clad in a long black dress that clung like a second skin to its wearer. Sacha had seen it before. It was Monica.

Sacha froze. From her hiding place she could see the woman convulse, attempting to penetrate the wood. It was as if the door fought against her. Where parts of Monica's body had squeezed through, the wooden slats dripped with a glistening blue liquid. By her right foot a pool of the viscous liquid had formed a puddle as it oozed from her flesh.

Sacha watched as the first layer of Monica's forehead was

forced through the door. Slowly, a long white nose appeared, and then bright red painted lips, followed by a perfect set of teeth. They sparkled in the soft light of the tunnel as a chin suddenly appeared, leaving yet more liquid to trickle to the floor. Sacha quickly got to her feet and, hugging the wall, began to make her way along the passageway, hoping that she could sneak away before Monica realised she was there.

But in a matter of moments, Monica's whole head had been forced through. She peered into the tunnel and saw Sacha trying to creep away.

"Don't think this door will keep me for long," Monica said. "Running away won't do you any good."

Sacha froze like a caught rabbit, trembling in fear. She huddled against the wall, hoping the stones would swallow her up. After a moment she tried to run, but suddenly realised that her feet were as heavy as lead.

"You're charmed, girl . . . You won't get far—feeling weaker?" Monica said, struggling to free herself from the door.

Sacha turned and looked at her. "I'll still get away; I've got to—"

"Get the boy? Felix?" Monica said with what looked like a disembodied head. "Is that what you want?"

"You can't keep him," Sacha shouted, pushing against the walls in an attempt to free herself from whatever power held her fast.

"And you can't move," Monica replied. "Caught like a fly in a web. Now, . . . what shall we turn you into?"

"Nothing!" Sacha shouted, her words echoing down the long tunnel. "I'll be turned into nothing! You won't make me a China doll like Scratty."

"So you know, . . . very clever . . . Who ya been speaking to?" Monica asked, her neck appearing to be stuck in the door. "You'd make a better waxwork than a China doll, or perhaps . . .

perhaps a *stuffed* child would look nice in my room. Covered in papier-mâché and painted bright pink. You could be a hatstand or a lampshade." Monica giggled.

"And you'll be dead if the kraken finds you," Sacha said, her feet rooted to the ground as if they had become part of the rock.

"The kraken? So, . . . you've found a new friend? How charming. Is he still pining for his companion? Still weeping for his lover? How romantic. I know many a man who would pay a golden guinea to have their lovers turned into ageless China dolls that sat in the corner and never complained or spent their money."

"He said you were a sea witch," Sacha retorted. A growing stench of brine filled the tunnel, billowing from Monica.

"And that I am, gloriously powerful and here for a purpose . . . to capture you." Monica stood one-legged, her left foot still stuck on the other side. Sacha glanced at her own feet and saw what looked like frost slowly climbing up her legs.

"Salting." Monica laughed as she tugged on her leg to release it from the door. "It'll hold you until I can get you myself."

With a final pull she freed herself from the wood and shook like a wet dog. Drips of bright blue liquid showered the tunnel. She stepped toward Sacha. The salting had crawled up to Sacha's waist, holding her fast.

Monica peered at Sacha through eyes that were milky white and covered with a thin membrane. She reached out a long, gloved hand, her red fingernails sticking through the black silk.

Sacha panicked as the hand came toward her face, the claws reaching to touch her skin. "Leave me!" she screamed, pulling away.

"Or what will you do?" Monica said. "Nothing, . . . you'll do nothing. Just like all you creatures."

Sacha cowered as Monica stroked her cheek and slid her hand around her neck. Then she noticed Monica's face begin to dry and crinkle. The pool of brine grew about her feet, and the stench of the sea became even more intense. It was the smell of dead fish. Sacha tried not to breathe. The sea witch peered at her through ever-milkier eyes, the membranes thickening as the fluid seeped from her body.

"It's Sacha, isn't it?" she asked quietly. "Worked for Bizmillah—he'll be sad you're gone."

"What'll you do?" Sacha asked, reeling from the stench.

"Otto's been looking for you. Who did you come with — there were two of you," Monica whispered close to her ear. "Don't tell me you came back on your own. Grimm and Grendel chased you from here this morning. I wasn't foggy eyed then, and I caught a glimpse of your friend." Monica stopped and thought, letting go and flexing each finger as if it were an eagle's talon. "Imagine, Sacha, what these could do to your pretty face. Was it Mariah Mundi who was with you?"

Sacha didn't speak, but her downcast eyes spoke the truth.

"I knew there was something troublesome about that boy. Otto should never have taken him on. I told him he was one too many, but he never listens to me," Monica growled, curling the long nails in front of Sacha's face like a cat. "Still . . . come midnight, Otto will have enough trouble of his own."

"He's gonna turn you into a waxwork," Sacha blurted. She grabbed Monica's hand and pulled as hard as she could, trying to knock her off balance.

"Never," Monica replied, pulling away.

"Saw it myself, hidden in his laboratory. You're done for— he doesn't want you anymore," Sacha announced fearfully. Slowly, the salting encasing her legs began to crumble. As Monica pulled against her, the glove slipped off of her hand.

Clutching the sequined black silk, all Sacha could see were fleshless bones tipped by painted fingernails. She stared, open-mouthed, her voice stuck in her throat. Monica smiled dryly as the moisture seeped from her painted face.

"So now you know. First one to see that in a long time. Can't have you tell anyone about this, my little girl. I was gonna take you to see your friend, let you stay with Felix and all the others Otto has got stuck in that hellhole of an oyster farm. Now . . . now it's a different story." Monica reached into the small purse that hung on her shoulder and brought out a shining pair of silver handcuffs. "Had other plans for these, but I guess you'll have to be the lucky lady."

"I won't tell. I didn't see anything," Sacha said, closing her eyes, not wanting to see any more.

Monica snatched the glove from her, then snapped a cuff upon her wrist. "Too late, far too late. I wouldn't want Otto to know his leading lady was rotting from the inside out." Monica sniffed. "But if what you say is true, then maybe he won't be around for much longer either." She slipped the handcuffs on Sacha's other wrist and squeezed tightly. "There. I think I *will* leave you with your friend and see what Otto has to say for himself before I deal with you."

Far down the tunnel, a slamming door echoed through the dusty passage. Monica muttered some strange words that Sacha couldn't understand. The salting crumbled from her feet, and the sea witch grabbed her by the arms and dragged her toward the oyster lagoon. Monica seemed distracted. Her misted eyes seemed more parched with each step, and flakes of powdered skin fell to the floor as she led Sacha on.

"We'll soon be there," the sea witch said as she turned the corner of the tunnel that led down a flight of steps and onto a gantry across the oyster lagoon.

"What about the beast?" Sacha asked.

"My little friend is locked away, ready for later . . . *and* to make sure you don't escape. One word to Otto and you die on the spot."

Sacha looked down at the steaming brown water, lit by a crescent of lamps that hung from the ceiling of the chamber. Far across the lagoon was the cell where she had seen Felix. All was quiet, the water still, broken only by the gentle simmering of the million oysters beneath the surface.

Monica opened the door of the small cell and pushed Sacha inside. "He's in there somewhere, him and the others."

The door slammed behind her. Sacha grabbed the bars in the small opening and looked out. Monica walked toward the lagoon, her skirt trailing behind her. She walked into the lake and slowly submerged herself, vanishing below the surface.

"Does it every day, has to bathe in the seawater or she'll dry up and die," a voice said behind Sacha. "Never thought I'd see you again, thought they had you." Felix rose to his feet.

"She's gonna kill me, Felix. I saw what she is, and she's gonna kill me."

CHAPTER

✹ 29 ✹

Imprimatur

The elevator was completely dark. It shrugged reluctantly from the lowest basement of the Prince Regent to the very top without stopping. Mariah had left Charity on the beach. He had told Mariah to find the fortune cards and meet him in an hour at the bar next to the theatre. Now Mariah stood in the darkness with his own thoughts and fears. He wondered where Sacha had gone. He thought of her in the hotel somewhere, alone. He wondered how she could just leave him behind and go off to finish their quest by herself. Her changeable heart reminded him of his own. She could be both brave and fearful in one breath, torn between duty and desire, never wanting to take things too seriously.

At least Mariah's own life was beginning to make sense to him. Charity made it better. At last there was someone Mariah could trust, an adult to talk to and spend time with. Charity was almost as good as family, nearly a father, though one fraught with trouble.

These thoughts comforted Mariah as the elevator chugged on. He felt a glimmer of excitement and hope for the future. Knowing that the captain was there made tonight's task somewhat easier; he was no longer alone. He also felt reassured by the three-bladed knife he carried in his belt, which Charity had insisted that he borrow.

By the time the elevator stopped on the top floor and the doors slid open, Mariah was convinced he would succeed. All he had to do was go to his room, get the Panjandrum and return to the ground floor, where Charity would be waiting at the theatre's Trisagion Bar with Cuba at his feet. "Simple," he said to himself as he opened the door to his room.

Everything was as he had left it. The lamp was dimly wicked and cast a gentle and welcoming light. The bed was neatly made and looked undisturbed. The window that overlooked the bay was half-open, the curtains gently blustering in the night breeze. Yet as he stepped inside he was aware that something was wrong.

A subtle smell hung in the room, something familiar. On the mantle was the smoking butt of a cigar . . . a Luger cigar. As he closed the door behind him and walked toward the bed Mariah suddenly became aware that he was not alone. He froze as the silence gave way to a gentle cough behind him and a cloud of smoke was breathed over him.

"Wondered how long I could hold it in," said a voice. "Been looking for you, Mariah; thought you'd left for good." It was Black. He stood between Mariah and the door.

Mariah stepped toward the window. "Mister Black . . . what would you want with me?" he asked. "Guests shouldn't visit the staff."

"Not you, but that which you were given at Kings Cross. Some playing cards?"

"I don't know what you're talking about," he replied, taking another step back and putting his hand on the windowsill.

"Surely, they were given to you by Perfidious Albion, a man you met before you boarded the train."

Mariah's eyes darted to the bed, giving away his thoughts.

"Hidden here, are they?" Black asked as he went to the mantle and picked up the cigar.

"I have nothing for you here. It would be best if you were to go," Mariah said, sitting on the narrow ledge, placing one foot upon it as he tried to lean casually against the frame.

"According to my friend and magic partner, Mister Bizmillah, you are no longer employed by the hotel. *Apparently,* two youths were chased from the establishment by a certain Grimm and Grendel this morning and are to be charged with theft." Black grinned, and for the first time Mariah noticed that his front teeth were tipped with gold. "*Apparently,* they have stolen something of value from Otto Luger and made off into town with the two detectives in hot pursuit."

"Hadn't heard. I've been in the company of a family friend. Saturday is my day off, and if Bizmillah chooses to sack me for that, then well and good." Mariah turned and now sat fully on the windowsill, stealing a glance at the small ledge and at the sea far below.

"So the cards are here?" Black insisted. He held out his fob watch, and it appeared to glow and vibrate in his hand. "They were given to you for safekeeping, but now I need them back. So tell me . . . what have you done with them?" Black kicked the bed.

The Panjandrum fell from their hiding place, the cards spilling from the pack across the rug. The joker slithered across the floor toward Mariah.

"Panjandrum . . . ," Black murmured, wide-eyed and short of breath, diving upon them as if to stop them from running from the room. "At last I have them back."

Mariah saw his chance. He scooped the joker from the floor and placed it in his pocket, and as Black attempted to gather up the rest of the cards Mariah jumped from the window to the narrow ledge below.

"No!" came a shout from inside the room. "It's not as you think!"

Mariah didn't listen; all he sought was escape. He held fast to the small ledge that ran just above his head, his feet gripping the row of narrow bricks beneath them. The gulls swooped upon him, seeming to think he was invading their territory. Mariah didn't dare look down. He knew that he stood above the sea. If he fell from his precarious footing, he would crash upon the rocks.

Hand over hand, Mariah made his way along the ledge to the slope of the roof. One gull flew close enough to bite his right ear. Blood seeped from the wound and across his cheek. He held tightly to the ledge, the pain intense, the gull diving again and again, trying to pull him from his grip.

Black called to him from the window. "Come back, Mariah . . . It's not as you think . . . I'm here to help you." He smiled and held out his hand.

Mariah pressed on, turning his face away. In two paces he jumped from the ledge to the roof, steadying himself against the balustrade that ran at waist height along the roof's edge.

"Come back, Mariah," Black shouted. "I need to talk to you; it really is not what you think."

Mariah glanced back at him, then set off across the roof.

He knew that to escape, he would have to break into the Prince Regent. The birds chased him as he ran, swooping with claws outstretched, pecking at his hands as he tried to fend them off. Soon he was at the far tower, and six feet above him was the porthole of Albion's room.

Mariah could see faint candlelight and a shadow cast upon the ceiling. He crawled up the grey slates and peered in. There was Albion, standing alone, chained to the bed by one hand. He reached out toward the mantel, a silver key left on it as if to torment him.

Wedging himself against the roof, Mariah took off his jacket, wrapped it around his hand and smashed through the window. The glass shattered, falling into the room. Mariah knocked the remaining pieces from the frame, draped his jacket over the edge and then slipped through the window.

"Albion," he exclaimed as he quickly took the key from the mantle and unlocked the chain. "I have lost the cards. A man has taken them. He's a magician."

Albion looked at the door. "I was kidnapped and brought here. There is a box of fortune in this place that has to be destroyed, . . . but I'm afraid that is all I can tell you."

"The Midas Box?" Mariah asked, turning the doorknob. The door was locked.

"How did you know?"

"Luger has it—it would seem everyone knows what the man is up to." Mariah smiled, looking Albion in the eye. "I have to meet someone by the theatre. He'll help us get the cards. Now, let's get out of this place."

Together they climbed through the window, slid down the grey slates and ran across the roof. By the high chimney that puffed the grey steam from the generator was a small black door surrounded by iron railings, a short flight of steps leading down to it. Mariah led the way, his shirt stained with blood from his wound. Black clouds sped across the sky as to the east a storm gathered over the sea.

The door opened into a long passageway flanked with guest rooms. At the far end, a flight of stairs led to another lamplit corridor that would eventually lead to the elevator.

Mariah ran, followed by Albion, unaware of the elevator descending toward them.

The elevator door slid open and Black stepped out, holding a short cane. At the sound of the approaching footsteps, he twisted its handle and pulled out a sword, stepping into the shadow of a doorway. He waited, unsure who approached but intent on defending himself.

Mariah and Albion kept running, not knowing he was there, lying in wait. He listened as the pounding feet echoed closer.

With a sudden shout Black leaped upon them, holding out the sword and, in the half-light, lashing out above their heads.

"Away with you!" he shouted, not yet realising whom he was shouting at.

"Isambard?" screamed Albion, staring up at him.

"It can't be . . . surely not . . . Perfidious?" He sounded as if he had discovered someone long lost. "Peradventure . . ."

"There is nothing of chance in this, Isambard," Perfidious said, holding out a hand to the man. "I have been saved by this young rascal, of whom a simple introduction should suffice. Isambard Black, meet Mariah Mundi."

Mariah's eyes flickered from one man to the other. He looked for a place to run but knew he would be cornered upon the roof. Black stood within a sword's length of him and could cut him down easily with one blow, should he desire.

"I've met him before . . . He's the man who stole the Panjandrum from me." He stepped behind Albion, unsure whom to trust.

"And you never told him, Isambard?" Albion asked lightly.

"He never asked, but I was about to when he ran off—jumped from the window and across the roof like a frightened rat." Black laughed.

"And you have the cards?" Albion asked.

Black held out a gloved hand and showed him the Panjandrum. "All except one that Mariah has in his pocket. The joker. Quite fitting for such a lad."

"You're in on this, Albion?" Mariah asked as he took a step away.

"In on it?" Black laughed. "He *is* it!"

Albion smiled. "Mariah, meet Isambard Black — my brother. Like you, me and Captain Charity, he's a former pupil of the Colonial School. In short, you have been followed from the day you left. Sadly, so was I. That is why I gave you the cards, knowing you would be in good company and that my brother would keep you safe."

"But he doesn't have your surname," Mariah said.

"No, a small matter of different fathers but the same mother. We were born in the same year, and the old colonel took us both in as his own."

"And you knew Charity when we were on the train?" Mariah asked angrily.

"Who could ever forget old Charity. Four years older than us, and still as stern now that we work together as he was then."

"So I'm being played by everyone?" Mariah asked indignantly.

"It is our job to track down items of . . . interest. Things that are *unusual* and whose presence in the world would cause . . . *alarm* to those who . . ." Perfidious paused, flustered.

"Those who are not used to the supernatural, such as cards that can foretell the future, boxes that change objects to gold," Black finished in a matter-of-fact way.

"The Midas Box?" Mariah asked.

"Precisely, the Midas Box. We are here to take charge of these items and revert any damage that may have been done," Black went on.

"So you're the police?" Mariah enquired, his mind racing.

"Not exactly—we're the Bureau of Antiquities," he replied, straightening his collar with one hand and sheathing his sword.

"Spook hunters," Albion said with a smile. "We have to find the Midas Box and destroy it before Luger can turn everything into gold. But . . . we don't think he is who he would like us to believe he is."

"The real Luger is dead," Mariah said, adopting their matter-of-fact way of speaking about such weighty things. "Found him in the foundations with a knife wound in him."

"Then it is as you thought, Isambard," Perfidious said. "It *is* Gormenberg . . ."

The two men looked at each other and then at the boy. Black nodded to Albion, seeming to say much with the raising of his brow and the look in his eye.

"But he looks just like the paintings of Luger that are around the hotel," Mariah said.

"He is an artist of a different kind, a sculptor and maker of the finest waxworks in Europe," Black explained. "What you see is a reconstruction of Luger's face, and not even his closest friends could tell the difference. We had been tracking him for many years when suddenly all went quiet and no one knew where he had gone. Then we heard that a man had found the Midas Box. Gormenberg had changed identities, stolen someone's life and become him. Easy really, if you know how. Quite a business he's running."

"How did you know I had the Panjandrum?" Mariah asked him.

"You were traced by your own curiosity. Remember when I fell to the floor on the train? I left the small skull, knowing you would find it. Inside the skull is a fragment of stone chipped from a larger block. When another piece from the same block comes near it and is mounted in gold, it vibrates.

How it works I don't dream to know, but with my fob watch I can track the vibrations. Look." Black showed Mariah his watch, the second hand glowing in the dark and pointing to his room. "I suspected that if you were involved, the Panjandrum and the skull couldn't be too far apart. Then Perfidious sent a telegram to say he had given the cards to you, and the rest was, shall we say, down to modern science."

"But I saw you talking to Bizmillah, and he works for Luger," Mariah argued.

"And I think it's safe to say that after my conversation, he is now of a different persuasion." Black laughed again.

"Not enough of a different persuasion to free me from my room when he came with my supper," Albion said.

"He didn't know of our relationship then, but before tonight's performance he told me where you were lodged. But this is enough talk; it is vital that our work be done by midnight." He stopped and looked at Mariah. "One thing," he said slowly. "The joker, . . . slide it back into the deck."

Black held out the cards and Mariah slid the joker into the middle of the pack. They shuddered as if they had suddenly hiccupped.

"I take it that your inclination *was* to see what they could do?" Black asked Mariah.

"Never again," said the lad.

"Good . . . It is always best to leave such things alone until you know what you're dealing with. The only way these can be destroyed is by being turned to gold—we need the Midas Box for that, and then it will meet a similar fate."

"Why destroy the cards?" Mariah asked.

"We can't have people looking into the future," Albion said. "Knowing what is to come does us no good, yet it is man's fascination. We cannot be content with here and now. The Panjandrum know that and tell us half-truths. They mix the facts with our imagination, and then spin the results before our eyes." Albion tapped the deck of cards in Black's out-stretched hand. "They have a life of their own, but soon they will be solid gold."

"How will you find the Midas Box? It could be hidden anywhere," Mariah said as the elevator left their floor, summoned from below.

"At midnight Gormenberg will try to use it again."

"And you'll steal it from him?"

Black and Albion hesitated and looked at each other, neither wanting to speak.

"We'll kill him first," Albion said quietly. "It's the policy of the Bureau of Antiquities—leave no one to tell what has happened."

"So what of me?" Mariah asked slowly.

"Your future was decided the day you left the Colonial School," Black said softly.

CHAPTER

✷ 30 ✷

Trisagion

The brass-studded door to the Trisagion Bar was locked. Mariah knocked gently, and a small silver letter slot was opened, a pair of dark eyes glaring through.

"Yes?" he was asked in a deep voice the colour of the stare.

"I have to meet Captain Charity," Mariah said. "He's expecting me."

The man scowled, but Mariah heard the lock turn, and the door slowly opened.

"Quickly," the voice said. "Visitors are not welcome, members only."

Mariah was hurried through. He stood in a large smoke-filled room that looked like the saloon of a gigantic oceangoing vessel. In the far wall were row upon row of portholes framed in brass. High above was the mast of a ship, festooned with flags of merchant vessels and men-o'-war. A hand-carved ebony bar ran along one wall.

The doorman pushed Mariah to move him along. Mariah searched the room for the captain. A sea of high-back leather chairs filled the room, resting on the polished wooden floor. From each came a plume of bright blue smoke. All was silent except for the occasional cough and the turning of newspaper pages.

The doorman pointed to a chair by a high marble fireplace on the far side of the room. On the mantelpiece was an ornate clock that merrily chimed the eleventh hour. Mariah walked past several chairs peering at the occupants, most of them reading newspapers. Each chair was equipped with its own candelabras attached to the wings. The candles burned brightly, shining through the newspapers and casting a shadow of the reader across the pages. Beside every reader was a small table, leather topped and ebony based. Some had a crystal decanter; all had a large tumbler of whiskey, a metal ashtray and a cigar scissor.

Waiters were positioned at the corners of the room, standing silently, trays in hand, waiting for a signal of some requirement. They eyed Mariah as he crossed the room. It was as if they knew whom he was there to visit, their glance going from him to the chair by the fire and then back again.

By the fireplace he found Charity sitting in shadow, the candelabra on his chair extinguished. He sat back, a blanket covering his legs and white gloves upon his hands.

"Mariah," he whispered expectantly. "Did you find the cards?"

Mariah hesitated.

"Did you find them?" he asked again, a little louder.

"Yes . . . no . . ."

"Have you got them or not?"

"I was found out. I was told to give you this." Mariah

handed him a small visiting card. Charity read the embossed gold letters.

"Isambard Black . . . Bureau of Antiquities."

"They told me to tell you that they would see you outside Luger's room just before midnight."

"*They?*"

"Yes, . . . they have the Panjandrum for safekeeping. They said you would know who they were. Black and Albion, . . . they told me they knew you all along, that—" Mariah stopped short. Something was wrong.

"Indeed," said Charity as he sat farther back in the chair. "They are here. Good . . ." He paused, then continued. "Now I want you to do something. Take this key and go to the cellar. The man at the door will go with you—don't worry, he can be trusted. Wait for me by the door to the sea, and when I have finished my business, I will join you. Find Albion and Black and tell them to go with you." Charity coughed, his voice somehow different. "Now go on; this place is members only."

Mariah stared at the shadowy face, not sure what to do. Charity attempted a half smile and nodded slightly. For the briefest of moments, Mariah thought he saw the skin on Charity's face move, seeming to suddenly melt in the heat of the fire.

"Go on," Charity said, putting his hand to his chin and fanning his face with a folded copy of the *London Times*. "My man will see you to the cellar. Go with him . . . quickly."

Mariah nodded and stepped away, unsure about whether or not his eyes had deceived him.

"This way," said the doorman. "I know where you have to go—do you have the key? We will take the elevator; it will save time."

They were out the door and moving along the corridor before Mariah could think about what was happening. He turned and saw Albion and Black in the hotel lobby, seated on a long couch with red tassels, Albion clutching a leather bag as Black rolled his walking stick between his hands.

Mariah looked at his escort, noticing the scar on the side of the man's face. It looked fresh.

"Must've hurt," he said, pointing to the scar.

"An accident; my own fault. I should have been quicker," the man replied.

"Known Captain Charity for long?" Mariah asked.

"Charity?" The man asked as he rubbed his chin. "Ah! Captain Charity," he snickered as he slid open the elevator door and made to step inside.

The doorman didn't know whom he was talking about.

"ALBION! BLACK!" screamed Mariah, trying to run.

"NO!" the man screamed, grabbing Mariah by the arm and pulling him toward the elevator. "You'll come with me."

"ALBION!" Mariah screamed, waving his hands to attract their attention. "HELP!" He fell to the floor. Albion looked up and saw him being dragged into the elevator, and sprang to his feet.

"Quickly, Isambard," he said. "He has Mariah."

The two men ran along the corridor as the door to the Trisagion opened and out stepped a stunted Captain Charity.

"Jack," shouted Black. "They have the lad."

Charity didn't move. He stood holding the side of his face.

"What's the matter, man?" asked Black. "They'll get away."

Charity reached into his waistcoat pocket, pulled out a silver pistol and pointed it at the two men.

"No farther," he said, slowly stepping back toward the elevator. "One more step and I'll shoot."

"Don't be a fool, Charity," said Albion as he got closer.

Charity aimed the pistol. "Gustav," came the voice of

276

Luger from his lips. "Hold the elevator — we have unwelcome guests." He pulled the melting wax mask from his face. "Not my best creation, but it worked well. Stay back, Mister Bureau of Antiquities, or you will be dead."

His true face looked younger than Mariah had expected, with a thick brow and razorlike jaw. His cheek was slashed with an old scar that ran from his right ear to just below the eye and looked like a crescent moon carved into his skin.

"Gormenberg," said Albion. "After all these years and halfway across the world, we finally meet. A different name in every city, and we find you keeping a boardinghouse at the end of the line."

"Not a boardinghouse, but the finest hotel in the world. And you will have to search again, for I am about to disappear. The Bureau of Antiquities will never find me."

"We want the Midas Box, Gormenberg. It should have been destroyed years ago."

"Gentlemen, gentlemen. If it were mine to give, then I would oblige, but only those with the highest ideals should keep such a thing. Is the Bureau so short of money that it needs to make its own gold?"

"If that were the case, Gormenberg, we would have used the philosopher's stone. That, we obtained many years ago," Black said, slipping the sword from the hilt of his walking cane. "We never leave empty-handed."

"How about empty-headed?" Gormenberg asked, aiming the pistol at Black.

Black and Albion walked toward him, steely faced.

"Then not for your own safety, but for his?" Gormenberg asked, turning the pistol on Mariah. "One more step and I will shoot the boy between the eyes."

"Do it, Gormenberg. Right here and now," Mariah shouted, kicking out at the doorman's shins.

"Do it, Mister Luger . . . Kill the little brat right now,"

shouted the doorman as he tried to dodge Mariah's sharp feet.

"Later," Gormenberg said, quickly stepping into the elevator and sliding the cage door closed. "Don't wait for us, *gentlemen* of the Bureau. All the doors to the cellars are now secure, and the elevator will be turned off. Or, as a matter of fact, stay right where you are, for when I close the steam valve for good, things should soon become quite . . . *explosive*?"

The elevator dropped suddenly from sight.

Gormenberg took Mariah by the ear. "So glad you could come; you'll have a ringside seat for the end of your world."

"Where's Charity?" Mariah asked, not caring about himself.

"Detained, indisposed and tied up. Not really an adversary of any worth. All I desire in life is to be challenged by a foe who is truly worthy." Gormenberg looked Mariah in the eye. "You had possibilities, boy. I didn't want to have you in the oyster farm—thought you could have worked for me in the real world."

"My father told me—"

"From what I've heard, your father is in no place to tell you anything," Gormenberg snapped as he twisted Mariah's ear even harder, dragging him from the elevator and through a narrow tunnel until he came to his laboratory and pushed him inside.

Seated at a long table, in chains, were Felix and Sacha. In front of them were bowls of dark brown porridge mixed with an abundance of bright white pearls. The two sat staring at the wall, turning slightly as Gormenberg and Mariah entered.

"Eat . . . I told you to eat," Gormenberg shouted, banging the table with his fist. "If I don't have time to use the waxworks, then I will have to use you." He crossed the room and lifted the lid of a metal vat. Cold steam oozed over its sharp lip and across the floor. "Once you've eaten, then—" He stopped and laughed to himself before turning to the doorman. "Shut him in the sarcophagus and make sure it's locked tight. Can't have him escaping, might have to use him as well. Now come on . . . eat."

Gustav pushed Mariah across the room before he could say anything to Sacha. The man shoved him face-first into a large painted coffin that was leaning upright against the wall, slammed the lid tightly shut and turned the key.

From his prison Mariah could hear footsteps leaving the room and the door shutting behind them.

"Mariah," whispered Sacha. "They have us all. Captain Charity is locked next door. Luger wants Felix and me to eat the pearls, and then he's gonna freeze us both and ship us to France. He showed us what's in the vat. It's a chemical that'll freeze anything faster than winter; we won't have a chance."

"You should have stayed, Sacha. We had a plan."

"Whatever plan you had didn't work," Felix said. "He got you, too."

Mariah ignored him and felt the inside of the sarcophagus with his hand. "Have you seen the kraken, Sacha? He followed you here."

"Just Monica—she *is* a sea witch; she can walk through doors and do magic."

"And so can I," Mariah said, appearing behind them, much to their astonishment. "It's Bizmillah's coffin; all you need to know is how to undo the back and hey-presto . . . I saw it yesterday."

"Still haven't gotten us out of here, though, have you, Mundi? Still as pathetic as ever," Felix said.

"Never expected to see you again, Felix. Once you'd left the Colonial School, I thought you'd be making your millions. That's what you always said, wasn't it?"

"You know each other?" Sacha asked.

"I know the dreamer," Felix said quietly, clearly unhappy

that his fate seemed to be in Mariah's hands. "Spent all his time with his head in the clouds, never good for anything—eh, Mundi?"

"At least I wasn't a bully, dowsing boys in water as they slept, filling their beds with cockroaches, putting a rat in a cooking pot," Mariah spat back.

"There's no time for this," Sacha shouted angrily as Mariah stepped toward Felix with his fists clenched. "Luger will soon be back."

"That's what I have to tell you—he's not Luger but a man called Gormenberg. He's a crook, and Black's from the Bureau of Antiquities, and so is Albion. And more than all that, Captain Charity is really—" Mariah stopped in midsentence and saw them staring at him incredulously. "There is so much I need to tell you, Sacha, so much. Look what Charity has given to me—there are only three in the whole world."

Mariah held out the three-bladed knife proudly. It glinted in the candlelight.

"Why did he give you that?" asked Sacha, rattling the chains that held her to the floor.

"Said that one day it would come in useful, and I think I know why." Mariah took hold of her chain and stabbed the fine point of one blade into the lock, twisting it back and forth. Soon she was free. Then he quickly undid Felix's shackles. Felix rubbed his wrist and ran to the door, peering through the keyhole.

"No use," he said desperately as he looked about the room. "There's a key in the other side."

Mariah didn't hesitate; pulling a piece of discarded newspaper from the shelf, he slipped it under the door and pushed at the keyhole with the knife. The key fell from the other side and Mariah pulled the sheet of paper holding the key back into the room. Felix smiled.

"Clever lad, this Mundi. I'll soon be out of a job." He tried to laugh.

"Learned it at the Colonial School—I was the one who trashed your room. Got the key from the caretaker's house just like this . . . and no one knew. Served you right for everything you did. I wanted to laugh when I saw you in that cage." Mariah clenched his fists, ready to fight.

"Then why did you come back?" Felix argued, his face flushing with rage.

"I came back for her, not you. You made my life hell. When you left the school, it was the best day of my life. Just cos you're a year older, thought you were the big man. But who had to save your skin? Me!" Mariah held the knife to his face. "You're a joke—I know that now. Always the joker, poking fun, hurting people. Never told her I knew you, didn't want to. A bad memory best forgotten."

"Stop it," Sacha shouted. "Luger will come back and you two will still be fighting."

"His fault," they said together, pointing at each other, clearly having done it a thousand times before.

"She's right," Mariah said reluctantly. "Let's save this for another day. It's waited this long, it can wait another hour."

"Likewise," Felix grunted.

"Gonna get us out of here, then, Mariah?" Sacha asked.

She spoke too late. The door shimmered as a body melted through it.

"My dear little friends," said Monica as she materialized before them, dripping blue liquid to the floor in a large pool at her feet. "You weren't thinking of leaving?" She looked at Mariah. "All together at last," she said, her eyes jumping from one to the other.

Mariah hid the knife behind his back and took a step toward Monica. A growing stench of salt water and dead fish seemed to emanate from the sea witch, filling the room. Monica appeared to steam, a haze of fog falling from her shoulders like a white cowl. Her face looked young and fresh, neatly powdered, her lips etched in bright red paint.

"You should've eaten enough of the pearls by now . . . Now I can dip you in liquid nitrogen to freeze you for your journey. Now, who shall go first?" She looked at Felix and Sacha in turn. "I think . . . Felix."

Before anyone could say a word, she grabbed the boy by his throat, her hands strong and powerful. She lifted him from his feet and dragged him toward the steaming vat of freezing steam.

Felix screamed and looked at Mariah, his eyes calling for help. Sacha tried to move and found her feet salted to the floor. Mariah too was held fast. Monica laughed as she dragged Felix toward the metal vat.

"Soon we'll have a boy who looks better than any of Otto's waxworks," she said.

"He's not Otto—he's Gormenberg," Mariah interrupted.

"What?" she asked.

"You heard me. He killed Otto Luger. I can show you his bones in the foundations. Otto's dead. Gormenberg lied to you, and he's gonna kill you too." Mariah spoke quickly as she took Felix closer to the vat.

"I would know if he were lying," Monica replied, intent on killing Felix, her grip tightening around his neck until he began to stop struggling.

The salting held Mariah and Sacha to the floor as her unspoken spell continued to do its work. Mariah could feel the brine cutting into his flesh as the crystals multiplied. Monica began to carry Felix up the steps that led to the top of the vat of freezing liquid. He had become limp in her hands. She laughed to herself, and Sacha's frightened sobbing filled the laboratory.

"I promise I'll be quick," Monica shouted. "Dying is easy—people do it all the time." She laughed again as Sacha scratched at the salt that now encrusted her up to her waist.

"Don't do it, . . . please," Sacha shouted.

As Mariah watched the sea witch he remembered the words of Captain Charity: "A triple blade for a triple death."

"Take me!" Mariah shouted as Monica dropped Felix onto the top step and readied to push him over the lip of the vat. She stopped, holding her hands against her waist and tipping back her head with a mocking laugh.

"Your turn will come," she said.

Mariah seized the moment. His hand flashed from behind his back, firing the triple blade through the air. It flew like a swooping hawk, taking on a life of its own, the air around it rippling as it sped toward the sea witch. It pierced her dress, sending sequins exploding across the room, and there was a flash of bright green light as the knife shot through her completely, embedding itself in the far wall.

Monica laughed as she put a hand to her chest and felt the fluid dribbling over her skin. "I'm not flesh and blood . . . I'm a sea witch . . . You can't kill me."

She leaned down to slide Felix into the vat.

"It didn't work—she's still alive!" Sacha shouted, the salting climbing higher up her body.

Monica stopped and gave Mariah a triumphant smile. Then fluid began to pour from her chest, and a look of concern flashed across her face. She looked at the triple blade embedded in the wall as minute orbs of green light burst from her. She gasped for breath, holding her hand across the rupture in her skin, trying to quench the flow.

Felix began to breathe again, and the salt melted from Sacha. The sea witch gasped harder, and a multitude of sparkles gushed from her wound like fireflies. She looked around the laboratory, holding out her hand as if she were reaching for someone, and collapsed.

Mariah walked toward her. His face was blank; there was not a single trace of emotion in his eyes. He had to make sure she was gone for good.

Sacha grabbed his arm to hold him back, but he shook free of her and made for the sea witch.

"You said someone had to be first, and it'll have to be you," he said, propelled by a force that welled up inside him.

He stepped up to the vat and took hold of Monica's leg. He pulled it around toward him, then stepped toward her, pushing her backward. Without a word he tipped her into the vat.

Like a graceful, silent swan, Monica the sea witch fell into the icy pool. In her final seconds of life, she looked at Mariah and smiled as if she knew something about him that he didn't. As she was consumed by the chilling fluid the sound of cracking bones echoed through the laboratory. She disappeared for an instant before floating back to the surface, her frozen, outstretched hand seeming to reach for mercy.

Mariah helped Felix up from the floor and gave him a harsh look. "Don't get any ideas, Felix. I did it for Sacha."

CHAPTER

❋ 31 ❋

Iqtar

In the faint light of the passageway, Mariah peered through the narrow slat that was cut into the cell door. In the corner of the room, he could see Captain Charity leaning against the wall, his head held in his hands.

"I can't open the door," Mariah said as he peered inside. "Albion and Black told me every-thing. I know who you are—and what's more, Luger is really Gormenberg."

Charity smiled as he went to the door. "Gor-menberg? I realised that when I was captured. If I cannot escape, then you'll have to go alone. Did you find Felix and Sacha? I heard their voices."

"They're safe, still in the laboratory. Felix is hurt. I . . . I . . . ," Mariah stuttered. "I killed Monica—she was a sea witch."

"Did you use the knife?" Charity asked. "It worked?"

"Yes—she's dead," Mariah said.

"I've never known the knife to fail in its task. Do you have it now?"

"In my belt," Mariah said softly, wanting more than this, wondering if everyone in the Bureau of Antiquities talked like this in times of great magnitude.

"Good . . . Find Black and Albion and the Midas Box. Sacha can help me. Go—go now."

"But Gormenberg has closed the steam valve and said the whole building is going to explode. You have to get out of here."

"Fear not, Mariah. I have no plans to leave this life. Find Gormenberg, and swiftly—he must not get away from the Prince Regent." Charity spoke quickly as the cell filled with a sudden gust of steam from a bursting pipe.

"But how will you get out?" Mariah asked. The sound of the generator suddenly stopped.

"That's not your concern, Mariah. Do as I say. Find Albion and Black. They will need you in what is to come." There was the sound of grating rock above their heads. The foundations seemed to jump, and they were showered in a pall of thick dust that fell from the ceiling.

"I can't leave you here," Mariah argued, rattling the cell door.

"I'll find a way to escape. You have to go, and go quickly," Charity insisted as more dust fell on him.

Mariah turned to leave and cast a glance through the laboratory door; Sacha was lifting Felix to his feet. Felix looked at Mariah and smiled.

"I judged you wrong. There's more of a Colonial boy in you than I thought," Felix said as he hobbled to the door, still holding his neck, his hands covering the bright blue finger marks around his throat. Mariah nodded. Somehow all that had happened between them before seemed so trivial now.

"Take Felix to the beach," he heard himself saying to Sacha. "And Charity needs you to help him escape. I have a task I must complete alone."

Sacha tried in vain to call him back, her words echoing along the tunnels as his footsteps sped off into the distance. Mariah ran until he came to the elevator. He pressed the button and waited, knowing in his heart that the machine would not come.

Wet sand covered the floor. Upon the wall the gas lamp burned dimly, its broken glass shield casting jagged shadows out and along the tunnel that led to the sea. He pressed the button for the elevator again. There was a long moan as the last breath of steam escaped from the ramrod far below. Mariah now knew for certain the elevator had died. Looking around him, he walked on, keeping to the tunnels that went upward toward the Prince Regent. It was lighter and drier here. The sea was left behind, the corridors covered in a fine sand that didn't show his footsteps but just shallow indentations marking his path.

The foundations trembled again, the earth shivering, the pressure mounting in the geyser deep within the rocks. He walked down a long passageway and came to a double door with salt-rusted handles. It was blocked with a pile of sand. Nearby was a discarded shovel with a blade that had broken in two.

Mariah pulled on the doors. They were jammed fast. He thought of going back, finding some other way through the labyrinth of tunnels that would lead him to the surface. But there was no time. And through the cracked pane of glass in the door, he could see the steps that led to the spiral staircase and eventually the lobby of the Prince Regent.

Taking the shovel, he smashed at the glass, only to find that it had been barred in place. He kicked the sand and then began to dig. In a short time he had moved the sand back into the tunnel, piling it as high as himself, but still there was more to be moved. He dug the shovel in deep until it cracked against something hard. He burrowed with his hands, moving away as much of the sand as he could until he came to something that felt as hard as iron yet as smooth as a silken handkerchief.

Mariah tapped on it three times. It sounded strangely hollow, ringing out with a dull thud. Then he felt the earth move slowly beneath him. There was no sound of a tremor or fall of sand from the ceiling, but he was sure he had moved. It stopped as suddenly as it had begun, and he knelt there, waiting. He tapped upon it again, smoothing away the sand, and saw the thick red shell of the pagurus.

It was as if there were an earthquake. As the creature woke and got to its feet, shaking the sand from its body, Mariah was tilted back and forth violently. Then the pagurus lifted him toward the ceiling. It snapped its claws and tasted the air, its one large red eye swivelling in its socket to stare at him.

For a moment he tried to think of what to do as the pagurus pushed him closer to the stone ceiling, hoping to scrape him from its shell and then pick him limb from limb.

Mariah dived to flatten himself upon its back, keeping one hand upon the shovel as the other grasped for the beast's eye. It snarled as he held the eye in his hand, wishing he could pull it from its socket. The pagurus leaned back, raising its claws high into the air as it snapped at him. It lurched from left to right, confined by the sand and the door.

Mariah hung on to its back, hand upon the shovel. He had run from the creature before, but now he felt compelled by powerful voices within him to stand and fight. The pagurus stopped and looked at him as he cupped its eye in his hand.

"I won't run this time," Mariah said.

The crab rattled its claws like jangling sabres, as if it had understood his words.

"You or me?" Mariah asked as he flashed the shovel back and forth.

There was another shudder of the rock, and a shower of fine sand exploded all around them like a swirling mist. The pagurus trembled, and the clatter of snapping claws echoed through the tunnel. Mariah stared at the beast, and the beast stared back at him. For a moment the pagurus hesitated. Mariah took the broken blade and swiped it underneath his hand, slicing off the creature's eye.

The pagurus hissed and moaned as it spun back and forth, grasping blindly with its claws. In one movement it threw Mariah to the floor and instinctively took hold of the door with its large right claw.

Mariah smashed at the creature as its powerful legs stabbed at him time and again. He thrashed it across its back, the shovel bouncing from it as if from the hardest steel. It backed against him, pressing him against the wall with its shell. He slid to the floor as it tried to step on him and impale him with its sharp feet. As he crouched beneath the beast he saw a nest of small red eggs clinging to its underside. As the pagurus darted its fat claw toward him, trying to pluck him from his hiding place, Mariah stabbed the nest. The eggs burst upon him like a fall of fresh cranberries. He scrambled into the light, and rammed the shovel's blade into the creature's mouth.

Like a madman, he twisted the shovel back and forth, driving it in as far as he could. The pagurus snapped with its mandibles and tried to reach Mariah with its claws. It started to back away, shuddering with every step. Then it froze in place, shuddered once more and fell to the floor . . . dead.

He wasted little time in opening the doors and walking through the dank tunnels until he found his way to the landing that led into the hotel. The sound of moaning and creaking pipes vibrated in the air around him. He felt truly alone for the first time. In the distance he could hear Gormenberg's croco-gon wailing in the depths. It roared like a caged lion.

Mariah pressed on, climbing the spiral staircase until his mind swirled. He jumped the stairs two at a time, his footsteps clattering against the stone. The brass banister pipe that coiled upward was cool to the touch, and the whole of the Prince Regent began to groan and creak as it contracted with the growing cold.

Soon he came to a door that would take him to the lobby and Gormenberg's office. It had been bolted from the inside, a broom wedged through the handles. Mariah quickly re-moved the broom and pulled the door open. He peered into the brightly lit foyer. Pinned to the ceiling was a gold clock face. It chimed the quarter hour and was echoed by the clocks throughout the hotel.

The lobby was empty except for an old janitor, who dod-dered back and forth with his brush and pail, sweeping cigar ashes from the floor.

Mariah walked as calmly as he could. He felt taller, almost a man. A painting of Luger, or was it Gormenberg, stared at him, its eyes following his every step, an outstretched finger pointing accusingly. Mariah smiled at the janitor as he walked past, turned the corner and stood before the door of Luger's office, near the entrance to the hotel. Through the revolving door Mariah could see a night porter standing on the steps outside.

There was no sign of Albion or Black.

On one side of the lobby, a grand staircase swept up-ward, its gold handrail shining in the dim light like a coiled serpent rising from the deep green carpet that stretched wall to wall.

Mariah heard footsteps coming from above, thumping slowly down the steps. He tried to follow them with his eye but in the dimmed lights could see no one. He stepped away from the door and into the shadows of a small alcove, pressing himself against the dark oak panel and holding his breath.

Gormenberg turned the corner and walked toward the office door. He seemed unconcerned, as if this were a night like any other night.

Mariah watched from his hiding place as Gormenberg fumbled in the deep pockets of his coat for a set of keys. He opened the office door and stepped inside. There was still no sign of Albion and Black. Mariah looked up at the clock. Nine minutes to midnight. Feeling the dagger in his belt, he knew he had to go alone. He opened the door and stepped inside.

"Mariah Mundi . . . how well you have escaped," Gormenberg said, seeming to welcome the lad into his office. "Of course, you now know Albion and Black." He pointed to the two men tied together and strapped around a large marble pillar that appeared to hold up the ceiling. "I thought I had taken care of everyone, but like a bad penny, you keep appearing. Whatever shall be done with you? I gave instructions to Monica to have you frozen, and yet you are here before me, alive and well."

"She's dead," Mariah said calmly, holding the knife behind his back. "Fell into the vat. Careless, really."

"And of course, you had nothing to do with it?" Gormenberg asked.

"Everything." Mariah looked at Black.

"Did you enjoy it, Mister Mundi? Did it give you a feeling of power?" Gormenberg asked.

"I felt nothing. It had to be done," he said. He sidled across the room to the marble pillar and leaned against it as Gormenberg sat in his leather chair, leaning over his wide desk.

There was no sight of the Midas Box. Mariah looked about the room hoping to see a trace of the artefact.

"So . . . what now?" Gormenberg asked.

"You killed Luger. I found his bones in the cellar; it was you, wasn't it?"

"What does it matter? You'll all be dead within the hour and I will be far away." Gormenberg yawned and glanced at the clock.

Mariah looked at Albion and Black, who struggled against the rope that bound them to the pillar. "How did you catch them?" Mariah asked, nodding toward the two men. "They'd come to get *you*."

"Our own fault," Albion said as he jabbed Black in the ribs with a sharp elbow.

"Was your idea to check his office before midnight," Black said.

"He was supposed to have been in the cellars," Albion protested.

"Grimm and Grendel saw to that," Gormenberg said. "They had chased you through the sewers and got themselves lost—they eventually came out at the castle and were back at the Prince Regent just in time to catch your two friends rummaging for the Midas Box where their greasy little fingers shouldn't be . . ."

"Grimm and Grendel caught you?" Mariah asked them.

"Not so much them, but the pistols they carried," Black grumbled. "Perfidious insisted that this affair would not require the use of firearms—didn't you, Perfidious?"

"It will soon be midnight," Gormenberg said as, much to Mariah's surprise, he pulled the Panjandrum from his pocket and began to take the cards from the box one by one. "You see, Mariah, I now have everything I desire. A device to make gold and another to tell the future. It would be unthinkable to allow these two buffoons to take them from me. You, my friends, will await the largest explosion this country has ever seen. They will say I was lost in a natural disaster of Icelandic proportions, a Pompeii beyond Pompeii. When the steam is trapped underground for too long and not vented through the hotel, heating the sea and the sand will seem like nothing. It will blow a hole in the side of the cliff that will engulf the hotel and half the town, and I will watch it all from the safety of the sea."

"You'd kill us for a box and a deck of cards?" Mariah asked.

"I'd kill you for less," Gormenberg replied. He rang a dainty bell on his desk. "Grimm . . . Grendel . . . All our guests are now assembled and I am to leave. Five minutes to midnight and I have one last task before I say good-bye to the Prince Regent." He put the Panjandrum back into the box and then into his pocket.

The door opened and the two detectives stepped into the room. Their fine suits were covered in mud and torn at the knees. Each held a small pistol. Grimm smirked.

"Nice to see you face-to-face. Chased you for so long, I wondered what you would look like."

"Suppose I'll be tied here to await my fate whilst you all escape?" Mariah asked.

"Suppose you're right, lad. Take your place and I'll see you right," Grimm said as Grendel hovered behind him.

From his position leaning against the column, Mariah began to secretly cut at his friends' bonds.

"I will see you on the steamship *Tersias* . . . Do not be longer than an hour or you will share their fate. I have to get the Midas Box. Don't be late." Gormenberg stood up and left the room.

The door slammed behind him. Mariah could hear the strands of rope snapping as he sawed through them.

"Careful, lad," Black whispered, faking a yawn. "Nearly through."

"Do you think you could show me the glasses—the ones you followed me with in the sewer? Show them to my friends;

it would be most interesting," Mariah said, playing to Grimm's pride.

The detective cast a glance at his companion and shrugged his shoulders. "Suppose it'll do no harm." Grimm pulled the spectacles from his pocket and put them on.

"So you can see where anyone has been?" Mariah asked.

"A vapour trail of red mist follows us all, unseen by everyone," Grimm replied.

"Even where Gormenberg has gone?" he asked.

"Even Gormenberg," Grimm said bluntly. "All I would have to do is take his handkerchief and hold it here," he continued, holding the white cloth to his face, "and then turn this dial, and once the frequency is registered, I could follow him forever."

"I must try them," Mariah pleaded as earnestly as he could. "Pleeeeze?"

Grimm looked at his sad, pleading eyes and lopsided smile. He took off the spectacles and placed them carefully upon Mariah's nose. "There," he said kindly. "The lad can go from this world knowing what they're like."

Mariah suddenly could see the swirling red mist that formed a trail of vapour from the seat behind the desk through the door. Across the floor were thick red blotches, like the footprints of a monster.

"And you got these from the Americas?" he asked.

"Yes, from a man who lived on a mountaintop. A stranger man I have never—"

"So, Mister Grimm. You are finally the victor and we the defeated," Albion interrupted.

"Quite so, quite so. A strange accident of fate," Grimm replied, seeming distracted.

"There are no such thing as accidents, Mister Grimm, no such thing," Albion said. He twisted his wrists and released the severed ropes. As if he were a wild beast, Albion threw himself at Grimm, knocking him to the floor. Grendel, stunned, raised the pistol to shoot.

Black leaped toward Grendel, landing on the detective like a leopard. "RUN, MARIAH!" he screamed. "Find Gormenberg before he escapes!" Black punched Grendel in the face and grappled with the gun in his hand.

Mariah hesitated. Albion held Grimm to the floor and looked momentarily at him, his brow sweating as he wrestled with the detective. "Go, lad . . . Find him and we'll follow."

The Prince Regent lurched suddenly with a fresh tremor, much stronger than the previous ones. Debris fell from the ceiling, and the sound of cracking oak walls ripped through the air. The deep silence of the dormant hotel was broken as the screams of guests in faraway rooms filled the night.

As Black and Albion fought, Mariah ran out the door and into the lobby. The staircase and the hallway were filled with panicking people escaping to the street clad in only their night-clothes. A trail of red footsteps led to the stairway. Mariah scoped the scene, the divining spectacles casting an auric glow around everyone he looked at.

The fleeing bodies left a trail like a living shadow; it was as if Mariah were staring upon a field of ghosts. Many were screaming in fear. He pursued the footsteps as fast as he could, the red vapour billowing about his feet. Far behind he heard four gunshots, and then complete silence.

CHAPTER

✦ 32 ✦

The SS *Tersias*

he chilling sound of the clocks striking midnight rang through the hotel. Their calls seemed different from any other night. The Prince Regent shuddered in time with each beat. As he ran, Mariah could hear the echoing of the carillon coming from all around him. He chased the red glow of Gormenberg's footsteps down and down. As the clocks struck the third chime of midnight he turned a corner into a long corridor. He had never been this way before. It was cold and damp, and smelled of cordite and pepper.

In front of him was a door that stood open a fraction, the light from inside shining into the dark corridor. The footsteps led to it; they were bright and fresh, and simmered with red vapour. He knew Gormenberg was near. From inside the room he could hear him set something heavy onto a wooden table. There was the click of a lock, and the man recited a charm under his breath. "Guardian of Gold, open the door to riches and grace."

Mariah listened, wondering what to do next. It was circumstances and not bravery that forced his hand. He was leaning against the door to hear more of what Gormenberg was chanting when suddenly he fell into the room and to the floor at the man's feet.

Gormenberg flinched, startled, but didn't look at him. Mariah could see that he held the outstretched wings of a plain lacquered box, the Panjandrum lying by its side.

"Don't move," Gormenberg said as he placed a piece of black coal into the box. "I must do this before I deal with you."

"I've come for the Midas Box," Mariah said, his voice trembling.

"Brave or stupid . . . I haven't decided which you are, but I'll soon find out." Gormenberg began closing the lid of the box over the lump of coal.

"Neither!" shouted Mariah, jumping to his feet, grabbing Gormenberg's hand, thrusting it into the Midas Box and slamming the lid on it.

Gormenberg screamed in agony, his face turning blue, then deep crimson. The box shuddered against the wooden table, vibrating as if it were alive as shards of golden light beamed across the room, a light so intense that it dazzled. Mariah struggled to hold Gormenberg's hand fast as they both became absorbed within the blazing light.

"You don't know what you're doing!" screamed Gormenberg. "I've succeeded at altering time at last—it will kill us both if you don't set me free."

His eyes bulged as if they were being pushed from his head, and as he screamed, darts of golden light shot from his mouth.

There was a sudden and terrifying explosion, and Mariah was blown from his feet and thrown against the wall. A thick layer of black smoke hung over the floor, and as Mariah got to his feet he saw Gormenberg rising from the mist. The man stood up, clutching his left hand. It glowed. It was solid gold, every finger frozen in bright precious metal.

"My hand," Gormenberg stuttered as he stared disbelievingly at it. "Look what you've done." He sounded like a child whose toy had been broken.

He had been showered in gold. Globules of the shining metal covered his coat, and his skin shimmered with fine gold powder. Droplets of gold hung from the ceiling, sparkling in the light. In fact, it was as if everything in the room had been bathed and outlined in gold, like a finely painted icon.

The Midas Box lay on the table, the cards close by. They appeared to have been undisturbed by the explosion. Mariah saw Gormenberg's eyes flash from box to cards and then to his golden hand, and he felt for his dagger.

"Your move, Gormenberg. Take them and I'll pin you to the table with this dagger." Mariah couldn't believe what he'd just said. His fear had gone. But as he clutched the dagger he heard the disturbing sound of soft metal against the hilt.

Mariah held the dagger in front of him and looked at his hand. The tip of his little finger to the second knuckle had been transformed to pure gold. It was perfect in every way and joined seamlessly to the flesh, as if the gold had grown from his skin.

Gormenberg saw the panic on the boy's face and laughed.

"Slightly less than mine," he said jovially as he grasped his own hand. "If we had fought much longer, we would both have been turned to solid gold." Taking advantage of Mariah's shocked state, he reached out, grabbed the Midas Box and raced from the room.

Mariah took the Panjandrum and ran after him. The mist

swirled red before his eyes as the divining spectacles followed Gormenberg. They ran down and down, Gormenberg leaving Mariah trailing far behind. All Mariah could see was the plod, plod, plod of red footprints in the sand that covered the stone steps. They headed into a long, tiled corridor that Mariah knew led to the beach.

Gormenberg darted quickly into a side passage far ahead as Mariah ran on behind. In the distance Mariah saw three figures coming toward him.

"Mariah," shouted Sacha, holding Felix's arm as Charity carried the boy.

"He's running for the harbour. Gormenberg is going to catch the *Tersias* before she sets sail," Mariah shouted, and kept running, knowing he couldn't stop.

"I'm with you, lad," Charity shouted as he laid Felix on the ground. "Sacha, take him to the beach. Can you make it, Felix?"

The boy nodded, leaning on Sacha as Charity joined the chase.

Once outside, Mariah took off the spectacles. He tried to catch up to Gormenberg, but the man ran like the wind, faster than Mariah had ever seen a man run before. It was as if his feet weren't touching the ground, and the distance between them increased with every step. A storm was mounting in the bay. The waves washed across the top of the North Pier, the buoys dancing in the water.

"CUBAA . . . ," shouted Charity, who ran far behind Mariah. "Get . . . the . . . man!"

Several yards away from Mariah, the soft white sand burst open and out sprang the crocodile, who had been basking in the warmth. The beast looked around, hearing the call of its master, and then, sighting Gormenberg, set off running.

"Go, Cuba . . . , go!" shouted Charity. He and Mariah

watched the beast chase Gormenberg through the mist and toward the pier.

Gormenberg turned and stole a glance behind him.

"Do you think a dragon can catch me, Captain Charity? Is that the best you can do?" His voice was shrill and angry. "You have no idea who I am, do you, Captain?" he shouted mockingly. Cuba raced toward him, getting closer.

She leaped the last six feet, launching herself through the air with all her strength. She dived toward him, snapping her teeth.

At the last moment Gormenberg sprang to one side. The crocodile fell into the surging water of the surf, unsure how it had missed him.

"Better luck next time," Gormenberg said, laughing, as he ran toward the pier.

"Head for the ship, Mariah," Charity shouted as Mariah ran, his lungs fit to burst and his throat burning.

The blackened, sooty funnel of the tramp steamer *Tersias* poked above the chimneys of the houses that lined the pier. A thick column of black smoke rolled upward into the night as its engine chugged and clanged, ready to set sail.

Gormenberg leaped up a flight of stone steps from the beach to the top of the pier as the crocodile continued to chase him. Mariah followed, more out of breath with every pace. He stumbled up the steps, slipping on the seaweed that clung to each tread.

In the faint gaslight of the pier's end, he could see Gormenberg leap from a stack of boxes onto the ship. Mariah pressed on as the *Tersias* put to sea, crushing the small boats that were moored to the side of the pier to matchwood. He ran along the pier, knife in hand as he caught up to the ship. Gormenberg stood aft, the Midas Box held proudly in his right hand. He waved to Mariah with his five golden fingers and shimmering palm.

"Next time, Mariah. I am sure there will be a next time.

Out of them all it was you who came the closest to capturing me. Imagine . . . just a boy. Keep the hotel . . . whatever is left of it." Gormenberg laughed as the ship slipped toward the mouth of the harbour. The vessel was drab and black, with dirty portholes that glimmered with meagre yellow light.

"I expected your escape to be on something finer than this," Mariah shouted back to him from the end of the pier.

"I have a bilge full of pearls and the Midas Box, what more could I ask for?" Gormenberg turned to walk away. "One more thing," he shouted. "The man who was killed outside the Three Mariners . . . I didn't do it. It was another."

"We'll find you, Gormenberg," Charity shouted as he caught up to Mariah.

Gormenberg waved his golden hand and laughed as the *Tersias* sailed clear of the stillness of the harbour into the turbulent open water of the Oceanus Germanicus.

"Lost to us," Mariah said. "He got away."

"But you fought well; you proved yourself."

"But Gormenberg got away with the Midas Box."

"Sometimes things don't happen the way we wish them to. Often it looks as if evil has triumphed and light is weaker than darkness. That is life, my lad." A panting Cuba came and wrapped herself around their feet like a dog.

"The Prince Regent," Mariah said. "I must go back. Gormenberg switched off the steam —"

"And I turned it back on. Sacha helped me escape — she did well. Together we found the valve, and the Prince Regent will shudder no more."

Mariah shooed the crocodile from their feet, and together they turned to walk away. Instead of being relieved, he felt as if the burden of the world had been thrust upon his young shoulders. None of what he had seen or done made any sense to him. It was as if life had become an opera and he a player against foul fiends.

He turned to cast a final glance at the sea.

"LOOK!" Mariah screamed. Just beyond the harbour mouth, the tentacles of the kraken had wrapped themselves around the bow of the *Tersias*, and were tearing the wooden slats from the steel hulk. The sea boiled as the creature took hold of the ship and pulled at its smokestack, ripping it from the ship and discarding it into the water.

"What did I tell you," Charity said as he watched. "Never trust a kraken; you never know what they will do."

As waves broke over the ship another beast came from below and gripped the craft's stern. Its gigantic tentacle broke open the bridge door and searched inside, and three crewmen ran out and leaped into the foaming sea. Gormenberg stood proudly on the top of the ship, shaking his fist at the shore in defiance, his screams drifting upon the wind with none to hear them.

In seconds the vessel was no more, the krakens pulling it to the depths below. Gone was Gormenberg; gone was the Midas Box.

"What's to be done?" Mariah asked Charity.

"Nothing, all has been done for us," he replied calmly as Albion and Black ran toward them.

"He escaped —," Mariah started before they could ask.

"Only to be caught again," Charity continued.

"We saw it, but couldn't believe our eyes. In all these years at the Bureau, we have never seen the likes before," Albion said enthusiastically.

"And the Midas Box?" Mariah asked.

"The sea will keep it safe . . . for the time being," Black said seriously. "Until it calls to be found again to ensnare some other madman."

"I have the Panjandrum," Mariah said.

"Then all is not lost," Albion replied, holding out his hand.

. . .

In the Golden Kipper, Smutch dusted the head of a stuffed elephant that was fixed to the wall. He stood precariously on a rickety old ladder, one foot propped against a covered bird-cage. The smell of fish wafted from the kitchen as the gathering sat waiting with anticipation. Sacha held her head in her hands, trying to stay awake as Mariah and Felix chattered.

"So you'll be staying, now that we've freed the other boys and everyone is safe and accounted for?" Black asked Mariah as Charity entered with a platter of steaming fried fish.

"At least a year," he said, smiling at Felix. "And Felix is staying too — he needs the time to get over the drubbing he got from the sea witch."

"And to keep an eye on you. Here less than a week and the whole town nearly explodes. Heaven help us if he stays longer," Felix said, jostling him with his shoulder.

"Then you'll take this?" Albion asked Mariah. He slid a felt-covered case across the table.

Mariah took the case as they all watched. It felt warm and soft in his hand. He opened the lid and looked inside. There in a silk sheath was a silver badge. It was imprinted with the shape of a caladrius rising from the sea, and around the image seven stars were cut through the metal. Along the outside edge were the words "Bureau of Antiquities."

"This is for me?" Mariah asked, wide-eyed.

"If you're up for the task," Charity replied. He placed the fish on the table and handed everyone a silver fork.

"Then I will take it," he said as they all smiled at him.

Inside the birdcage, snug and warm, the caladrius warbled and chirped quietly to itself. In the light of the moon, it had been revived. By the fire Cuba flicked her tail back and forth as she dreamed of an ocean far away.

Beyond the harbour, past the headland, the two krakens swam contentedly together, the spell of the sea witch broken.

The bodies washed from the *Tersias* lay on the beach like wax-works in the light cast by the Prince Regent.

There, in the steaming sands, the sea had taken the sacrifice it was due. Gormenberg lay in the ebbing surf, his golden hand shining in the moonlight, his face looking to the stars. Slowly, as the last train whistled its departure from the end-of-the-line, he turned his head, stared out to sea and smiled.